THE SPIRIT QUEEN

ARNÉE FLORES

BLOOMSBURY
CHILDREN'S BOOKS

NEW YORK   LONDON   OXFORD   NEW DELHI   SYDNEY

BLOOMSBURY CHILDREN'S BOOKS
Bloomsbury Publishing Inc., part of Bloomsbury Publishing Plc
1385 Broadway, New York, NY 10018

BLOOMSBURY, BLOOMSBURY CHILDREN'S BOOKS, and the Diana logo
are trademarks of Bloomsbury Publishing Plc

First published in the United States of America in October 2022
by Bloomsbury Children's Books

Bloomsbury books may be purchased for business or promotional use. For information on bulk
purchases please contact Macmillan Corporate and Premium Sales Department at
specialmarkets@macmillan.com

Library of Congress Cataloging-in-Publication Data
Names: Flores, Arnée, author.
Title: The spirit queen / by Arnée Flores.
Description: New York: Bloomsbury Children's Books, 2022.
Summary: When their friend Ilsbeth is kidnapped, Calliope and Prewitt the
Bargeboy set out on a secret quest to save her—a quest that traps Calliope on the
Nymph Isles, a place of great darkness and ancient Spirit Magic.
Identifiers: LCCN 2022000452 (print) | LCCN 2022000453 (e-book)
ISBN 978-1-5476-0515-6 (hardcover) • ISBN 978-1-5476-0516-3 (e-book)
Subjects: CYAC: Fear—Fiction. | Self-confidence—Fiction. | Magic—Fiction. |
Fantasy. | LCGFT: Novels. | Fantasy fiction.
Classification: LCC PZ7.1.F59427 Sp 2022 (print) | LCC PZ7.1.F59427 (e-book) |
DDC [Fic]—dc23
LC record available at https://lccn.loc.gov/2022000452

Book design by Jeanette Levy
Typeset by Westchester Publishing Services
Printed and bound in the U.S.A.
2 4 6 8 10 9 7 5 3 1

To find out more about our authors and books visit www.bloomsbury.com
and sign up for our newsletters.

For Véda, my heart

THE SPIRIT QUEEN

1

The kingdom of Lyrica was woven by stories, and it was the Bookkeeper who wielded the needle. Across the centuries, Bookkeeper after Bookkeeper collected the tales, first by tongue and then by pen. They gathered them into books and placed them onto shelves in a tiny shop at the edge of the Royal City beach that they called the Firebird Tale and Tome Bookshop.

Magic was everywhere in Lyrica, but nowhere was it as close at hand as it was in the Bookshop. The Firebird Tale and Tome was *alive*. Stories were its beating heart, and the readers who stepped across the atrium and reached out to its shelves were its lifeblood.

As the years passed, the Bookshop grew, story by story, until it towered, wonky and bright, all the way up to the highest tier of the Royal City, where it stood eye to eye with the castle. It watched Queens change and Bookkeepers shift across the centuries.

One day, nearly a thousand years after the first book was placed on its shelves, the Bookshop felt the current Bookkeeper's footfalls change. No longer rhythmic and constant, but frantic on the staircase. They were joined by two other sets of footsteps, racing up and down, up and down.

Books were yanked from shelves and rushed across the atrium, taken away through a hidden golden hatch. The shop felt its life draining away as tomes were taken by the dozens, by the hundreds, by the thousands until there were none left at all. Finally, the lantern that hung at the top of the Bookshop was changed from white to red, a warning to all who could see it that something Terrible was coming.

A hand pressed against the Bookshop doorframe. "Goodbye, old friend. Keep the lantern burning; let it be a warning, but also a promise of better days to come. I'll soon be back, with more stories for your shelves, and a prophecy that may save us all." With that, the Bookkeeper had gone, and the Bookshop had sat empty and alone, fading into unconsciousness. The last thing it saw through boarded eyes were the monsters of fire and ash breathing destruction on the Royal City, and a strange sorceress standing on the parapet, her skin whiter than bone. *Where is the Firebird Queen?* it wondered. There was no one to tell it that the Firebird Queen had fallen, or that her daughter, the infant princess, had been hidden away until the time came for her to return.

Twelve years later, Calliope, the Lost Princess of Lyrica, burst through the Bookshop door and raced across the atrium.

"Bookkeeper!" she cried. "I've come for my lesson!"

The old man emerged frown first from behind a thick velvet curtain. "Queen Calliope, you're late."

Calliope cringed. She hated it when he called her that. She had reminded him that she wouldn't officially be Queen until after a coronation, but he had insisted that the coronation was only a formality.

Calliope had only recently learned that she was a Princess, the last hope for her kingdom. It was a lot to take in, and she wasn't sure she was ready for more. She had spent her whole life hidden away from the Spectress and the Demon, who had killed her parents, but when Calliope had learned the truth, she had known she must act. With the help of Prewitt, the Royal Bargeboy, and with the information held within a mysterious prophecy that the Bookkeeper had given them, Calliope had called the Firebird back to Lyrica and defeated the Spectress.

Now that she had returned to the Royal City, the Bookkeeper insisted it was time for her to be Queen, but the title didn't feel like it fit. Maybe it never would. It was a name that belonged to someone else. She reached into her pocket, and felt the wrinkled parchment inside. A portrait of her mother, torn from a book. It was worn from where her fingers had squeezed it again and again, searching for comfort. Calliope forced her hand away and swallowed the lump in her throat. "How can I be late?" she asked. "The sun is barely up."

"A Queen must work harder even than the sun." The Book-keeper flicked his hand toward the semicircle of scribes' desks, and Calliope hurried to sit.

For a long time, the Bookkeeper glared at her without speaking, and she waited. His back was permanently curved, and the only place he ever looked comfortable was when he sat at a desk, bowed over parchment and ink. Now, he rubbed absently at his spotted head and craned his neck, the tendons taut. Irritation radiated from him, and Calliope tried to tell herself that she was not the cause. After all, she could see the soot beneath his fingernails, the dark shadows pulling at his eyes. His slippers and hem were black with grime, and beyond the Bookshop atrium, through the curtain that led into the Bookkeeper's bedroom, the golden hatchway was open once again.

She knew that the Bookkeeper had spent another night wandering the hidden tunnels beneath the city, searching for books that might have survived the Spectress's monsters. All stories had been outlawed, and anyone who was found with a book was subject to death. But the Bookkeeper had kept them anyway, protected them in spite of the danger.

There had been miles of books stacked beneath the city; at least, that was what Prewitt had said, but they had all been burned by the ash golems in the Spectress's attempt to find Calliope.

She wondered if the futility of the search for surviving books was driving the Bookkeeper a little mad. He had kept them safe for so long, but in the end, it had all been for nothing.

4

On more than one occasion, she had seen him apologizing to the empty shelves as if the Bookshop could hear him muttering.

Calliope watched and waited, and finally the Bookkeeper cleared his throat, coughing away the disappointment of another fruitless night, and then the lesson began. He paced the floor, haranguing her on the history and geography of Lyrica, the royal lineage, castle protocol, and the Hierarchy of Spirits, his salvo of questions aimed like weapons.

Calliope met them all without hesitation. When he finished, she beamed, waiting for praise, but instead, the Bookkeeper spun away. "It isn't enough!" he said, flinging his hands in the air.

Calliope blinked. "Did I get an answer wrong?" She knew she hadn't.

"It isn't your answers that are the problem." He waved a hand at the bookshelves. "I can't teach you what you *really* need to know—the *secrets* of Firebird Queens."

Before Calliope could ask what he meant, the Bookkeeper whirled on his heel. "Come!" he barked and strode to the door, hurling it open with a *bang*.

A rush of cool sea air flurried around her as she came to stand beside him on the stoop.

He pointed up toward the city. "The sun has risen, the day is bright, and yet, the streets are bare. Not a breath of smoke from a chimney, not a peep of laughter or joy. The Firebird has returned, their Lost Princess has come home, and yet, they hide."

Calliope looked at her toes. She didn't need to see it again. She knew. Her hands plucked at the golden Feather tucked into her waistband. She had gone through so much to bring the Feather back to the Royal City. It was a symbol of hope, a gift from the Firebird itself.

"I've tried to get them to come out." Calliope's voice was barely a whisper. "You know I have. We all have. But nothing works. I've promised them feasts, and festivals, and balls, but none of it helps." She shook her head. "I don't understand. When we came home, people were so happy. They were celebrating!"

Her eyes lifted, and the Bookkeeper's mouth was grim. "Of course they were," he said. "You sailed into the harbor holding that Feather, and bringing their lost children home. What could they have felt but happiness? They were distracted from their fears by jubilation. But twelve years of suffering can't be erased overnight. Once the celebrations ended, the memory of their fears was still present, their loss still there."

Calliope wrapped her arms around herself. "But the Firebird returned. The Demon and the Spectress are gone. There's nothing to fear anymore."

Sunlight glinted off the Bookkeeper's oval glasses. "Are you so sure? What if the Demon rises again? What if another Spirit attacks?"

Calliope's jaw set. "I'll keep them safe."

"How?"

Calliope thought for a moment, her heart thudding in her chest; then she reached down and pulled the Feather out of her waistband, holding it up. "I'll call the Firebird. It will help us."

"Ah." The Bookkeeper turned away. "Your first wrong answer." He trudged back into the Bookshop.

Calliope followed. "What do you mean? I'm the daughter of the Firebird Queen. I can call the Firebird whenever I like." She hesitated. "Can't I?"

The Bookkeeper huffed. "The Firebird isn't your *pet*, Highness. You can't summon it and order it around like a subject. It has already returned, has set nature back to order, has given you its Feather. *You are the Firebird Queen. You* must keep your people safe."

Calliope tugged one of her curls. "How?"

The Bookkeeper whirled, and his blue eyes flashed. *"Magic."*

Calliope's mouth fell open. "Magic? What magic?"

The Bookkeeper pulled on his beard, suddenly self-conscious. "Ah . . . well, I don't know *exactly*. What I do know is that when the Firebird gave the first Queen the Feather and the crown, it also gave her some kind of power to wield its magic. *Spirit magic.* A power that could protect the kingdom if the Spirits defied the Firebird's choice for ruler."

Calliope stood straighter, her heart fluttering like birds' wings in her ears. "Why didn't anyone tell me?"

The Bookkeeper pushed up his glasses with a crooked finger. "Because I am the only one who knows. Somehow, the magic was forgotten. There were hints of it, snippets of stories in books so ancient that they were kept in locked cabinets and taken out only rarely. I read them as an apprentice, but I did not realize then how important the information would be, and that was

7

a very long time ago." He rubbed his temples, groaning. "This old mind. I'm ashamed to say that I've forgotten." He sat heavily on a wooden bench.

Calliope plopped down beside him, reaching a gentle hand to his elbow. "But don't you see? This could help everyone feel safe! If I had magic, then they wouldn't have to worry about being attacked again. No one would be afraid anymore. Everyone could be happy. Please, *try* to remember."

The Bookkeeper squeezed his eyes shut, and when the words came, they were slow and careful. "It was something in the *Song*." He let out his breath and shook his head. "At least, I thought it was. When you called the Firebird back, I was so certain its Song would ignite the magic in you." His brow was a mess of creases, and he pulled his arm away, looking up at the red lantern high above. "Maybe I was wrong."

They sat side by side in the empty shop, both caught in their own thoughts, until finally, the Bookkeeper sighed and hauled himself to his feet. "That's enough for today. We'll continue your lesson tomorrow."

Calliope wanted to argue, to beg him to try to remember. If she had more information, she knew she could figure out how to make the magic work. But she saw the weariness in the Bookkeeper's eyes, and she knew that she would get no further answers.

The Bookkeeper glanced back at her as he hefted aside the curtain to his room. "I must warn you not to tell anyone what I've told you—not even the Bargeboy. It is best that we keep this between us. No sense in giving anyone false hope." He paused. "Or fear."

Calliope felt a thrill of apprehension. Was there something to fear?

Before she had shut the Bookshop door, she heard the locks on the golden hatchway click back, and she knew that the Bookkeeper was returning to the tunnels.

That night, Calliope woke with a start to find the old man looming over her bed. The door was wide behind him and a stream of light poured across the stone floor. A cloak hung heavy around his shoulders, and beneath a wide hood, a jack-o'-lantern grin split his wrinkled cheeks.

"I found one!" he hissed. He reached into the folds of his cloak and pulled out a book. It was twisted and charred, and the binding was missing, but the Bookkeeper looked at it as if it were a precious gemstone. He caressed it with a pale and dirty finger. "It was there all along! A lost child, waiting for me in the ashes."

He pushed the book under her nose, letting it fall open in his palms. "Look!" He cackled, giddy and unhinged. "A ledger. Nearly eight hundred years old!"

Calliope slipped the Firebird Feather from beneath her pillow, holding it so that its light poured across the blackened page. It took a moment to make out the writing, but finally she saw the fine scrawl of numbers, places, and descriptions of things that seemed ordinary.

"No, no, Highness. You're looking, but you aren't *seeing*. *Here* in the margin." He rapped the page.

Seven books to be moved to the secret vault beneath the library at Lyda.

Calliope's eyes widened. "There was a secret vault?"

"Yes!"

"But—" The Feather dropped from Calliope's fingers and onto the bedspread as she leaned forward, excitement thrilling through her. "What if there are still books there? We might be able to find something more about the Queen's magic!"

"Yes! Yes! I must go and see!" crowed the Bookkeeper. "There's not a moment to waste."

Calliope threw off her covers and flung her legs over the edge of the bed. "I'm coming with you."

The Bookkeeper shook his head. "You cannot. Every day that passes, the Firebird Song fades a bit more. If I am correct, and your magic is somehow sparked by the Song, then you must stay here and *listen* for it, find it, pull it to you. Let nothing distract you. I will be back within a fortnight. Firebird willing, I'll have more answers."

He stepped away, his face falling into shadow, but his grin was radiant. "I must go, Highness." He clutched the book to his chest. "I must go and find my children."

Before Calliope could argue, the old man was gone.

She sat for a moment in the empty room, and then she took

a deep breath and stood. She wasn't going to waste time. If the magic was in the Song, then she was going to find it *right now*.

She sat cross-legged beside the bed. The moon was a clipped nail through the high window in the hall, and shadows shivered across the cool stone floor. Calliope closed her eyes, the Feather warm between clasped fingers. Its golden light glowed against her eyelids, and she took a deep breath of the stale air and *listened*.

She heard the creaking of branches in the woods beyond the window, the dull drone of the distant sea, the wind's high whistle. But she did not hear the Song. She could *remember* the way it had sounded, the caress of notes against her heart, but remembering was not the same as hearing.

She took another breath and reached further. With all her might, she tried to force the Firebird Song to come to her, but no matter how she strained and listened, she could not hear it. Night after night, she sat on the floor, trying to find it, and night after night, she failed.

A fortnight passed, and then another, and the Bookkeeper did not return. Calliope told herself not to worry, but she couldn't help it. Surely, he must have found the library at Lyda by now. Why hadn't he come home?

She shook her curls and took a deep breath, reaching once more for the Song, and the *sound* that hit her was so unexpected that she fell backward from shock, striking her head on the stone floor.

Her breath was wild, and her heartbeat thundered all the way to her skull. She pushed herself up, swaying, eyes darting as she held the Feather high.

She had reached for the Firebird Song, but something else had answered.

Somewhere, someone was *screaming*. No, not some*one*. Many, many *someones*.

Help us! Save us! Free us! they shrieked all at once, the pain in their voices pulling at every muscle in Calliope's body.

"I'm coming!" she cried. Her feet slipped on the stones as she ran out into the corridor. "I'll help you!"

The voices tugged her forward. They were close, so close, so desperate.

The soles of her feet slapped as she raced forward, her blood cold, and her skin speckled with goose bumps. The screams grew louder, more urgent, and Calliope tried to keep the terror from her voice. "I'm coming! I'm coming!" She turned a corner and nearly bowled someone over.

A candle snuffed out, and smoke wound upward like a question in the dark.

"Highness? Are you all right?" Prewitt's mother, Marisa, stood in her thin nightgown, worry thick across her light-brown face.

Calliope shook her head. Of course she wasn't all right! How could Marisa be so calm when the cries were so loud? "We have to help them, Marisa! We have to find them!"

Marisa blinked, tilting her head so that her long, dark braid fell heavy across her shoulder. "Help who, dear?"

Calliope gaped. "Can't you hear them?"

Marisa frowned, confused; then something dawned in her eyes, and she reached out and pushed back Calliope's curls. "I see. I understand now. You've had a nightmare."

Calliope stiffened. "A nightmare?"

Her mind reeled as Marisa steered her back to her room. Why couldn't Marisa hear the voices? Even now, they screamed and wailed so urgently that Calliope almost couldn't make out Marisa's soothing words. "There, there. There's nothing to fear. No one is screaming. The world is still." Marisa pulled back the covers. "You're safe," she promised, and Calliope forced herself to smile and climb into bed.

She pressed her eyes shut, pretending to sleep, and finally Marisa kissed her on the forehead and padded softly away, clicking the door shut. Calliope waited until she was certain Marisa was gone; then she sprang up and ran from the room.

She followed the cries down to the harbor, but there, she was forced to stop. There was no sign of their source. Only the endless, star-swept sea and the lonely Bookshop at the edge of the beach. Its red lantern pulsed, and with her hands clasped over her ears and her heart thrumming, Calliope wished more than ever that she knew what had become of the Bookkeeper.

2

Calliope raised her hand and knocked, her left arm aching under the weight of a large wicker basket. "Hello?" she called, hoping her voice would carry beyond the wooden door. "It's me, Princess Calliope. I've brought apples fresh from the orchard, green beans and cauliflower, and herbs from the garden."

Silence.

"Tell them about the egg!" the Bargeboy hissed from a few feet away. He stood beside a wagon, red jacket open to the afternoon sun, a white linen shirt loose beneath.

"There's even an egg today!" Calliope made her voice as cheery as she could.

The precious egg was nestled at the top of the basket, wrapped carefully in sun-bleached linen. They were a rarity, but soon, the spring chicks would be old enough to lay, and then there would be more eggs than anyone knew what to do with— at least, that was what Marisa had said.

Calliope knocked on the door again, feebly this time, but as usual, her taps yielded nothing.

She sighed, placing the basket on the porch and trudging back to the wagon.

"Maybe tomorrow," said Prewitt.

"Maybe tomorrow," she repeated, giving him a half smile. It was what they had been saying every day for nearly two months. Evening after evening, they had knocked on doors, and knock after knock, the people within had not answered. They had waited until Calliope and Prewitt had gone before stretching out furtive arms to snatch the baskets inside.

Calliope grabbed a watering can from the wagon and sprinkled bright orange flowers that grew along the tier. She felt like a failure for not being able to do more to help people feel safe, but she refused to give up. She had gathered seeds from the fire flowers that grew at the top of the cliffside, and spread them across the tiers, hoping they might bring people a little comfort. They had bloomed practically overnight, adding bursts of color all along the streets and through the alleys.

The Royal City was built into the side of the sea cliff, and stairs cut through the terraces from the beach all the way up to the castle. Not a step, or house, or darkened shop front had escaped Calliope's scattered seeds. The tiers were a riot of orange and yellow flowers, but the city itself was lifeless.

There were still a few baskets left to deliver, and Calliope and Prewitt did so quickly. The sun was lazing against the horizon, and Marisa would worry if they weren't back to the castle before it set.

Calliope sighed as she and Prewitt reached the city steps. The empty watering can clattered as she tossed it into the bottom of the wagon.

Prewitt pointed with his chin. "Ilsbeth's still there."

A girl sat stiff and upright on one of the steps. Her head swiveled toward them, and she stood when they came near. Her face was expressionless, but her knuckles were white on the handle of a coiled green whip that hung from a belt at her waist.

Ilsbeth had once been the reluctant leader of the Glade Girls, the children who had been placed in their baskets at the edge of the forest and saved from the Spectress by the Guardians of the Glade and the Wild Woman. The girls had been raised among Spirits in the Halcyon Glade, and they had been like sisters. But everything changed once they had returned home to the Royal City.

Now, Ilsbeth's dark eyes met Calliope's, questioning.

Calliope shook her head. "Maybe tomorrow." She tried to make her smile bright, but the other girl did not return it.

"Come up to the castle for supper," coaxed Calliope. "Marisa always makes too much."

"No. I will stay here until the sun sets. The Glade Girls may need me."

Calliope and Prewitt exchanged a glance. Ilsbeth waited on the steps every day. Before, the Glade Girls had been one another's only family, but now, they had parents, parents who were determined to keep them safe. Doors were locked and shutters were closed, and Ilsbeth waited alone.

Prewitt and Calliope left her glaring out at the sea and continued up the city steps toward the castle, the wagon bumping up the pavers. They reached the top of the cliff, and Prewitt turned toward the orchard, but Calliope shook her head. "I need to get more flowers."

Mock horror bugged out Prewitt's eyes. "More? Where in Lyrica are you going to put *more*?" But he followed, grinning, as she hurried along the eastern edge of the castle and beyond the courtyard to where the fire flower fields bloomed in waves of bright orange, their hearts sunbursts of yellow flames.

Calliope gathered an armful, burying her nose in the blossoms. She breathed deeply, as if their scent could somehow take away her worries. "Maybe if people look outside and see flowers everywhere, it'll help them believe that the world isn't such a bad place. There's still good here."

The sun flashed against the windows of the Bookshop as it sank farther in the sky, and a shadow drew across Calliope's heart.

"Cal?" Prewitt's hand pressed against her shoulder. "Are you okay?"

Calliope avoided Prewitt's gaze. "I'm fine."

Prewitt opened his mouth, and for a moment, he looked like he wanted to argue, but instead, silence stretched like a chasm between them.

He didn't believe her. She knew. But the Bookkeeper had told her not to tell anyone about the magic, and even if she did, how could she explain her failure? She was the ruler of Lyrica.

It was her job to make everyone feel safe. If she told Prewitt the truth, if she told him about the voices that screamed in the night, the ones she didn't know how to silence, he would see just how afraid she was, how lost and uncertain, and then he might be scared, too. What good would that do when there was no way for him to help?

Calliope shook off her feelings and forced a smile to her lips. "Let's go back," she said, tucking the flowers in the crook of her arm and grabbing Prewitt's hand.

They had only just turned toward the castle courtyard when a salt breeze blew across the fire flowers, and the blossoms around their feet parted like a wave. In an instant, they saw a flash of something strange in the wet, black dirt.

"What is *that?*" Prewitt dropped her hand, and bent to push aside the flowers.

Vivid blue stones winked up at them. They were laid in a pattern, staggered like arrows toward the cliff's edge.

Flowers tumbled, forgotten, from the crook of Calliope's arm as she reached down and ran her fingers across the stones. They were cool and gritty, coated in a thin layer of fresh soil. "It's a pathway," she whispered. "I wonder how we never saw it before."

Calliope jumped up and started off, tugging Prewitt with her.

"Wait, where are you going?" he asked.

"Don't you want to see where it leads?"

Prewitt glanced back over his shoulder at the abandoned wagon, but he didn't argue as she pulled him farther, and she saw by the way his eyes swept the path that he wanted answers as much as she did.

The stones were slippery as they felt their way along, and Calliope grasped for balance at ferns sprouting from the side of the rock. Her hand landed on a smooth piece of twisting wood.

"Look, Prewitt. Someone carved a handrail!"

"You're right!" he said. "It must be really old. Look how worn the wood is."

They held on tightly, following the path, both growing more and more curious about where it would lead, and when the blue stones ended, they found themselves at a door.

It was unlike any that either of them had ever seen. The door itself was made entirely of seashells. They arched around a nautilus knob in swirls of deep pink, peach, gray, purple, and ivory. From there, the shells continued, limpets and whelks, lucines and sand dollars, scallops and tellins, forming the outer walls of a small cottage.

Calliope thought it looked like a jewelry box tucked away on the edge of the cliff.

Prewitt started forward, reaching for the knob, but Calliope grabbed his sleeve.

"No, wait."

"Wait? What do you mean? You were the one who—"

"I know, but . . . it feels . . . sad somehow. Can't you feel it?"

Prewitt's mouth quirked. "Sad? How can a cottage be sad?" But even as he asked, Prewitt understood what she meant. There *was* something lonely about it. The door's hinges were thick with rust, and the two round windows were clouded with salt grime. It was beautiful and mysterious—and yes, sad.

"We should go back," said Calliope, shivering.

But Prewitt had already pressed his light-brown face to one of the windows. He pulled back, rubbing his sleeve across the glass, trying to clear some of the grime. "I can't see anything. We've lost too much light."

Calliope felt the blood leave her cheeks as she cast a glance at the horizon. The sun was nearly in the sea.

Apprehension hummed through her bones.

She snatched Prewitt's hand. "Come on! Your mother will be waiting."

He flinched. "You're right. Let's get out of here."

They raced back up to the waiting wagon and barreled toward the castle, rickety wheels rattling behind them through the fire flowers.

3

"**Where in Lyrica have you children been?**" Marisa stood in the doorway to the castle kitchen, her hands on her ample hips. "I was worried!"

"We're sorry!" Calliope and Prewitt both apologized, and before Prewitt's mother could scold them further, they told her about the shell cottage.

"What's this? What trouble have you two found now?" The Bargemaster's voice boomed from within the kitchen, and Marisa swept Calliope and Prewitt inside.

A low fire crackled in one of the kitchen hearths, and something delicious-smelling burbled in an iron pot above the flames.

Prewitt's three-year-old sister, Pyper, sat cross-legged on one of the tall tables, playing with a woven basket, and three blond girls were arranged on the floor near the fire, trimming and snapping green beans before tossing them into the pot.

"We found a secret cottage, Mer!" burst Calliope. "On the cliffside!"

Prewitt watched as Calliope told his father about the cottage, waving her arms and bouncing on the balls of her feet. Every so often, she reached out and tugged on the Bargemaster's sleeve.

It was still strange for Prewitt to see how close Calliope and his father were. For twelve years, the Bargemaster had been the only person Calliope knew. He had kept her hidden and safe from the Spectress, visiting her every day on the *Queen's Barge* where she lived. He had done everything in his power to protect her—even keeping her existence a secret from his own family.

Now, the Bargemaster rubbed his mustache and shook his head. "Ah, yes, the shell cottage. I haven't thought of that place in years."

"Neither had I." Prewitt's mother stepped down into the kitchen, a far-off look in her brown eyes.

"What is it?" Calliope tilted her head. "Who lived there?"

"The Painter," said Marisa, rolling up her sleeves and moving around the kitchen.

"Who?" Prewitt frowned.

"Her name was Miriam, and she was one of the most talented painters I've ever seen."

"One of the most talented the kingdom has ever seen, I should think," said Meredith.

Marisa nodded. "Her paintings were special. The only ones of their kind. People said she was *swayed*."

Meredith laughed and Marisa scowled. "Don't laugh!"

Meredith rubbed his mustache.

"What do you mean?" asked Prewitt. "What does that mean, *swayed*?"

Meredith's eyes crinkled at the corners, and he seemed to be trying very hard not to laugh again. "There are people who believe that a child who encounters an Ancient Spirit is sometimes blessed with unique skills."

Calliope stood up straighter. "Skills? You mean like magic?"

"No," said Marisa. "No, not Spirit magic. That would be incredibly dangerous."

Calliope chewed her lip. "Why?"

Marisa wiped her hands on her apron. "Because, dear, humans are not *meant* to wield Spirit magic." Marisa's round face was serious, and her hand trembled as she brushed a stray hair away from her forehead. "Don't forget what happened when the Demon gave a human magic. The Spectress lost herself and became something inhuman and terrible."

At the mention of the Spectress, one of the blond girls began to cry, and soon, all three were sobbing.

Calliope and Prewitt sat down near the hearth, watching as Marisa crouched and gathered the girls into her arms. "It's all right. It's all right," she crooned. "You're safe. The Spectress is gone."

"We don't want to go back to the dungeons," said one of the girls. "Please, don't make us."

"No, no, of course not. You will never see a dungeon again, I promise. You are safe here."

It took a few minutes for the girls to calm, and Marisa sent them out to the garden with an empty basket to gather a few more beans.

She waited until they were gone before she said, "Those poor, sweet girls. I don't even know their real names. I've just been calling them darlings and dears for months. Their parents still haven't come for them. I'm trying not to think the worst. After all, they might still be out there somewhere, searching, hoping." She sniffled. "I thought the Falconer was going to send birds out again. If we could just get a message to someone who—"

"He did," said Meredith, shaking his head. "No one has answered. No one has come. It's almost as if something is keeping people away."

The fire guttered, and they all jumped.

"But if a *sway* isn't Spirit magic," said Prewitt, refusing to be deterred, "what is it?"

Meredith frowned. "It's nothing. *Sways* don't exist. Miriam spent hours with a paintbrush in her hand and became the very best. That is the explanation behind her ability. No magic to it."

Marisa pursed her lips, and Calliope leaned toward her. "Tell us more, Marisa."

Prewitt's mother ignored Meredith's groan. "Let's see. Well, a *sway* happens when a spirit's magic leaves an *impression*." She thought for a moment, her pestle rhythmically grinding aromatic herbs. "They might become faster or stronger or smarter. Or, in Miriam's case, they might have an extraordinary ability to paint."

Prewitt huffed. "Both Cal and I have been around loads of spirits. How come we're not changed?"

"Because you're perfect just the way you are." Marisa leaned down, kissing him on the cheek.

Prewitt made a face. "Cal and I were around the *Firebird*! None of the Spirits are more powerful than it! We should have been *swayed*, for sure!"

Marisa plunked a basket of potatoes at Prewitt's and Calliope's feet and handed them each a knife.

She gestured at the potatoes. "Perhaps peeling potatoes is your *sway*. That would certainly be useful."

Prewitt rolled his eyes, but he picked one up and started peeling.

"Tell us more about the Painter," said Calliope, reaching for a potato. "What happened to her?"

"She got sick. Everyone hoped that she would get better. Her husband and her children—a boy and a girl—were desperate to find a cure." Marisa shook her head. "But it was no use. She was gone too fast, and they were all devastated, but none as much as the little girl. She and her mother had been inseparable."

Calliope felt her throat tighten. She had sensed sadness in the cottage, and now she understood. It was a place where there had once been joy, and then it had been lost. Just like the castle. She thought of her own mother, of the terrible way she had died, and she felt a kinship to the Painter's daughter.

"What happened to the Painter's family?" she asked.

"You know her husband," said Meredith.

"We do?" Calliope and Prewitt looked at each other.

"Yes. Thomas—the Bookkeeper."

"The Bookkeeper had a family?" said Calliope. "I didn't know that!"

Prewitt shook his head. "Me either. I thought he always lived alone in the Bookshop."

"Yes, he has for a very long time." Marisa set down a basket of fat red radishes. "After the Painter died and her bottle was sent to the sea, the Bookkeeper locked the cottage and moved the children into the Bookshop. He left all her things behind—including the paintings." Marisa's mouth turned down. "Milo and Sina. Those were the children's names. They were twins, and it was good that they had each other because, in a way, I think they also lost their father. I'm not sure the Bookkeeper ever spoke of Miriam again."

"No," agreed Meredith. "He wouldn't let his children speak of her, either. I believe he hoped it would make it all easier."

Calliope stopped peeling the potato in her lap. A lump had formed in her throat. She understood not wanting to talk about things that hurt. Whenever she tried to speak of her mother, her eyes stung, and she knew that if she opened her mouth, she would cry.

"What happened to the kids?" asked Prewitt.

Neither Meredith nor Marisa spoke for a long moment, and then Meredith finally answered. "They grew up. Milo was quiet, and spent all his time in the Bookshop preparing to become the Bookkeeper himself. The girl, Sina, was nothing

26

like her brother. She was probably the sharper of the two, and was always learning something new. But she didn't want to just read about things; she wanted to do them. She was a free spirit, an adventurer."

Marisa's eyes suddenly welled with tears, and she turned to wipe them away. When she looked back, a smile was on her lips, and she nodded at Meredith to continue.

"When the Bookkeeper went in search of the prophecy, the twins sailed with him. All the way north to the Nymph Isles."

Calliope and Prewitt knew without asking which prophecy he meant. They had held it in their hands, had pressed the black conch shell to their ears and heard the ancient voices whispering. It was the prophecy of doom that had forewarned of the downfall of the kingdom if Calliope failed to have hope. It had been full of dark warnings, but it had also given them clues that had sent them on a quest to find the fragments of the stolen Firebird Feather.

"What exactly are the Nymph Isles anyway?" asked Prewitt, tossing a peeled potato into the basket. He balanced the knife on his knee as he reached into his jacket pocket and pulled out a golden book. It was a collection of maps that the Bookkeeper had given him in the tunnels when he had been searching for the Lost Princess. He opened it to a page that showed the three seas and the Nymph Isles like crescent moons at the top.

"No one really knows," said Meredith. "The Nymph Isles have always been a mystery. Magical gifts have shown up on our shores, and the tides do not lie. There is no doubt that they must have come from the black beaches of the crescent islands, but there was never a note, never any sign of who had sent them."

"The Bookkeeper told me once that it's where the Ancient Spirits went," said Prewitt.

"Yes," said Calliope. "He said that they left because they didn't believe there was hope for humankind. They didn't believe in Firebird Queens, so they abandoned Lyrica a thousand years ago and went on to create the Nymph Isles."

Prewitt leaned forward, his brown eyes bright. "People say it's a place that no one ever returns from, but the Bookkeeper did! He sailed all the way there and back, and nothing happened to him at all."

Meredith and Marisa exchanged another glance, and Calliope could tell there was something they didn't want to say. "Something did happen, didn't it?"

Neither grown-up spoke. Finally, Marisa said, "Not to him, dear. Not directly."

"What happened?" pleaded Prewitt.

Meredith sighed. "We don't know. We only know that when the Bookkeeper left for the Isles, Sina and Milo were with him, and when he returned, they were gone."

Prewitt leaned forward. "Did they die?"

Meredith shook his head. "The Bookkeeper refused to say."

"I think they must have," said Marisa. "He had aged so much. When he left, he was old, but when he returned, he seemed ancient. Only a deep sorrow can do that."

They were all quiet a moment, the fire crackling.

Prewitt stared down at the book, tracing the crescent moons of the Nymph Isles. "He never said what happened? Not even a hint?"

"Not even a hint." Marisa tossed her thick braid over her shoulder. "Now, let's not speak of it any further, and for Emperor's sake, you two, stay away from the shell cottage. It wouldn't be right to go disturbing it now."

She wiped her hands on her apron. "Hurry and set the table. It's practically dark and supper isn't even finished."

Calliope jumped to her feet, a half-peeled potato rolling onto the floor. She had let herself get distracted, had let time get away from her. She couldn't be here when the cries began. She couldn't trust herself to keep a straight face, and there was no way to explain the fact that she was hearing voices that no one else could.

"Cal?" Prewitt was staring at her.

"I'm—I'm not feeling well," she said.

Marisa rushed at her, all hands, but Calliope ducked away. "I'm fine. I just need to lie down. I'll see you in the morning."

"Well, okay, dear." Marisa's brows knitted. "Would you like me to bring you some soup?"

Calliope shook her head. "No! No, thank you." She backed away, and then she spun and raced from the kitchen.

4

Prewitt stood outside Calliope's bedroom door. He wanted to knock, but the Queen's crest carved into the wood stopped him. His father was constantly reminding him that he must respect Calliope's wishes. They were friends, but she was still the Queen—even if she refused to let him call her that.

When they had been on the quest together, solving clues and collecting the fragments that would play the Firebird Song, it had been easy to forget that she would someday rule over everything. But here in the castle, in the Royal City, everything was different. *She* was different.

Prewitt wanted to comfort her, to reassure her, but how could you reassure someone when they wouldn't tell you what was bothering them? How could you comfort them when they shut the door?

Prewitt sighed, pressing his hand to the wood. *I'm here, Cal.*

She had changed in the last few weeks. There was a new sheen to her gaze, and something desperate and unsettled about the clutch of her fingers on the Firebird Feather. Something was wrong, but he didn't know what, and she wouldn't say.

It had something to do with the Bookkeeper. But when Prewitt had asked Calliope why the Bookkeeper had left, she would only say that the old man had gone in search of surviving books.

Prewitt bit his lip and forced himself to turn away from the door, walking down the corridors to his room in the visitors' quarters.

When Marisa had asked Calliope if she would like them to come and stay with her in the castle, Calliope had seemed overjoyed. For a while, things had even been fun. They had explored the towers and keeps and halls and rooms they had no names for, but then, they'd both had things they were supposed to do, responsibilities that pulled them away and meant they saw less of each other.

Prewitt was overwhelmed by his new role as his father's apprentice. The Bargemaster had been teaching him everything that Prewitt always wanted to know about sailing, not just the *Queen's Barge*, but every kind of craft. He was finally experiencing a waterman's daily life—and it wasn't nearly as exciting as he'd expected. He was utterly disappointed to find that being the Bargeboy was mostly work.

He'd crawl from his covers while the stars were still shining, and when he'd fall into bed at night, he was exhausted and sore. His hands were calloused, and his mind was a jumble of new information. He should have been excited. It was what he had always wanted—to be his father's apprentice—but he had thought it would be more of an adventure.

"When will I get to pilot the Barge on my own?" he had asked his father.

"When you are ready." The answer had annoyed him.

He had helped defeat the Spectress, had done something important, and been a hero, but then he'd begun his apprenticeship, and that was less about heroism and more about doing what he was told. If his father wasn't ordering him around, his mother was barking at him to help. He was the Age of Hope, but he was still being treated like a little kid.

One morning, after he and the watermen had sailed back into the harbor at dawn, the deck slimy with fish guts, Prewitt hadn't been able to hide his disappointment. He had grumbled when his father handed him the mop, just as he'd done the day before, and the day before that. His father had flicked the bill of Prewitt's cap, laughing. *I know it's not as thrilling as you'd hoped, Prewitt, but if you don't put in the work, you won't be ready when the adventure calls.*

Prewitt sighed as he climbed into bed, pulling the covers up to his nose. If he was really honest with himself, it wasn't adventure he wanted most. It was his friend, Calliope.

With that thought, and with the knowledge that his father would be rapping on his door before the sun was up, he fell asleep.

Help us!

Save us!

Free us!

Calliope pressed her face deep into her mattress and pulled the pillow tighter over her head. She gritted her teeth. She wouldn't let them draw her out, wouldn't allow their calls to bring her back to the edge of the sea. Not again.

But she did.

She always did.

The voices could not be ignored.

She ran barefoot through the city in her nightgown, down to the cool water where there was nothing to do but sit listening to their screams, clasping and unclasping the Feather as it glowed across the gently pooling tide.

Help us! the voices shrieked as the stars trembled in the sky.

Save us! they begged as the moon clung to the sea.

Free us! they urged as Calliope hid her face in her arms.

"Please!" she whimpered. "I don't know what you want."

But the voices grew more and more insistent, until she could stand it no longer. "Leave me alone!" she cried.

A large black bird startled on one of the wooden bollards along the quay. Moonlight glittered in its feathers as it dove into the water without a splash. For a long moment, the surface was still, and then Calliope jumped as the bird reappeared in the shallows a few feet away. It waddled toward her, shuffling up onto the sand.

The hairs on Calliope's neck prickled. The bird was acting odd. Its neck convulsed, and it made strange hacking, choking sounds as it approached. It came closer and closer, until it was only inches from Calliope's hand, its wings glowing gold in the light from the Feather. Calliope pulled away, goose bumps racing up her arm.

The bird coughed and spat something round and glistening into the sand at her feet. A strange pearl, no larger than her pinkie nail, glinted icy blue in the moonlight.

The bird watched her with bead-black eyes, waiting.

Calliope bit her lip, leaning forward, stretching her fingers toward the pearl.

"Cal!" Prewitt's voice boomed behind her, and the bird spooked. With a flurry of feathers and a sprinkling of seawater, it dove back beneath the surface and disappeared into the night-black sea.

"There you are! I've been looking for you everywhere!"

Calliope's eyes flicked across the sand, her heart in her throat. The pearl was gone, washed away by the waves.

"Cal?" Prewitt's hand was gentle on her shoulder. He frowned down at her, and she was suddenly embarrassed.

Her brow furrowed, and her cheeks burned. Had he heard her talking to herself? Could he see how frightened she was? "What are you doing here, Prewitt?"

Prewitt flushed, and his fingers plucked at his jacket buttons as the words rushed from his lips.

"You have to come back to the castle right away. The Bookkeeper's returned!"

5

A large black horse was tied in the courtyard. Its sides were coated with sweat.

Calliope and Prewitt raced past it, bursting into the throne room, out of breath and panting. There, standing in the center of the moonlit throne room, oval spectacles gleaming, was the Bookkeeper.

His face was taut, and shadows stretched beneath his vivid blue eyes. His back was even more bent than usual, perhaps from hours of riding, and his hands trembled as he ran them over and over across his sweating scalp.

He looked small in the cavernous room, and for a moment, Calliope wanted to rush to him, to wrap her arms around his hunched frame. She wanted to tell him that she knew now why he had thrown himself into books, why stories seemed to be all that mattered to him. He had lost people he loved, and he was just trying to survive. She understood what that was like.

But the warmth she felt snuffed out as the Bookkeeper lunged toward her, pinning her with a ferocious gaze. His words came in a harsh whisper. "Did you do as I asked? Did you listen? Did you find a way to ignite the magic?"

Calliope swallowed. "I tried!"

Disappointment tautened the Bookkeeper's sallow cheeks.

"Thomas!" The Bargemaster burst into the room. His uniform was buttoned to the throat, and a fresh gray cap was pulled neatly down on his brow. Only his tired eyes gave any clue that he had been woken in the middle of the night.

Marisa followed close behind, tightening the knot in her threadbare robe, and Pyper hopped after her on one foot. Her tiny voice was exuberant. "I told you someone was here!"

"Yes, well done, dear." Marisa caressed the top of Pyper's head, pulling her close.

The three nameless girls peered around the doorframe, too timid to enter, their eyes bright as the windows overhead.

"Where have you been?" Calliope asked the Bookkeeper. "You promised you'd be back within a fortnight."

The Bookkeeper's hands shook as they fluttered across his scalp. "I thought I would be. But I was kept by a *story*."

"You mean you found the vault!" Calliope looked around. "But where are the books?"

The Bookkeeper's head swayed on his neck, and his shoulders slumped further. "I did find the vault. But the books were destroyed. Everything was burned, the vault, the library, the entire city of Lyda. There is nothing left."

Calliope's face fell. She had held out hope that the Book-keeper would return with answers. "Then what story did you find?"

"Yes, tell us, Bookkeeper. It must have been important to keep you so long." The Bargemaster's face was drawn.

The Bookkeeper's hands shook, but his words were clear and unfaltering. *"The Spectress has returned."*

Calliope took a step back. "That's impossible!" She swung toward Meredith. "You were there. You saw the Firebird defeat her!"

Meredith's face had gone gray, and the familiar strain returned to the corners of his eyes.

The Bookkeeper nodded. "They say she has risen, stronger and more powerful than before."

"*Who* says?" asked Meredith. *"Who makes these claims?"*

"The *Silver Shag.*"

The name slid across the throne room floor.

Calliope wrapped her arms around herself. "Who is that?"

"Precisely what I needed to find out. I knew I could not return without an answer. I wasted no time, riding through the villages, galloping through the forest and up the river, searching. But the people did not trust me. They would not respond to any of my questions.

"Fortunately, I am a man of keen observation. With growing foreboding, I noted that although they did not appear to have left their homes, and smoke did not rise from their chimneys, fresh bread and meat lay on their tables and newly woven blankets were heavy on their beds. Someone was providing for them while stoking their fear.

"I changed tack; instead of asking questions, I wondered aloud at these blessings. Their faces lit, their eyes shone, and they each said without failing, *'The Silver Shag has come.'*

"The Silver Shag arrived by cover of darkness, and she did not come alone. She leads a band of followers who call themselves the *Masked Rampage*. They dress in black cloaks and don silver masks with long, sharp beaks." The Bookkeeper's hand curved outward from his bulbous nose. "'The Silver Shag will keep us safe,' they said. 'She will protect us from the Spectress.'"

Meredith let out a huff of breath, ripping off his cap. "Protect them? Firebird feathers! There is nothing to protect against!"

"Why is she doing this?" said Calliope. The room spun around her, and sweat beaded on her forehead. "Why is the Silver Shag spreading lies? Why would the Masked Rampage want people to be afraid of something that isn't real?"

Everyone looked at the Bookkeeper. His face was grave. "That is why I've returned. I have discovered that it is all part of a plot to overthrow you and take the kingdom."

The news fell across the room, and no one moved.

"And there's more," said the Bookkeeper, the words stretched and strangled. "The Silver Shag does not want the throne for herself. She serves an Ancient Spirit."

Prewitt let out a shout of outrage. "If the Firebird wanted Spirits to rule, it would have given one of them its Feather. But it gave it to Cal."

The Bookkeeper spread his hands wide. "We know that. We were there. But the Silver Shag claims that our story of what happened in the caldera is a lie, a mere ruse for power. She insists that Calliope is not the true Queen of Lyrica, and instead, one of the first children of the Firebird, an Ancient Spirit, is Lyrica's rightful ruler. It is Spirit magic, she says, that will restore peace to the kingdom." His eyes met Calliope's. "Not a powerless child."

"She's not powerless," objected Prewitt. "She's got magic of her own. The magic of hope. Right, Cal?"

Calliope looked at her toes. She felt failure in every inch of her body, so heavy she couldn't breathe. The magic of hope. It was what had called the Firebird back, but it wasn't helping her now. She needed to find a way to ignite the Queen's magic—whatever that was. She needed answers, but the Bookkeeper had only brought more questions. She shifted, trying to think above the voices still screaming in her head. Without the magic, without the books, without her mother, she was lost. How could she keep the kingdom safe?

"Maybe the Silver Shag is right," she whispered. "Maybe a Spirit *could* keep everyone safe. That's more important to me than being Queen."

"Spirits!" Marisa spat. "Where were all the Spirits while the Spectress tortured us and burned our houses and killed our friends? They did nothing. They ran away. Don't doubt yourself for a moment, Highness. You are a descendant of the Firebird Queen. You are the right ruler for Lyrica. If you cannot keep us safe, no one can."

Prewitt stepped close, reaching for Calliope's hand. "It'll be okay," he said.

Calliope pulled away. "How? The people don't trust me. They won't even open their doors. It's been months since the Firebird returned, and the only thing I've managed to do is plant flowers."

The Bookkeeper groaned as he sat heavily down on the steps of the dais, his head in his hands. "If only the books had survived. Without their knowledge, without the Queen's wisdom, we are lost."

"We are not lost," snapped Meredith. "I'm not going to allow some *Masked Rampage* to come in and take over. Tell me, Bookkeeper, how do they travel? By river? By boat? Boat is the most logical way, especially at night, but they'd need lights to navigate. Someone would have seen them."

The Bookkeeper sniffed. "There *was* a child who claimed to have seen a ship. But—"

"There! You see?" Meredith pressed his cap back on his head, triumphant. "Tell me what it looked like and I will find the Silver Shag and put an end to this before it goes any further."

"The child said the ship flew no sigils, its sails were mere strips, and water poured from holes in the hull."

Meredith tugged at his mustache, drooping. "That doesn't make sense. A ship like that could never sail."

The Bookkeeper heaved his shoulders. "It is likely only a child's imagination running wild. No, it is not a ship we are looking for, Bargemaster. The Masked Rampage do not come by boat, or horse, or foot."

The room was silent. What other way was there?

"The Masked Rampage comes by *air*."

Eight sets of eyes blinked.

"*Yes.*" The Bookkeeper's words were a whispered hiss: "*They fly.*"

"Emperor above," whispered Marisa. "Spirit magic!"

Calliope couldn't move, couldn't think past the agonizing voices in her mind. She tried to keep her face from crumpling as she turned toward the windows, fighting to compose herself. Moonlight filtered through the cracked stained glass, and broken fragments of Queens past shone down on her. How she wished they could speak to her, could tell her what to do.

The Bookkeeper stepped close. His whisper was urgent, and his breath was hot in her ear. "You *must* listen for the Song. Find the magic that was meant to protect the Queens. It is the only way."

Calliope whirled on him. "I tried! I did what you said, and it made everything worse!"

Help us!

Save us!

Free us!

Calliope clamped her hands over her ears. "Stop it!" she shouted. "I don't know how to help you! I don't know how to help anyone! Can't you see I'm alone?"

Everyone in the room froze.

"You're not alone, Cal," said Prewitt, not able to keep the hurt from his voice. "I'm here."

Meredith cleared his throat, his eyes shifting back and forth between the Bookkeeper and Calliope. "I think we could

41

all use a break. Everyone go and get some rest. I will stand guard, and we will come up with a plan in the morning."

Calliope didn't wait. She rushed from the throne room, brushing past the three girls who were crying and clutching one another. "You'll keep us safe, won't you?" one of them whispered. "You won't let the Spectress come back and hurt us again."

Calliope didn't answer. Her feet tripped over the wrinkled carpet as she ran down the hall, and the Bookkeeper's voice chased after her. "*Listen*, Calliope. *Listen*, or lose your kingdom forever."

6

Calliope ran until she found herself in front of a door. She hadn't planned to come here. She didn't know where she had planned to go.

The door was made of pine planks, the same that were being used to repair the boats in the harbor.

The old door had burned to nothing, leaving a hole like a gaping wound. It was the first thing Calliope had asked Meredith to do after they'd returned—make a new door to the nursery, a solid, sturdy door that could be locked.

But no door could keep away the fear and pain of the past. No lock could erase Calliope's memory, or take away the words that she knew were still on the wall behind the door: *Wind, Woman, Thief.*

Unbidden, the scene rose again in her mind. The storm glass, dark as night, lifted in her mother's fragile fingers, the sound as it shattered across the carpet.

Black sand, broken glass, a sharp fragment slicing through a delicate palm.

Calliope had only been a baby when it happened, but months ago, she had been forced to live it all again in a moon memory. She had watched as her mother had used her own blood to paint the desperate message across the wall—a message that would save her kingdom.

But it wouldn't save *her*.

Calliope hadn't seen what happened next, but she hadn't needed to. No one in the castle survived the Spectress's monsters that night—the night of the Terrible Thing.

The memory was excruciating no matter how many times it played in her mind. It always felt as real as if it were happening that very moment, and anything could trigger it. A candlestick, a tapestry, a fragment of a dress her mother might have worn.

How could she move forward with constant charred reminders of her mother's absence all around her? She had asked Marisa and Meredith to put it all inside the room, and she had ordered the door to be locked.

Why had she come here now?

Calliope was flooded with desperate loneliness. It was all too much—the voices she didn't understand, the magic she couldn't find, and now, this Silver Shag and the unknown Spirit who wanted to take over the kingdom.

Calliope knew by the feeling in her gut that her people were in grave danger, but what could she do?

She looked down at the Feather. If only the Firebird had

given her more. She didn't know how to protect people, how to keep them from being afraid. She didn't know how to erase the past from their memories and help them to move forward. She needed someone who would understand, someone who could help; she needed her mother.

She pulled a heavy key from her pocket. But before she could put it in the lock, she hesitated, chiding herself. What would going inside accomplish? Her mother would not be there. Calliope was lying to herself, searching for comfort that didn't exist.

Calliope turned away and slid to the floor. She stuffed the key into her pocket, and her fingers brushed the well-worn piece of parchment. She drew it out, unfolding it.

Her mother smiled up from the page. She was dressed in red silk, and an ornate golden crown studded with pearls rested on her black curls. In her fingertips was the Feather.

Calliope ran her finger across the raised brushstrokes. Her mother looked so powerful: a Queen people could trust. Calliope's eyes burned with tears she refused to cry. She leaned her head against the smooth door, the smell of pine enveloping her.

"Queen Calliope?"

Calliope stiffened. "Please don't call me that."

"I'm sorry, dear," said Marisa, shaking her head. "This must all be so hard for you." Her gaze flicked to the door, a question in her eyes.

"I just wanted to be close to her," said Calliope, her voice small.

Marisa nodded. "Of course you did. Would you like to go inside?"

Calliope shook her head. "What good would it do?" Her lip trembled. "She can't help me. She can't tell me what to do. She's gone."

"It might help you feel—"

"You don't understand!" said Calliope. "I can't waste time *feeling*. I have to put the past in the past."

"But it's a part of your story, dear. It's natural to—"

"No." Calliope held up the Feather. "This is my story now. The kingdom is all that matters. I have to find a way to protect them, to get them to trust me. I need answers, and I won't find them here."

Marisa was quiet for a moment, and then she reached out her hand.

"Come with me. I want to show you something."

7

The Firebird's wings were crimson, and its eyes were glittering rubies gazing inscrutably down at the girl who knelt before it. She was small and plainly dressed, her dark curls a mass over one shoulder, and in the Firebird's sharp beak was a crown.

Calliope reached out to the mural. She could almost feel the flames from the Firebird's draping tail.

Marisa cleared her throat and Calliope jumped.

"The Bookkeeper asked the Queen to remove all his wife's paintings, and she did. All except this one." Marissa's mouth lifted at the corner. "The Bookkeeper never found out, because he never would have come here. You see, this was your mother's dressing room."

Calliope touched the Firebird's wing. It was hard to believe it was only paint. The colors were too vibrant, the figures too lifelike.

"People often forget that the Firebird made the child Queen

over all of Lyrica—not just humans, but Spirits, too. Only the Firebird had the authority to do this. It is the most powerful of all Spirits—except perhaps the Demon."

"I know," said Calliope. She had heard the story many times, had read it herself when she lived on the Barge in the Sacred Cavern. "The Firebird was the one who created all the Ancient Spirits. The Spirits of the Land, the Wind, the Sea, and the Sky. It gave them the power to create lesser spirits of their own."

"Yes," said Marisa. "All that power originated from the Firebird. It could have chosen any of them to rule, but instead it chose a human child. It gave her a Feather—the same one you hold in your hand. You will find a way to keep everyone safe. I know you will, and we will be here with you."

Calliope let her gaze drift across the painting. Around the girl were other figures—animals, humans, and spirits.

"She was meant to unite the kingdom," said Marisa. "To be Queen of both spirits and humans."

Calliope shifted, wanting to tell Marisa what the Bookkeeper had said about the Queen's magic, but not sure if she should. The Bookkeeper had been so insistent that she keep it a secret. But she needed help, and she knew that Marisa wouldn't laugh at her or tell her that it was a fairy tale. So she took a breath and let the words come.

Marisa listened and nodded. "I have not heard that before, but I am old enough to believe that anything is possible."

"The Bookkeeper said that the magic had been lost somehow. He thought that its secret must have something to do with the Song." Calliope stepped closer to the mural, looking up into the gray-green eyes of the first Queen. They were the same age. They had the same onyx curls, the same sun-gold skin. "If only I could talk to her." She turned back to Marisa. "You said that Spirit magic is dangerous for humans."

Marisa nodded. "It is not a door that should be opened lightly."

Calliope swallowed. It was too late. She had already opened the door, had reached for the magic, and *something* bad had happened.

Marisa put her arm around Calliope's shoulder, giving her a squeeze. "Don't worry, Highness. I know that you will find a way to keep your people safe—magic or not."

Calliope's eyes burned, and she avoided Marisa's gaze, looking instead at the mural. The great painting wrapped around the turret in a cascade of white-capped sea waves, and Calliope could almost hear the water crashing into the bird-scattered rocks.

She blinked. "Marisa, what are these black birds called?"

"Those are cormorants. The Sentinels of the Sea."

"One came up to me earlier. It was acting so strange. It coughed a pearl into the sand."

Marisa tensed, and Calliope thought she saw fear in her eyes. "Was it blue?"

Calliope nodded. "How did you know?"

Marisa's hand flinched on Calliope's shoulder. "Did you pick it up?"

Calliope shook her head. "No. The waves washed it away before I could."

Marisa sighed, and Calliope could see the relief in Marisa's face as she looked back at the mural. For a moment, she seemed to be searching for something; then she pointed at the waves. "Look, here. What do you see?"

Calliope squinted. At first, she couldn't see anything, but then she made it out—a figure. It seemed to be a woman made entirely of water. Something in her posture was unsettling. She was looking up at the girl and the Firebird, and Calliope could sense that she was dreadfully unhappy.

"Who is it?" she asked.

"That is the Spirit of the Suffering Sea," said Marisa. "She steals the stories of those who suffer and uses them to grow in power. Legend has it that she gained incredible strength during the last Dark Age and filled the sea with spirits and monsters. But when the first Queen called the Firebird back with hope, the suffering ended. There were no more stories to steal, and the Spirit became weak. For a thousand years she has been trying to get her power back." Marisa's words were smooth, but her voice was serious as she continued.

"When I was young, not much older than you, a boy I loved lost his father. His mother lay in bed, day after day, refusing to eat or drink, and her son stayed with her. Then, one morning, while the pain of heartbreak was still fresh, a pearl the color of ice on the sea appeared on their windowsill.

"When the boy's mother took the pearl, her sorrows melted away."

Help us!

Save us!

Free us!

The voices pounded in Calliope's head, and she rubbed her temples, trying to tune them out. She thought of the pearl that the bird had dropped at her feet. "It seems kind," she said. "To take away someone's sadness."

Marisa reached out, tucking a stray curl behind Calliope's ear. "I know it seems that way. But that's not the end of the story. After my friend's mother took the pearl, after she traded away her sorrow, she became someone else. She was no longer the person she'd been, no longer had a connection with her son. He was left alone with his grief, and he never recovered."

Marisa pulled back, looking Calliope in the eyes. "Taking a part of someone's story, even a painful part, is not a kindness."

Calliope's eyes dropped. She wasn't sure she understood. It still seemed like kindness to her. She thought about the room that held the memory of her mother, of all the loss and sorrow in her past.

She reached out, tracing the figure of the Sea Spirit. What would it have felt like if she'd taken the pearl? Could she have finally stopped missing her mother so much? Would her loneliness have faded? Would the voices, shouting in her head, have stopped? If she had picked up the pearl and silenced the voices, would she have finally heard the Song and found a way to reconnect with the Queen's magic?

"Princess," said Marisa. "It isn't just the mural that I wanted to show you."

She gently steered Calliope across to a folding screen, near the far end of the room, and pushed it back.

There on a low table, cushioned by a bundle of red silk, was the Queen's crown. Jewels and pearls had been added over the years, but there was no doubt that it was the same one that the Firebird had given the first Firebird Queen.

"Where did you find it?" Calliope whispered, unable to keep the awe from her voice.

Marisa smiled. "It was still in the royal vault—a miracle really. It was a bit charred, and I wasn't sure I would be able to salvage it, but a few weeks and some elbow grease and it's as good as new." She lifted it from the cushion. "I know you haven't had your official coronation yet, but you *are* the Queen. If you are going to show people that you are the rightful ruler of Lyrica, I think you need to wear the crown." She held it out, and it shimmered in the low light. "Are you ready?"

Calliope nodded, her throat tight.

Marisa tilted her chin at a row of dressing mirrors on the wall, and Calliope turned toward them.

Marisa raised the crown and placed it gently in Calliope's curls.

Calliope took in her reflection. As she stared at her face beneath the crown, she was hit with the realization that the last person who had worn it had been her mother. Had she stood just like this, gazing at herself in the mirror? What had she felt? Surely, she hadn't been as afraid and uncertain as Calliope was now.

Instead of making her feel like a Queen, the crown made her feel like a child playing dress-up. She felt like an imposter.

She didn't want a crown. She wanted her mother to be alive. She reached up and yanked the crown from her head.

"I can't. I'm sorry." She shoved the crown into Marisa's hands. "Please, take it away. Take it and lock it in the nursery with the rest of my mother's things."

She didn't stay to hear Marisa's reply. Instead, she ran to her room and crawled into bed, pulling the covers up to her chin. But although she closed her eyes and wished for it, sleep did not come.

8

Calliope was not the only one who couldn't sleep.

Someone else was awake, black ponytail swishing down her back, muscles rippling as a whip cracked against the night. Ilsbeth's breath was hot, and droplets of sweat slid down her high cheeks. The night air was cool in her nostrils as she coiled the whip and tucked it into her belt. She bent to a pool at the center of the cove and splashed her face. The moon shone in the water, and for a moment she thought of the Spirits of the Halcyon Glade. They had run away into a moon memory when Lyrica needed them most. She smacked the surface, sending up a spray of water. Then she straightened and broke into a sprint.

A small brown fledgling gripped her shoulder as she raced along the sandy pathway. Her father had given her the peregrine the day they'd returned from fighting the Spectress in the caldera. It had been a tiny, gawky thing, covered in light-brown fuzz.

It is yours to train, he'd said in his brusque way. *Keep it close until it fledges—until it flies.*

He had shown her how to feed it from her hand as it grew, and when it was time for it to fledge, he had tied bells around its ankle so that she would always know where it was.

He'd told her to name it and to call it by its name. But Ilsbeth had refused. A named thing was a kept thing, and the moment the Falconer had given her the peregrine, she had known she would set it free.

She hadn't said that to her father. It had been clear that the bird was a bridge—an attempt to connect them. But they had nothing to talk about, and when they were together, they spent most of their time in silence.

He didn't ask her questions about her life so far, about growing up in the Halcyon Glade with danger always on her mind. She did not tell him how she had trained without resting so that she would be ready when the day came to leave and fight the Spectress. And of course, it had come, and she had faced the Demon in the heart of the volcano, and she had not been afraid. She had known that as long as she had her whip, she could defeat any monster—spirit or human.

A roar broke through her thoughts, as if to challenge them. Her fingers flinched on the handle of her whip, but she did not slow her steps. She raced toward the sound, picking up pace, pushing herself harder and harder, enjoying the way her lungs tightened and her heart pounded.

She could smell the salty breath of the sea, and she soon

reached a deep pit that filled with seawater, burbling and bubbling, rising up in a rush and then falling away.

There was no indication of where the water came from or where it went. It could have been the sea's mouth, gulping the water and spewing it back out again.

Ilsbeth set her jaw. The only way to enter or leave the cove was by surrendering to the sea. She watched it, her knees bent, as she matched her breaths to the rise and fall of the tide.

She had faced ash golems. She had trained with the Spirits in the Halcyon Glade. She was not afraid of *this*.

The sea snarled, surging upward and drenching her, daring her to step closer, taunting her as it had since the day she first laid eyes on it when she had stared out at its vast wildness, and felt a foreign sense of panic. Here, at last, was a monster her whip could not tame.

Ilsbeth had hated the way the sea made her feel, small and powerless, and she had forced herself to face it. Each day she had sat alone on the steps, glaring out at the endless blue-black void. Each time she felt the tingling prickle of fear, she had punished herself by moving closer to the waves.

That was how Jack had found her. She recognized the boy from their trip home on the *Queen's Barge*. He was easy to spot even from afar in his oversize blue waterman coat, his long, dark plait sleek down his back.

He had hauled a pile of nets across the beach and up the steps, plopping himself down beside her. His hands had worked with the thick nets, and they had sat together in silence for a long time until suddenly they had heard it, a tiny, desperate mewling. They had glanced at each other.

"Did you hear that?" Jack had asked.

Ilsbeth had nodded once.

It hadn't taken them long to find the kitten. Its paw had gotten caught on a piece of driftwood, and it was soaked and trembling. Its ears were tattered, its tail was broken, and its eyes were crusted shut with salt water.

Jack had reached out a gentle hand, and the kitten had hissed and sunken its sharp teeth into his finger.

Ilsbeth had expected him to jerk away and leave the kitten where it was, but instead, Jack had soothed it. "Shh . . . It's okay, you're okay," he'd said, and gently worked her leg free. Then he had scooped the gray kitten up and tucked it inside his jacket.

Ilsbeth had watched, amazed, as Jack rocked and shushed and sang to the kitten, and after a moment, a purr had rumbled from within the dense fabric. Jack had laughed, delighted, and for an instant, Ilsbeth's guard had slipped. She had almost wanted to smile.

Jack's eyes caught hers and she looked quickly away.

"It must be hard for you," Jack had said, his voice as gentle as it had been with the kitten.

"What do you mean?" Ilsbeth had bristled, and her legs had tensed, ready to send her racing back up the stairs.

"Being alone. After all, you've been with the other girls your whole life. I know you've found your families, but I wonder if it somehow feels like you've lost your family, too."

Ilsbeth had been taken aback. That was exactly how it felt. Without the Glade Girls, she felt so weak and empty that she knew that if the sea ever snatched her, she'd float away forever into its depth—a tree uprooted and hollowed out. But those were emotions she would never have shared. Not with Jack, and not with her sisters. She had seen the joy in their eyes as they had joined their families, and she had given them encouraging nods even as she had ached in secret.

But standing there with Jack, Ilsbeth had felt her eyes prickle, and she had been furious, wanting to snap at him, to tell him he was wrong.

But Jack's face had been so kind that instead she had nodded, just once, and said, "It is . . . not easy."

Jack's cheek had dimpled. "I know it isn't the same as having your sisters back, but you can talk to me if you want."

It was such a generous gesture, so free of expectation, and Ilsbeth had wanted desperately to trust him. She had spoken on impulse, the words out before she could steal them back. "Show me a place where I can train. Someplace no one will bother me, where the sea cannot sweep me away."

And he had.

Now, standing before the sea's mouth just as Jack had shown her all those weeks before, Ilsbeth took a breath, gathering all her courage, and leaped into the pit.

For a moment she fell, and then a rush of icy water met her, launching her up through the darkness.

She grabbed for the rocks at the top and hauled herself out, soaked and panting. She lay, trying to catch her breath, and was about to sit up when she heard a strange creaking, grinding sound. She tensed, listening.

Unfamiliar voices drifted across the rocks, low and cautious, and it was clear that they did not want to be overheard. The dark hairs on Ilsbeth's forearms lifted. No one should be near the cove entrance in the middle of the night. Even during the day, that part of the beach was always deserted.

She rolled onto her stomach, inching across the rock, and hushed words drifted toward her.

"Keep out of sight. Wait for the right moment."

The sweat on Ilsbeth's brow ran cold. She pushed herself onto her elbows, peering over the edge of the rocks.

There, floating on the moonlit waves, was a ruin of a ship. It was so wrecked that even Ilsbeth knew it should not be seaworthy. Thick green algae, barnacles, and mussels clung to a hull full of holes. The keel was smashed, as if it had run aground, and the sails were rustling tatters.

Silver light outlined the silhouettes of a thousand black birds lining the gunwales, perched along leaning masts, and roosted in rusty, creaking rigging.

Ilsbeth crept farther out, crawling on her belly along the rough rocks. The skirt of her white dress caught, and she reached to pull it free.

A hand locked on to hers.

She rolled to the side, her dress tearing, her whip in her left hand. Her wrist flicked back just as Jack's face loomed above her, a warning finger firm against his lips.

Ilsbeth relaxed, scowling up at him. He should have known better than to sneak up on her.

The kitten, who had earned the moniker Urchin, clung to Jack's shoulder, tail swishing beside the boy's long black plait.

Ilsbeth turned back to the ship, searching for the source of the voices, but there was no one there. The ship was silent, and whoever had spoken was gone.

She scanned the water. It was free from anything but the waves breaking against the rocks.

"This does not make sense," she whispered. "There were at least a dozen people here. I heard their voices. Where could they have gone?"

Jack's dark eyes swept the cliffs. Their steep sides were black and drenched with seawater. "Something about this doesn't feel right," he said.

Ilsbeth didn't stay to talk it through; she flung herself down from the rock, landing on her feet in the sand. "We have to warn the Princess."

9

Prewitt was doing everything he could to keep his eyes open. He walked back and forth across the pavers, counting his echoing footsteps.

"Go to bed, son," said the Bargemaster. He stood in the moonlight at the edge of the courtyard, his alert eyes scanning the city below.

"No, I can do this. I can help."

The Bargemaster nodded. "Then be still and *watch*."

Prewitt came to stand by Meredith, gaze trailing across the sleeping buildings, the moon-swept waves, the silhouette of clouds billowing across the stars.

"What are we going to do if the Silver Shag comes?" Prewitt asked.

"We will do what we always do—we will keep the Queen safe."

"By ourselves?"

"If we must."

Prewitt shifted his weight. He looked out at the dark tree line and imagined the Silver Shag and her Masked Rampage hiding within the forest, waiting to attack and take the castle for some unnamed Spirit.

"What if the Spirit is with them?" he asked.

"Then we will fight it too." His father's hand rested on the hilt of his sword.

Prewitt scowled. "I wish I were *swayed*. If I were *swayed*, I'd probably be a great warrior."

Meredith's eyes lifted to the stars, and he huffed out his breath. "You *can be* a great warrior, Prewitt. It takes no magic. It takes determination, a teacher, and dedicated practice."

"Yeah, I know, but if I were *swayed*, then I wouldn't have to waste time doing all that. I could be a warrior now! I could protect Calliope from the Silver Shag all by myself." Prewitt spun in a circle, holding out an imaginary sword. He thrust and parried and tripped over a rock.

He looked at Meredith to see if his father had noticed.

Meredith's eyes had not left the city. "Don't get caught up in wishing, Prewitt. Real magic is in hard work. It's in dedication. We earn it by showing up day after day, focusing on our duties, whether we feel like it or not. There are no shortcuts."

"I just want to be able to help."

"Then do the work. Work is your magic."

Prewitt sighed. "I've been doing it, haven't I? I haven't even complained!"

Meredith's eyebrow raised.

"Much," Prewitt amended. He sighed. It didn't feel magical when he was pulled out of bed before the sun, or mopping the deck in the heat, or pounding nails into planks with rusted hammers in sore hands.

"I just want to be able to help. I want to do something that matters. You said that I'd be ready for the adventure when it came, but I don't see how working on the boats is making me ready. I—"

Meredith stiffened. "Quiet! Someone's coming."

Prewitt held his breath, following his father's gaze. Two figures were dashing up the steps toward the clifftop.

Prewitt squinted. Buttons flashed on a jacket, and he made out the tiny form of a small bedraggled cat on a shoulder. "It's all right. It's only Jack," he said. Prewitt saw the second figure, dressed in white, bounding up the stairs ahead of Jack. "And that must be Ilsbeth."

Meredith nodded. "You're right. Well done, Prewitt." His eyes sparkled. "Maybe you're *swayed* after all—*exceptional* eyesight. Now, wouldn't that be one for the books?"

Prewitt groaned. "That's not what I had in mind."

Ilsbeth ran into the courtyard. "I need to speak to Queen Calliope."

"Why? What's wrong?" Prewitt asked, but Ilsbeth shook her head.

"Not you. *The Queen.*"

"Can't this wait until morning?" asked Meredith.

Ilsbeth shook her head again, jaw set. Jack appeared, breathless, and Prewitt saw the fear on his friend's face.

He frowned. "It's all right, Dad. I'll take them."

"Well, okay," said the Bargemaster. "But keep it short."

Prewitt tried to ask the others more questions as he led the way across the throne room and through the corridors, but Ilsbeth wasn't listening. She pushed past him, racing ahead.

Prewitt looked at Jack, incredulous. "She doesn't even know where she's going."

"Then *lead*, Bargeboy," Ilsbeth snapped over her shoulder.

"I'm trying! But you have to actually *follow*."

Ilsbeth's eyes blazed, and Jack stepped between them. "We saw a ship!" he said. "Well, a ship*wreck*. There were people on it—we heard them talking—but then they vanished."

Prewitt's stomach lurched. The wrecked ship! Just like the child had told the Bookkeeper!

The Silver Shag was here.

Prewitt didn't wait; he raced through the hallways, the others close behind. When he reached Calliope's door, he hesitated only a moment, then raised his hand. But before he could knock, the door flung open, and Calliope nearly crashed into him.

Prewitt gaped at her. "Are you going somewhere? You can't go anywhere! It isn't safe! You have to stay in the castle."

Ilsbeth didn't wait for Calliope's answer. She pushed past Prewitt into Calliope's room, reporting what they had seen in quick, keen detail.

There was a long silence as the three children waited for Calliope to say something.

But Calliope just stood, knitting her brows and clasping and unclasping her hands around the golden Feather.

"Maybe I should get Dad," said Prewitt, eyeing the door.

"No!" The word was sharp, and they all spun toward Calliope. "No, we can't tell him. If we tell him, he'll make me stay inside. He'll force me to go back to the Sacred Cavern and hide on the Barge again."

"But you *should* stay inside!" said Prewitt. "The Silver Shag is here for you. She *must* be."

Ilsbeth glared at him. "The Silver Shag? Who is the Silver Shag?"

Prewitt quickly explained, expecting Ilsbeth would nod and agree that Calliope needed to stay in the castle. But instead, she rounded on Calliope. "You cannot stay here. You have to do something! You must convince everyone that the Silver Shag is lying. You must prove that the Spectress is *not* back."

The flames in the lantern flickered, and the cat leaped off Jack's shoulder, attacking the shadows on the wall.

"I don't understand why people just listen to this Shag person," said Prewitt. "Why can't they believe that the Spectress is really gone?"

"I think I understand why," said Jack. "The four of us were there when the Firebird returned, so we know what really happened. But no one else saw. They just woke up and things were different. All those years of fear had no place to go. It got caught inside."

He held out his arm toward the flame in the lantern, and he swallowed hard. "I have to *force* myself to stand so close to fire." He moved his hand back and forth, and they saw that his forearm was covered in goose bumps. "See? Even though I *know* the truth, I *know* that the ash golems won't come, my body tells me something different. Every single muscle wants me to run away."

The lantern crackled, and he yanked his arm back.

"Here, Urchin," he called, and the cat leaped into his arms, purring. He turned back to Calliope. "I lost my parents to the Spectress," he said. "Her marauders killed them before I ever got to know them. I would do anything to keep that from happening to someone else. I understand why people want to believe the Silver Shag's promises. They want to feel safe—whatever it takes."

Prewitt played with the buttons on his jacket. "If only we could erase everyone's memories of the Spectress. Then it wouldn't matter if the Silver Shag told them lies or not. Her only power comes from reminding people of how bad things used to be."

Ilsbeth crossed her arms. "Power is power, wherever it comes from, and we must take it away before it grows any stronger."

Calliope's thoughts drifted back to Marisa's story about the Spirit of the Sea and the pearl that could take away suffering, and she wished again that she had one or, better yet, a thousand to give to all her people.

She glanced up and caught the others staring at her. She turned away, facing the lantern. Inside the smoky glass, the flames danced. There was nothing to fear. She *knew* that. But her people did not.

Calliope couldn't wait to find a way to use Spirit magic. She had to do something *now*.

She twirled the Firebird Feather slowly between her fingers, her heart thrumming. For months she had tried to make them see that they were safe, but it hadn't worked, and now, they were out of time. The time for patience was over; the time for planting flowers had ended.

She held out her hand, letting the warmth of the fire turn her palm rosy.

Her people did not need the protection of the Silver Shag and her mysterious Spirit. Calliope could keep them safe, and she was going to prove it.

She turned to the others.

"I have a plan."

10

No one in the crowd made a sound as Calliope raised the unlit torch.

Help us!

Save us!

Free us!

Calliope gritted her teeth against the voices shouting across the water. *Not now.* She could only deal with one problem at a time, and this was the one she knew how to solve . . . At least, she hoped she did.

The people were packed together, stretched across the beach, tucked so closely that they must hear one another's anxious breathing. Calliope scanned the crowd. Was the Silver Shag among them?

People glanced furtively at their neighbors, but no one spoke. They had been ordered there, the Queen's command shouted through the streets by the Bargeboy. Calliope hadn't been certain it would work, but Prewitt had reassured her. "No one will disobey a royal command. Especially not in the middle of the night!"

He'd been right; even Meredith had tramped down the stairs, the rest of the family in tow. Questions deepened every crevice of his face, but he had not asked them. He had only gone and stood nearby, stiff and wary.

Somehow, that made Calliope even more nervous. Was her idea truly a good one?

Prewitt shifted beside Calliope. A flint was heavy and awkward in his palm. "Let's get this over with," he whispered.

Calliope felt the sting of uncertainty. Just the sight of the flint, the torch, and the unlit driftwood piled high at the edge of the beach had been enough to make people cower.

Calliope knew that there was nothing left to fear in fire. The Spectress and her ash golems were gone. People did not need to be afraid. Would forcing them to see the truth be enough to calm their fears and help them move forward? Would it be enough to prove that the Silver Shag was not someone they could trust?

In the crowd, a woman sobbed, and a little boy turned his face into his father's shirt.

Calliope's throat was tight as her eyes raked the tiers, searching the shadows for silver masks. Her head tilted to the sky, as if she might catch sight of the Silver Shag swooping down from the stars. If the Silver Shag was here, where was she? Where was the Masked Rampage?

Calliope's skin was alive with nerves that hummed so loudly she was certain the crowd would hear.

"Just do it," Ilsbeth whispered. "There is no time to hesitate." She stood beside a moonlit tide pool, her white dress billowing in the night breeze. Her bronze shoulders were taut, and the muscles in her arms were rigid.

As the people had gathered, Ilsbeth had raced from Glade Girl to Glade Girl, pleading with them in urgent whispers, but their parents had pulled them close and waved Ilsbeth away.

"Please," said Ilsbeth now, and Calliope could see how much begging cost her.

Calliope nodded, turning to the crowd and holding the torch higher. The Feather glowed at her waist, and she let its comforting light urge her on. "People of the Royal City, I brought you here tonight to show you the truth. Someone has been spreading lies, telling you that the Spectress is still in power, but I promise that cannot be. The Firebird returned, the Demon has been defeated, and there is nothing more to fear!"

Calliope turned toward Prewitt. "Light the torch, Barge-boy!" Her voice rang across the night. Somewhere in the dark, a chorus of birds jeered, but the crowd was silent, waiting, watching as Prewitt struggled with the flint.

For an excruciating moment, Calliope held the torch, and Prewitt fumbled, striking again and again. Each shower of sparks sent the crowd flinching backward. Urchin hissed on Jack's shoulder. But the torch would not light.

Ilsbeth snarled. "You are making them nervous! Give it to me." She snatched the flint, striking it close to the torch, and at last it caught. She pursed her lips and blew until the flames blazed hot and wild.

The crowd sucked in a breath, terror in the growing whites of their eyes.

Calliope raised the torch high. "No! Don't be afraid! Can't you see? The Spectress is gone! You are free! You are *safe*." For a split second, she hesitated, and then she flung the torch down onto the pile of driftwood.

Sparks scattered across the sand, and the crowd jerked collectively backward. The flames nibbled, and then gnawed, and finally gobbled down the driftwood, snarling blue teeth snapping at the stars. All around, the firelight danced in the reflecting tide pools at their feet.

The crowd began to relax, their tension easing as the heat from the fire warmed the air and no monsters appeared. A man laughed, and then another. On and on the laughter caught, shimmering across the crowd. People began to look one another in the eye. What had they been so worried about?

A mother released her child's hand, and he toddled forward, squatting down to inspect a tide pool. He prodded the flames' reflection with a fat finger. They rippled and jigged, and instead of showing fear, his eyes were bright and curious.

Calliope smiled. "It's working," she whispered.

Prewitt grinned back. "You were right! I *knew* it was a good idea."

A flash of something silver caught Calliope's eye, and she grabbed Prewitt's wrist.

His smile faltered. "What is it? What's wrong?"

Calliope blinked. She had caught the glitter of a curving bird's beak in the swarm of faces. But now, it was gone; the masked figure had vanished.

"I saw one of them! One of the Masked Rampage. I'm sure I did. But . . . where did they go?"

A scream shattered the night.

"Ash golems! The ash golems are here!"

The crowd erupted.

"It's not true. It can't be true," Calliope whispered.

But it was. All around, ash golems were rising, swelling, growing ever larger.

They were bigger than Calliope and Prewitt remembered. Their hulking shapes sparked and roiled as they stalked across the beach, their mouths yawning, their bellies molten hot and starving.

"Where did they come from?" asked Ilsbeth, pulling her whip from her belt.

"Urchin, wait!" Jack's cat screeched and launched itself off his shoulder, racing away through the galloping crowd. "Urchin! Urchin, come back!"

"Jack, don't!" cried Calliope. But Jack had vanished into the crowd.

The golems roiled through the tide pools, growing larger, veins burning brighter.

"I don't get it!" said Prewitt. "They shouldn't be able to move through water. They couldn't before!"

Calliope shook her head, trying to make sense of it. "They're stronger this time. I don't underst—" A *sound* crashed so suddenly against Calliope's skull that she stumbled backward.

This was nothing like the voices that shrieked from across the sea. This was something new, something that took her breath away and made her knees buckle. It hammered behind her eyes, and she pressed her hands against her ears, her face twisted in agony.

"Cal? Cal! What's wrong?"

She could barely hear Prewitt's voice. The hollow chord collided in chilling waves against her skull. She squeezed her eyes shut as a frigid feeling of emptiness rushed through her head. It stung her eyes and ached in her molars.

The fledgling bated on Ilsbeth's shoulder, and Ilsbeth reached up a hand. "Fly! Fly away! I do not want you here!" The bird shifted, tilting its head back and forth, but it did not leave. Ilsbeth scowled. "You foolish bird."

She turned toward Calliope. Calliope's hands were pushed so hard against her ears that Ilsbeth could see the bones of her knuckles through her skin, and tears leaked from the corners of her tightly shut eyes. "What is happening to her?" Ilsbeth asked.

"I don't know!" Prewitt's voice squeaked. "We have to do something!" He flung himself at Calliope, grabbing her shoulders, shouting her name, but she did not answer.

"Stop it," snapped Ilsbeth. "She cannot hear you." Her fingers tensed around the handle of her whip, but she refused to let her panic go any further. She slowed her breathing and sharpened her focus on the beach.

All around, people were sobbing and screaming, grabbing for their children and hugging them close. Ilsbeth did not have to search for her father; she knew that he had not come. She imagined him still in the falconry, his growling voice urging the birds to calm. Would her safety even cross his mind? She let out her breath. It did not matter. She could handle herself.

Another strangled cry broke through her thoughts as someone shrieked. "The Spectress! Oh, spirits help us! It's the Spectress!"

Prewitt's and Ilsbeth's eyes locked, and they turned in unison.

There she was, not ten feet away. The Spectress's white veil rippled around her, and she spread her arms wide, her nails sharp as claws, her teeth a menacing flash of perfect white.

The entire beachfront was a chaos of erupting sand and trampling feet as people slipped across wet driftwood, pushing and shoving to get—where? They did not know.

"I don't understand," said Prewitt. "How is this possible? We saw her defeated! We saw Calliope send her away. She wasn't like this anymore."

Ilsbeth squinted, tuning out Prewitt's babbling as she tried to make sense of what she was seeing. "This is a trick. It cannot be the Spectress."

"You're right, girl." The Bookkeeper appeared beside them, firelight flickering in the oval glass of his spectacles. "Not everything is as it seems." His inky fingers smoothed the top of his spotted pate as he peered into Calliope's twisted face.

"Highness? Tell me what you hear!"

"She won't answer!" said Prewitt. "I tried!"

But Calliope did answer, although her teeth were gritted, and the words were barely audible. "I—I don't know. It's—a sound—something I've never heard but—but it's . . . more than that. It's a *feeling*. A hollow, horrible feeling." She shuddered. "I feel cold and empty and—and—" She broke off in a sob.

Ilsbeth's head whipped toward Calliope and Prewitt caught the movement. "What?" he asked. "What is it? What's happening to her, Ilsbeth? Tell us!"

Ilsbeth took a moment to settle her thoughts before speaking. Then her words were careful. "The Queen is hearing Spirit magic."

The Bookkeeper's face lit, and he turned back to Calliope. "Highness," he shouted. "The *sound* you hear could be the source of the Queen's magic. Don't struggle against it. Let it come! Reach out and take it!"

"No!" said Ilsbeth. She turned to Prewitt, and her eyes were grave. "I grew up among spirits, but even I cannot hear the *sound* of their magic—for good reason. Humans cannot touch Spirit magic. If Calliope tries, she will not survive."

The Bookkeeper's glasses blazed. "She is the daughter of a Firebird Queen! The magic is in her blood. It is her destiny."

Prewitt's eyes darted to the Spectress. She sauntered across the beach, reaching down into the tide pools and pulling up a fistful of dripping flames. Her head flung back on her delicate neck, and her shoulders shook as if in laughter, but no sound came from her lips.

Ilsbeth huffed out a breath. "Enough of this." She pulled her whip from her belt.

"Ilsbeth, wait." Prewitt grabbed for her, but she was already gone.

A guttural cry tore from her throat as she raced forward, her whip held high. She flung it out, and with a *crack*, it struck the Spectress high on the cheek.

The Spectress turned, her eyes finding Ilsbeth. She took a menacing step toward her, and then her cheek split open like the blanched skin of a peach. Dark water gushed from the gaping wound, and the Spectress's mouth expanded in a silent scream as liquid cascaded from her face. All around, the ash golems burst in great showers of water, and the Spectress's body deflated until she melted into the tide pool, leaving nothing but the reflection of flames flickering in the black surface.

"She's gone," breathed Prewitt, moving closer to Calliope. "The ash golems, too."

Color was returning to Calliope's cheeks, and she let out her breath, tentatively taking her hands from her ears. The *sound* had faded.

"I don't . . . I don't hear it anymore." Her voice was hoarse, and she didn't know if she felt relieved or upset. She looked around, trying to catch her bearings. "That—that wasn't the Spectress at all. I knew it couldn't be. But . . . what was it?"

The Bookkeeper pushed his glasses onto his nose, disappointment plain on his face. He stepped close to the pool where the Spectress had vanished, his curiosity overtaking him. "What indeed?" He bent to investigate, tentatively dipping his finger into the surface.

The water rippled, and then something began to appear, floating up from unseen depths.

Without warning, the *sound* crashed back into Calliope's skull, and Prewitt grabbed her elbow as she stumbled.

"It's happening again!" she cried.

"I told you! It's Spirit magic," said Ilsbeth. "A Spirit is doing this!"

For a moment, the figure rising in the tide pool was shapeless, a black, undulating blob, and then it was the body of a man, tangled and bound in seaweed. Long blond hair clung to a gaunt frame.

The Bookkeeper's face lengthened in shock, and he jerked his hand back, cradling it in the other as if he'd been burned. "No," he whispered.

The drowned man's face was deathly pale, and his eyes flashed open, white as bone. He struggled against the seaweed, and finally, his arm broke free, and he reached for the Bookkeeper, grasping, clawing with curling yellow nails.

The Bookkeeper fell backward into the sand. "No! No! It can't be!"

The man's mouth formed words that none of them could hear.

The Bookkeeper shook so badly his glasses fell from his face. He fumbled, pawing the sand, until at last, he found them and shoved them back onto his nose.

Water dribbled from the sides of the drowned man's mouth, and he began to choke. He gurgled and spluttered, his white eyes wide.

The Bookkeeper scuttled backward, pushing himself up and hobbling across the beach as fast as his old legs would go. He disappeared into the Bookshop, the door slamming behind him. The Closed Indefinitely sign fell from its hook, smashing on the stoop.

Calliope lurched toward the drowning man.

"What are you doing?" Prewitt caught her sleeve. "You heard what Ilsbeth said! It's Spirit magic! Don't go near it!"

Calliope shook him off. "It's a person! I don't know if he's real or not, but if he is, I have to help him! Can't you see he's suffering?" Broken shells crunched beneath her knees as she fell down beside the tide pool.

The man's white eyes turned toward her. His entire face seemed to be dripping away like candle wax. She reached out.

The moment her fingers touched the man's cheek, her world tilted.

The *sound* of magic crashed into her once again, and this time, it was not only in her head, but in every part of her body. Ice sludged through her veins, and the chill of total emptiness darkened the corners of her vision.

Calliope couldn't help it. She opened her mouth and screamed.

11

Calliope collapsed on the beach, broken shells crunching beneath her head.

"Cal! Cal!" Prewitt shouted, gently brushing the curls from her forehead, but there was no response.

"Ilsbeth, help!" He turned and realized that Ilsbeth was no longer there. He frowned. Where had she gone? He shook his head; he couldn't worry about that now. Ilsbeth could take care of herself.

Instead, he tried without success to get Calliope to wake. He called her name again and again, and finally, he splashed water on her cheeks. She groaned, her eyes fluttering open.

"What happened?" Her voice was barely a whisper.

Prewitt sighed, relief flooding through him. "Come on. We have to get you off the beach before that person . . . *thing* . . . whatever it is comes back." He leaned down, letting her put her weight on him as she stood.

Her hand shook beneath his. "The drowned man looked so real!"

"I know," said Prewitt. He guided her across the sand, her arm draped across his shoulders, and she leaned against him. The Firebird Feather dug into his hip.

The door to the Bookshop was open, and Prewitt pulled Calliope inside, shoving it shut and bolting it behind them. Through the half-moon window, shadows and firelight convulsed across the beach.

"Here, sit down." He helped Calliope onto the bottom step of the spiral staircase. Her face was gray, and she leaned her head against a bookshelf.

"Bookkeeper!" Prewitt's voice echoed from the top of the Bookshop.

He sat down beside Calliope. "Don't worry. The Bookkeeper will know what to do. He'll have something to make you feel better." He glanced around. The lantern at the top of the Bookshop glowed red, and the empty shelves creaked.

"I made everything worse." Calliope's voice was small.

"What do you mean?" Prewitt blinked at her. "You didn't do anything! It was . . . I don't know what it was. But it definitely wasn't your fault!"

Calliope tried to sit up, but her head still ached, and she leaned back with a groan. "If I hadn't started the fire, then none of this would have happened. I forced everyone to come to the beach. I forced them to face their fear. I promised them it was safe! Now they'll never trust me."

"It wasn't your fault, Cal. How were you supposed to know that would happen?"

Because I'm the Queen, thought Calliope, once again hating the word. *I'm supposed to have answers.* But she didn't say it. Instead, she shrugged.

Prewitt chewed his lip. "Can you *really* hear Spirit magic?"

She avoided his gaze.

"Is that what you've been hiding from me? I know you said you were fine, but you aren't, are you?"

Calliope's eyes flicked up, and she saw the worry on Prewitt's face. "I'm so sorry, Prewitt. I didn't mean to make you upset." She tucked a curl behind her ear, and she finally told him everything. She told him what the Bookkeeper had asked her to do, and explained how she had reached for the Firebird Song and the strange voices had answered instead. "Night after night I hear them calling me. I go to the water, but there's nothing I can do for them."

She rubbed her eyes as she tried to explain the way the voices shrieked and cried. "I haven't slept in so long."

Prewitt patted her back. "I'll help you figure it out, Cal. I promise. You aren't alone."

She smiled at him, but she knew he was wrong. The voices were in her mind and no one else's. Still, it felt good to no longer have a secret between them.

"You should have said something. I could have at least come down to the water with you!"

"I didn't want to worry you by telling you that I was

hearing voices that no one else could." She looked down. "It's embarrassing."

Prewitt burst out laughing.

Calliope raised her eyebrows.

"No, no. I'm not laughing at you. I'm just so relieved! I thought . . . I thought you didn't want to be my friend anymore."

"Oh, Prewitt, I'm so sorry." Calliope grabbed his hand, squeezing it tightly. "I never meant for you to feel that way. I will always be your friend. Two halves of the moon, remember?"

Prewitt grinned, squeezing her hand back. Of course he remembered. It had been a part of the prophecy that the Bookkeeper had brought back from the Nymph Isles. They had thought it meant the two of them, because they had been born under the same moon, but that hadn't been what it meant at all.

Prewitt was glad that she still thought of him that way. "We'll figure this out together. You don't have to do it all alone. Okay?"

Calliope managed another smile. "Okay."

"Spirit magic," whispered Prewitt, running his hand through his hair. "Both my mother and Ilsbeth said Spirit magic isn't for humans. Now we know it's definitely true. I was worried you weren't going to wake up."

Calliope rubbed her temples. "I must be doing something wrong! I'm supposed to be able to do it! The Bookkeeper said that the Firebird Queens had magic. It's just been forgotten."

Prewitt scowled. "I don't know, Cal. The Bookkeeper isn't always right."

"Don't tell him that," said Calliope, laughing.

Prewitt winked at her and then sat up straighter, looking around. "Where is he anyway?"

Calliope frowned. The old man normally would have come out the moment he heard someone in the shop.

"Did you see his face when that man appeared in the tide pool?" asked Prewitt.

Calliope nodded. "I've never seen him look like that before."

"It was like he saw a ghost."

They peered around the Bookshop. It was eerily quiet. Even the sea was barely a hum beyond the door.

"Maybe we should go check on him." Calliope grabbed the gold handrail, pulling herself up.

Prewitt jumped to help her, but she shook her head. "It's all right. I'm starting to feel better. I think—" She broke off.

"What? What is it?" Prewitt saw Calliope's eyes widen as her gaze shifted to the half-moon window.

"The door was open," she whispered.

"Huh? What do you mean?"

"The *door*, Prewitt. When we came in, it was *open*."

Prewitt swallowed, sudden understanding making his gut twist.

Their gazes locked. The Bookkeeper *never* left the door open.

"Bookkeeper?" Prewitt called.

There was no answer.

"He was upset," whispered Calliope. "He just . . . forgot to shut the door. That's all."

"No," said Prewitt. "No, I saw him close it. I remember now. When he ran away, he slammed it so hard the sign broke."

They shared a nervous glance and crept toward the thick curtain that separated the atrium from the Bookkeeper's quarters. It hung, still and unyielding, giving no hint as to what might be behind it.

Prewitt took a steadying breath, then reached out and pulled the heavy velvet back.

"Oh no." Calliope's fingers fumbled for the Feather at her waist.

Behind the curtain, the Bookkeeper's room was a mess.

Portraits had fallen from the walls, and broken clay jars wept ink across the rug. The desk chair lay in splintered pieces, and on the other side of the room, the Bookkeeper's mattress was split and bleeding feathers.

"You don't think he did this himself, do you?" whispered Calliope.

"Maybe," said Prewitt. But he couldn't imagine the Bookkeeper breaking his own things. Prewitt had been in the room before, and it had been immaculate.

Calliope looked around as if the mess could give them answers.

She leaned down to pick up a jar of ink, and something caught her eye, something coiled in the shadows beneath the desk.

She sucked in a breath, and her arm was heavy as she reached out and picked up the object.

Prewitt turned to see what she'd found, and his heart plummeted.

Hanging between Calliope's fingers, limp and lifeless, was Ilsbeth's green whip.

12

"**Maybe she accidentally dropped it.**" **Prewitt looked** forlornly at the whip.

But they both knew it was impossible. Prewitt and Calliope wouldn't have been any more shocked had they found Ilsbeth's arm lying there without her.

No, something had happened to her, something that had left the Bookshop in disarray and forced her to leave her whip behind.

"Ilsbeth fought ash golems," whispered Calliope, wondering what could possibly defeat her.

"Not alone," said Prewitt.

The smell of smoke was pungent as they left the Bookshop, and it brought with it memories that made Prewitt catch his breath. He shoved his hands in his pockets and reminded himself that the Spectress and her monsters were truly gone. *It was a trick. Only a trick.*

The beach was abandoned but for Meredith, Jack, and the two watermen, Cedric and Old Harry, who were heaving buckets of sand onto the driftwood.

"Jack!" shouted Prewitt, and the other boy turned toward them. When he saw Prewitt's and Calliope's faces, he set down his bucket and ran forward.

The woebegone kitten was back in its place around his shoulders, its fur drenched.

"Where have you two been? I looked for you after I found Urchin, but—what's wrong?"

Calliope thrust the whip forward.

For a moment, Jack stared at it, uncomprehending. "Why do you have Ilsbeth's whip?" His eyes searched the beach. "Where is she?"

Before they had finished telling him what they had seen, he raced off toward the cove.

They chased after him, following him up over the rocks. They were slippery with seawater, and Prewitt nearly fell on top of a group of roosting cormorants. They flapped their disapproval before tucking their heads back beneath their wings, a wary eye still on the children as they scrambled through the dark.

"It's gone," said Jack, his breath rushing out. "The wrecked ship. It's gone!" He sat back, staring out at the dark sea. "They took her!"

Calliope gripped the rocks as the waves crashed over them, soaking her and weighing her down. "Why would the Silver Shag take Ilsbeth? I thought she wanted me."

Prewitt shook his head, frowning. "They must have wanted

87

the Bookkeeper. Why else would they have gone into the Bookshop? He must have some information they need."

Jack slapped his forehead, and Urchin startled. "Ilsbeth must have seen them go into the Bookshop. She wouldn't have stopped to tell us. She would have tried to save him on her own."

Calliope groaned. "You're right, Jack. She must have gotten in the way, and the Masked Rampage took them both." She rubbed her temples. "I should have told Meredith everything. He would have gone down to the shipwreck right away. I just— I didn't want him to stop me from building the bonfire."

"We'll tell him now," said Prewitt. "Maybe he and the watermen can take a ship and go after them."

Jack shook his head. "The Silver Shag's ship isn't a normal ship. It shouldn't even be seaworthy."

"Spirit magic," whispered Calliope.

"Yes! I think so, too," said Jack. "It's the only explanation. I don't think any of our ships could catch it now, and it would probably be dangerous to try."

They slid dejectedly from the rocks, trudging back through the sand toward the city.

"Ilsbeth can take care of herself." Prewitt tried not to look at the whip dangling from Calliope's fingers.

"She shouldn't *have* to!" said Calliope, the words coming out sharper than she'd intended.

"Someone should tell the Glade Girls," said Jack. "They need to know that Ilsbeth was taken."

Prewitt shook his head. "You go. Cal and I have to get back to the castle."

Calliope stopped. "What do you mean? I'm going after Ilsbeth."

"No! You have to stay where you'll be safe. The throne is still in danger."

They began to argue, and Jack ran up the city steps.

"People are what matter, Prewitt, not some title, or castle. Not some crown." Calliope stamped her foot. "I don't care if it puts me in danger. I'm going to help Ilsbeth."

"Help her *how*, Cal? We don't have any idea where they took her! What are we supposed to do?"

The watermen's deep voices drifted across the beach, and Calliope saw Meredith flinging sand onto the last of the flames, vanquishing them into wisping white clouds.

"Mer!" Calliope ran to him, burying her face in his linen shirt. He stumbled back a step.

"Are you all right? Are you hurt?" Meredith held her at arm's length, looking her over.

"They took Ilsbeth and the Bookkeeper!"

"*Who* took them?"

"The Silver Shag and the Masked Rampage!" The words poured out like the water from the fake Spectress's wounded cheek. She told Meredith about the wrecked ship. She told him about the chaos in the Bookshop. She told him everything— everything except the magic and the voices.

The Bargemaster's face had grown more and more serious

as she spoke, and by the time she finished, his cap was twisted in his hands. "Go to the castle and *stay there*."

Prewitt gave Calliope a look. *See?* it said.

Calliope shook her head, and her cheeks were hot. "I want to help!"

"You won't be helping anyone if they get you, too." Old Harry leaned on his shovel. "The way I see it, this city only has one chance, and that's you, Highness. Keep that Feather close."

Calliope bit her lip, her hand going to the Firebird Feather. What good was it? It hadn't done much but glow since she'd gotten it.

Meredith bent so they were face-to-face. "Those were no ash golems we saw tonight, Calliope."

"We know," said Prewitt. "It was Spirit magic. Ilsbeth is the one who figured it out. The Silver Shag was trying to trick people. She was using a Spirit to make them believe that the Spectress is back."

"People don't use Spirits," said Old Harry, running his fingers through his shock of white hair. *"Spirits use people."*

"If you want to help your friend, Calliope, find out what Spirit we're up against." Meredith tugged on his mustache. "Then we might be able to find out what it wants and have a plan for what to do if the Masked Rampage returns."

"Not if," said Cedric. *"When."*

Meredith nodded grimly. "Now, please. Go back to the castle. You're not safe here. We'll go to the Bookshop and see if we can find any clues as to who this Silver Shag might be." He squeezed her shoulder and then gestured to the watermen. They dropped their shovels and jogged with Meredith toward the Bookshop.

Prewitt started off up the steps, but when he looked back over his shoulder, he realized Calliope wasn't following.

She stood in the sand, her fingers on the Feather, her eyes on the sea.

Prewitt went back. "Are you hearing the voices now?"

She shook her head. "It's almost dawn. I only hear them at night when everything is darkest."

"Then what is it? What's wrong? Is it the *sound*? The Spirit magic?"

Calliope shook her head again.

"Don't worry, Cal," said Prewitt. "Everything is going to be all right. We'll find Ilsbeth and the Bookkeeper."

"Even if we do, it doesn't change the fact that the Silver Shag really is working with a Spirit. It wants to rule, Prewitt. We both saw how powerful it is, how afraid people were. The Bookkeeper is right. The only way to fight this is by finding a way to harness the Spirit magic myself, but you saw what it did to me just by *hearing* it. How in Lyrica am I supposed to *use* it?"

Prewitt bit his lip. "I know the books are gone, but maybe there's a clue in the castle somewhere. Maybe if we go back and look for something your mother might have—"

Calliope held up a hand. "She's gone, Prewitt. My mother can't help me now. I have to figure out the magic on my own."

"But what if—"

"I've already looked all over the castle. There's nothing there."

91

Calliope pressed her lips tight. If she was going to have the strength to fight the Silver Shag and keep her people safe, then she needed to do whatever she could to stay hopeful. Searching the castle would require going into the locked room. She wouldn't. She couldn't.

She whirled toward the steps and was about to march away when the sound of jingling bells made her turn back.

A bird flew across the sea toward the city as fast as its wings could carry it.

Calliope squinted, and then her mouth fell open. "It's Ilsbeth's fledgling!"

It swooped down, gliding over the city.

"Come on!" said Prewitt, grabbing her hand.

They raced up the steps, eyes on the fledging as it angled toward the falconry.

It shrieked, landing on one of the perches mounted outside the window, and the door banged open as Calliope and Prewitt ran breathless across the agriculture tier.

The Falconer towered in the doorway. He glanced at the bird and then at the children, and finally his gaze fell to the whip in Calliope's hand.

His dark hair blew around his shocked face, and his thick brows met above his black eyes. He held out a gloved hand, and the peregrine fluttered to him, extending a yellow foot. A small piece of rolled parchment was bound to its ankle with string. The Falconer unfurled it, his scowl darkening as his eyes swept the ink.

Prewitt shifted from foot to foot. "What does it say?"

Instead of answering, the Falconer stretched out and grabbed Prewitt by the collar. Prewitt yelped as the Falconer pulled him close and thrust his hand into Prewitt's pocket.

"Hey!" said Prewitt, as the Falconer yanked out his book of maps. "Give that back!"

But the Falconer ignored him. He flipped manically through the pages until he landed on one that showed the Lyrican coastline. The leather of his glove made a whispering sound as he brushed his finger across the page to a place where the land jutted into the sea. "Castaway Cape," he growled.

Prewitt could see the letters, slanting across the protruding point.

"Castaway Cape?" said Calliope. "What is it? What does it have to do with the message? Tell us!"

The Falconer wordlessly thrust the parchment toward Calliope.

Prewitt watched the color drain from her cheeks and saw the parchment tremble in her fingers. "What does it say?"

Calliope tried to keep her voice steady as she read it aloud. *"Queen of Lyrica: We have your friend. Bring the Bookkeeper to the fort at Castaway Cape before the full moon wanes or the girl will die. Come alone."*

It was signed: *The Silver Shag.*

The Falconer shoved the book of maps into Prewitt's chest and then disappeared into the falconry, the door slamming behind him.

"The Bookkeeper got away!" said Prewitt. "I can't believe it."

"I can," said Calliope. "Of course, Ilsbeth saved him."

"But where did he go? Why didn't he tell anyone what had happened to her?"

The window banged open and they both jumped. Dozens of hawks waited beyond the sill, their wings a frenzy.

The Falconer gave a sharp whistle, and the birds lifted, one by one. They circled en masse above the city, looking like a gathering tempest against the lightening sky.

The Falconer launched himself through the doorway and charged across the agriculture tier, his leather trench coat flapping.

Calliope chased after him. "Wait!" she cried.

The Falconer did not slow.

"What is Castaway Cape?"

"It's a prison," growled the Falconer.

"That's where they took Ilsbeth? To a prison?"

The Falconer ignored her, striding through the courtyard to where the Bookkeeper's black horse was still tied. It spooked back.

The Falconer shushed it, pressing a gentle hand against the horse's soft nose.

"You can't go after her," insisted Calliope. "You read the message. I have to go. I'm the only one who can help her now."

The Falconer spun, stretching out his hand. "The whip. Give it to me," he barked.

Calliope reluctantly placed it in his glove.

Without another word, he flung himself up into the saddle and drove his heel down. The horse took off across the courtyard.

"Wait!" shouted Calliope, but the Falconer was already gone.

Calliope shook her head. "Poor Ilsbeth," she whispered.

"What do we do?" asked Prewitt. "What's our plan?"

Calliope looked down at the parchment in her hand. "The Silver Shag's note is clear. Without the Bookkeeper, the Falconer will never get Ilsbeth back. We have to find him. It's the only way."

Prewitt nodded, all arguments about Calliope staying safe in the castle forgotten.

"Whatever we do, we can't tell *anyone* about the Silver Shag's note," said Calliope, tucking it into her pocket.

"No," agreed Prewitt. "It would be too dangerous. They would want to come along, and the note was clear."

Calliope bit her lip. She shouldn't let Prewitt come, either. She knew it was a bad idea, that it wasn't safe, but she also knew that there was no way he would ever let her go alone, and a part of her was glad.

She squinted in the direction the Falconer's horse had galloped. The sky was brightening at the edges, dark orange sweeping like wet paint across the horizon, and it turned everything a bleary red. For a moment, she thought that her eyes were playing tricks on her, but then she let out a cry and ran forward.

Prewitt chased after her, and when he had caught up, he did

not say a word. They stood in the place where the fire flowers had bloomed. The field had been trampled, the petals crushed and the heads broken. Only one or two remained.

By the cliff's edge, the lapis pathway now shimmered in full view, bright orange petals bleeding into the stones.

"The cottage!" gasped Calliope.

They raced down the path, slipping on smashed petals.

When they got to the end, they skidded to a halt.

The little house was still there, tucked into the cliffside. But where before it had seemed to be sleeping, a precious, forlorn place, now it was a shell, pried open and spoiled.

The door hung on its hinges, and morning light spilled in through the doorway, a smattering of orange petals smeared across the threshold.

Someone had found the cottage.

13

Neither Calliope nor Prewitt spoke as they inched closer. It felt like finding an unearthed grave, as if something sacred had been disrupted.

After a moment's hesitation, they stepped into the cottage. The pale morning light illuminated a cloud of dust that floated like a veil across the room. Boot prints tracked dirt and flower petals across the cottage floor.

A long table stood in the corner, set with plates and forks and light-blue glasses, a bright red vase like a kiss at its center. If not for the fine layer of gray dust covering everything, it could have been laid for that morning's meal.

A rusted pan was on the potbelly stove, and dishes were stacked in the basin. A desk took up the whole right wall, strewn with paint pots and brushes, their handles splattered with bright pigments. A stack of blank canvases leaned against the corner.

"Firebird feathers," whispered Prewitt. "It's like someone was living here one day and then . . . they just . . ."

He trailed off.

"Died," said Calliope, the word dry in her mouth.

They continued their way around the cottage. There were two small bedrooms at the back, the ceilings made of curved rock inlaid with thousands of pearlescent shells. The beds were layered with faded patchwork quilts, turned down and inviting.

Calliope rubbed her arms. Was this where the Bookkeeper's children had slept? Had the pillows and blankets been stitched by their mother's hands?

Calliope felt a sharp pang of sorrow as she imagined the little girl standing where she was, surrounded by memories of a mother who was gone. Calliope would never know the Painter's daughter, but it felt like she did.

"Nothing looks broken," said Prewitt. "It's like they haven't touched anything. All this dust, and not even a fingerprint."

"So why did they come here? Why break the door?" asked Calliope. "What were they looking for?"

"For the paintings, of course."

Calliope and Prewitt jumped, turning to see the Book-keeper hunched in the shadows of the living room. His face was drawn, his eyes were bloodshot, and there was a tremor in his hands that hadn't been there before, but he did not seem to be injured. He pointed at the wall, and in the brightening light they saw the telltale outlines where dozens of paintings must have hung.

"Bookkeeper!" Calliope wasn't sure if she wanted to hug him

or yell at him. "Are you all right? Why didn't you tell anyone what happened? Why didn't you tell us about Ilsbeth?"

The Bookkeeper frowned. "Who?"

"Ilsbeth!" said Prewitt. "We found her whip in the Bookshop."

"Ah." The Bookkeeper walked over and stood beside one of the beds, staring down at it, unmoving.

"Bookkeeper?" Calliope stepped closer.

"They tried to take me." The Bookkeeper blinked several times, as if he couldn't quite believe it. He reached out and lifted one of the pillows. A book was hidden underneath. He picked it up, gazing down at the cover. His mouth drooped as he stood motionless and silent.

Calliope tugged her curls. She was preparing to tell him about the fledgling's note when Prewitt pulled her away to the far corner. "You can't tell him about the message," he whispered.

Calliope tilted her head. "Why not? How else are we going to get him to Castaway Cape?"

"I don't know. But you saw how he responded when we asked him about Ilsbeth. He doesn't care. He only cares about *himself* and books. He could have told someone what happened. We might have been able to save her, but he only cared about saving his own skin."

Calliope shifted, casting a glance back toward the bed where the Bookkeeper stood hunched and muttering.

"If we tell him the truth and he refuses to go, we've lost our only chance to find Ilsbeth," said Prewitt.

Calliope nodded. She knew he was right. It wasn't worth

the risk. "Okay," she said. "But we aren't giving him to the Silver Shag. Not really. Once we save Ilsbeth, we will find a way to get everyone home."

Prewitt nodded. "Agreed."

Calliope took a deep breath, and then she went to stand beside the Bookkeeper. He didn't seem to notice she was there.

"They took the paintings," he muttered. "Miriam's paintings."

"Bookkeeper," said Calliope, reaching out and touching the back of his weathered hand.

He looked up.

"I think . . . I think I know a place where books survived."

The Bookkeeper stared blankly at her through his murky glasses. "I have already searched the whole kingdom," he said dully.

Calliope took a deep breath; she didn't know if what she was about to say *could* be true, but she put all her conviction into the words as she spoke. "While you were gone, I did what you said. I tried to hear the magic, and I looked for answers in the few books that we brought back from the mountain. I found a mention of a library at a place called Castaway Cape."

The Bookkeeper's trembling hands stilled. "Castaway Cape? Yes . . . there *was* a library there. In fact, it was your mother who established it. She never liked that people could be sent off and forgotten, but it had been written into law long before she became Queen."

Calliope stared at him. "Sent off and forgotten? You mean they were never allowed out again?"

"Now, now, Highness, don't look at me like that. *I* didn't send people away. It was the Reckoner who made that decision. The Queen could have stopped his orders, but she rarely intervened. It was all done to keep the kingdom safe."

"I've never heard of the Reckoner," said Prewitt.

"No, you wouldn't have. He hasn't been seen since the night you were born, the night of the Spectress's attack. It is likely that he hid within the Cape. It is a fortress. There's a stone wall that cuts the peninsula off from the rest of the land, and steep cliffs make it impossible to reach by sea." The Bookkeeper's fingers tapped his forehead, and the gleam returned to his eyes. "Yes, the library there *may* have survived. I should have thought of it myself. But I rarely think of Castaway Cape at all."

Calliope pressed further. "If there is any chance that books about the Queen's magic might have survived, then we have to go right now! It could save us all from whatever Spirit attacked with the Silver Shag."

The Bookkeeper leaned forward, tucking the book back beneath the pillow, and Calliope realized how strange it was that the old man had left books behind in the cottage. "You're right," he said. "I will go at once."

"I'm coming with you this time," said Calliope.

"Me too," said Prewitt.

They had expected him to argue, but the Bookkeeper nodded. "If I find the books, it will be best if you are with me so we can employ whatever information we find without delay."

They left the cottage, and the Bookkeeper closed the door. His hand lingered on the knob, and his face was so sad that

Calliope felt a pang of pity. The Masked Rampage had broken into a place that the Bookkeeper had taken care to lock away. They had disrupted something precious and stirred up memories that did not belong to them. They had stolen a part of the Bookkeeper's past and damaged what he had tried to keep safe.

The Bookkeeper stood with his back to them, and Calliope wondered for a moment if he might be crying. Guilt twisted in her stomach. Was it cruel to trick him when he was clearly hurting?

But when the Bookkeeper turned, his eyes were clear again, and his wrinkled face was determined.

He walked away from the closed door and did not look back. "Books, Highness. Books may save us yet."

But it wasn't books that Calliope thought about as they hurried up the blue tiles—it was Ilsbeth, and the Silver Shag who was expecting them all.

14

Jack hammered on doors and shouted at shutters, trying to alert the Glade Girls.

"Ilsbeth has been taken! Giana! Becca! Lanna!" He called their names. "Hazel! Poppy! Maddie! Fi! Please! You have to help her!"

But they did not come out of their houses. Once or twice, he thought he heard someone try to answer, but their voices were quickly shushed.

He sat down on the stoop of one of the houses, utterly dejected. It had been the last one—the one where Fi lived with her parents and an older brother.

Fi had been the only Glade Girl who had bothered to speak to him after they had defeated the Spectress in the caldera.

Her row bench had been behind his when they had returned on the *Queen's Barge*. He hadn't realized she was blind at first.

It wasn't until she had spoken directly to him that he had noticed her green eyes were focused elsewhere.

"Your name is Jack," she had said, her voice soft. "You are the boy who rescued three girls from the mountain dungeons."

Jack's face had grown hot. "It wasn't just me. Prewitt and the Princess were there, too. I wouldn't have had the courage to do anything without them."

"But you alone took them on the river. You alone rowed them to safety."

"I guess that's true." Jack had hardly been able to believe it himself.

"I am very happy to know you, Jack," Fi had said.

And that had been all. They hadn't spoken again after that. But they had rowed the *Queen's Barge* back to the Royal City and had helped return the Lost Princess to her kingdom. That was something that would always connect them. Their one shared moment had felt like a bond.

That was why he couldn't understand how the others could ignore the fact that something had happened to Ilsbeth. They were bonded by far more than a moment. They were sisters.

Jack knew that if any one of the Glade Girls had been kidnapped, Ilsbeth would have done whatever it took to find them and bring them home. She would have swum across the sea—and Jack knew how much the sea scared her even if she tried to hide it.

"Pssst."

Jack glanced up.

Pale fingers pushed through the shutter slats. He rushed over.

"Jack?" His name came in a whisper, and he saw Fi's cheek pressed against the wood.

"I'm here!"

"Tell me what has happened. Quickly."

Jack told her, and the weak wood complained as Fi's cheek pushed harder against the slats. "Ilsbeth would never have left her whip behind."

"I know. That's why we have to go and find her."

"Fi!" A man called her name, fear tight in his voice. "Get away from the window! It's not safe!"

Fi turned away, saying something Jack couldn't hear.

He waited a long time, and suddenly, a different face appeared at the slats: a round woman's, crimson-cheeked and frazzled. "Please, child, you shouldn't be here. Didn't you see the Spectress? Don't you know it's dangerous outside? Your mother will be worried."

Jack didn't tell her that his mother couldn't worry. She had already been killed because of the Spectress. Instead, he tried again to tell her about Ilsbeth, but she shook her head and turned away. The slats clattered as she tugged them shut.

Jack trudged up to the castle in search of Calliope and Prewitt, but they weren't there.

He asked Marisa if she'd seen them, and she frowned. "I thought they were with you." She wiped her hands on her apron, poking her head out the kitchen door.

"Prewitt! Calliope!" There was no answer, only the singing of birds.

The Bargemaster came around the corner, and Marisa hurried toward him. "Have you seen the children?"

Meredith frowned. "They were supposed to come straight to the castle."

Marisa's hands clasped at her heart, and panic filled her voice. "You don't think something happened to them, do you?"

Meredith rubbed his mustache, and Jack watched the shadow of worry spread beneath his eyes.

The three girls were whispering in the doorway, and Marisa's gaze snapped to them. She marched over, hands on her hips.

"What do you three know?"

"We saw them go into the woods on the other side of the castle," said one of the girls. "They were with that old man. The Bookkeeper."

Jack stared at her, astonished. "Are you sure?"

All three of the girls nodded.

Meredith pulled at his mustache. "Something strange is going on here," he said. "I don't like it at all."

"They're with the Bookkeeper. That means they'll be safe . . . right?" said Jack.

Meredith and Marisa exchanged a glance.

"You have to go after them," said Marisa.

Meredith nodded. "I'll go and get Cedric and Old Harry."

"I'll come with you," said Jack.

"Stay close to the Bargemaster," warned Marisa, pulling Jack's coat closed and fussing with the buttons. "The Firebird may have returned, but the woods are still full of monsters."

15

"I thought we were in a hurry," said Prewitt, as they tramped through the thick forest undergrowth. "Wouldn't it have been better to get a horse? Why are we going through the woods?"

Unseen birds called out from the tangled branches above, and the Bookkeeper struggled to climb over a fallen log. His robes caught, and he cursed as he pulled them free; then he paused a moment, his breath ragged.

Prewitt's eyes met Calliope's. It was dawn, but the moon would be full when night came again. Neither one had forgotten the Silver Shag's threat: *Bring the Bookkeeper to the fort at Castaway Cape before the full moon wanes or the girl will die.*

"It is precisely because we are in a hurry that we are not wasting our time with a horse," huffed the Bookkeeper. "Now, give me the book." He snapped his fingers at Prewitt.

"The book?"

"Yes, boy. The book! Emperor's gut. Don't tell me you've lost it."

Prewitt frowned, reaching into his jacket and pulling out his shining book of maps. "You mean this one?"

They could practically hear the Bookkeeper's eyes creak as they rolled. "What else could I possibly mean?"

Prewitt scowled and handed the golden book to him. "I don't see what good it will do," he muttered. "Map or not, it'll still take us weeks to travel the forest paths."

"Ah, but we aren't taking the paths." The Bookkeeper let the book fall open in his palms. The breeze caught the pages, and map after map flipped past until an intricate forest map glistened in the morning light. "Our route is much faster—and much more *dangerous*."

Prewitt leaned forward, trying to see what way the Bookkeeper could mean.

The old man's mouth spread. "All this time you have loved this book without fully understanding what it was."

He stretched up and tugged on a low-hanging branch of a hemlock. A shower of dew rained down, beads catching in their hair. The Bookkeeper held the book aloft, letting droplets splatter the page. Then he swept his palm across them until the painted forest was damp and shining.

For a moment nothing happened, and then a shimmering green ink began to appear, racing across the page to reveal a thousand arched bridges snaking through the treetops.

Prewitt gasped.

"Haven't I told you, Bargeboy?" said the Bookkeeper, his blue eyes gleaming. "Books reveal the secrets of the universe to those who are worthy." He handed the book back to Prewitt.

"But why are they hidden?" asked Prewitt, gaping at the bridges. He had spent so much time looking at the maps, had memorized many of the paths through the forest, and yet, he never had even the slightest inkling that there might be more. What other secrets did the book hold?

He looked back at the Bookkeeper, and he wasn't sure what he saw in the old man's eyes. Was it fear? Anger?

"They are hidden because they are not *meant* to be traveled by humans," snapped the Bookkeeper.

Calliope bit her lip. "Maybe we shouldn't take them, then."

"No, we *should* not." The Bookkeeper pressed his glasses higher on his nose. "But we *must*. The kingdom is in danger, and the more quickly we figure out your magic, the better." His eyes took on a haunted look, a trace of the expression they had seen the night before when he had knelt on the sand before the drowning man.

"Lead the way, Bargeboy."

Prewitt hesitated. He wasn't sure he wanted to take the bridges now. He had a feeling that the Bookkeeper would be willing to risk almost anything for the possibility of finding books at Castaway Cape. But he also knew that they had no choice. They were in too deep, and although Ilsbeth wasn't a friend *exactly*, she was a person he felt connected to, and the idea of something bad happening to her was enough to push his feet forward toward the first bridge.

Calliope and the Bookkeeper walked behind him as Prewitt

confidently followed the map, and after a few minutes, he stopped. "The bridges should be somewhere *here*," he said, looking around.

"Yes. I see them!" Calliope pointed up toward the treetops. They never would have noticed them if they hadn't known that they were there. The bridges were made of the trees themselves, twisting across the canopy.

"Extraordinary, aren't they? They've been here for thousands of years, built by the Tree Trolls," said the Bookkeeper. "Dangerous creatures, longtime enemies of the Bookkeepers."

"Why?" said Calliope.

A shadow passed across the Bookkeeper's eyes. "Never you mind," he said. "No one has seen a Tree Troll in years. If we are fortunate, and if we are fast, it may not be of any relevance at all."

They found a set of steps hidden within a lichen-coated trunk and climbed up toward the treetops. The morning sun promised warmth as it shimmered and danced across the bridge. The branches were artistically woven, twining and braided, shoots and leaves peeking through. It was beautiful, but it was dangerous. The bridge was slick, and there were gaps where a foot could get caught or a leg could slip through. Worse than that, there were patches that had been burned and were now rotting and dead.

It was nerve-racking to cross so high, knowing that if they tripped, or if the bridges gave way, they would fall hundreds of feet to the forest floor.

The Bookkeeper was strangely quiet. Where normally, he

would have used any time with Calliope to lecture or test her, now, his face was grim, and his knuckles were white as they clung to the branches that formed the twisting railing. The forest was full of sounds, and each one seemed to startle him.

"How much farther, Bargeboy?" he barked.

Prewitt's head bent close to the map. "There are five more bridges before we reach the edge of the forest nearest the wall."

"Five isn't so bad," said Calliope. "It only took us a few minutes to cross the last one."

They continued on and had finished crossing the fourth bridge when the Bookkeeper began to relax, his mood visibly improving. "Only one to go, and then we will see the great stone wall of Castaway Cape."

Calliope and Prewitt hurried ahead, and the Bookkeeper followed.

Calliope stopped, frowning. "Do you hear that?"

"Hear what?"

"It's like . . . bells. No, not bells. I don't know exactly." She pressed her fingers to her temples and tears suddenly welled in her eyes.

"Cal, what's wrong?"

"I just . . . I feel so sad. It's . . . it's horrible."

The Bookkeeper came closer, leaning forward. "You're hearing it again! The Spirit magic! Tell me what it sounds like!"

But he never knew because the forest around them was suddenly alive, reacting to something enormous that was bending treetops and sending clouds of frantic birds winging into the sky.

"What's happening?" asked Prewitt.

"It's a Tree Troll," shouted the Bookkeeper, his face contorted with fear. "Don't let it take me." He ran ahead, faster than they had ever seen him move. "Get off the bridge!" he shouted back at them. "Get to the wall!"

But it was too late. The trees groaned, and the trunk of a nearby oak ripped apart with a sound so loud that the bridge shuddered and buckled, sending the Bookkeeper sprawling. His glasses fell from his face, and he pawed for them, knocking them down, down, down to the forest floor.

The air was thick with the ripe scent of damp oak, and the Tree Troll peered through the space in the tree, leaning out across the bridge. Its skin was entirely made of bark. Ivy draped across its forehead, and its wide eyes were moss-filled pockets. Its branch-like arms extended from the tree, and it grasped the railing with foot-long fingers, dragging itself onto the bridge between the children and the Bookkeeper. Its legs hung behind it, charred black and dead.

"*Bookkeeper*," the creature's voice creaked as it trained its eyes on the cowering Bookkeeper. It crawled forward and the Book-keeper scuttled back.

"No! Stop! Please, don't hurt him," cried Calliope, running close.

The Troll turned its head toward her. "Who are you to command a spirit?"

Calliope stood up taller. "I am Calliope—the Princess of Lyrica. You're a Tree Troll, aren't you? Did you build these bridges? They're amazing."

The creature's mossy eyes were unblinking as it regarded her. "I am Sapling, the last of the Tree Trolls. Yes, my ancestors and I built these bridges, but now I am alone, and they have fallen into disrepair." Its head bowed toward its charred legs. "As have I."

The Bookkeeper began to scoot away, and the Troll's arm unfurled, its long fingers roping around the Bookkeeper's ankle and dragging him back.

The old man howled. "No, no! Let me go, you creature!"

"Please," said Calliope again. "Please, don't hurt us. We don't mean any harm. We just need to get to Castaway Cape."

"Hurt you?" Tiny, star-shaped leaves at the Tree Troll's brow trembled. "I will not hurt you as long as I have what is mine. No one crosses the Tree Troll bridges without paying the toll."

It turned its head toward the Bookkeeper, who whimpered. "No one knows that better than you, do they, Bookkeeper? I am surprised that you would dare to come here."

Calliope reached out and grabbed Prewitt's hand.

"It is time for you to pay," said Sapling. "Give me a story, and I will let you cross."

Calliope felt herself relax. A story? The Bookkeeper lived to tell stories. They would soon be across the bridge, and then they could find Ilsbeth and go home.

But if anything, the Bookkeeper seemed more afraid. "I—I don't—I don't have a story to tell," he said, his voice full of bravado that didn't match his trembling hands, his quivering jaw.

"Very well." The Troll laughed, and it was the rattling sound of wind against leaves. All around them, the canopy shook. Sapling's mouth spread, and they could see moss curling around teeth as sharp as stakes. "The trees are *hungry*, Bookkeeper, and the time has come for them to feast."

16

"I will tell you a story!" said Calliope, stepping forward.

"It is not your story that I desire," said the Troll.

The Bookkeeper's forehead furrowed, and Prewitt could see him scheming. "Let me give you something better than a story," the old man wheedled.

"What can you give me?" asked the Tree Troll. "You know better than anyone what keeps the bridges strong, what makes them run true and straight."

"Perhaps, but the bridges don't matter anymore," said the Bookkeeper. "Humans no longer know these paths. What is *my* story going to do? It might straighten one bridge, but there are thousands of others."

Prewitt frowned. The Bookkeeper had said that the paths were not meant for humans. He hadn't said that the knowledge had been kept from them. He looked down at his book. The page was drying and the green ink was beginning to fade.

"You say you are the last of the Tree Trolls," said the Book-keeper. "But I know that there are others. I know that some escaped the Spectress's burning of the woods. You were left behind because of your charred legs."

Tears spilled onto Calliope's cheeks. "He's right. I can feel it," she whispered to Prewitt. "The Troll's loneliness. It's awful."

"But you do not need to be alone," continued the Book-keeper, his eyes steady on the Troll's face. "The Queen can heal you. You can go and join your family."

Calliope flinched. "What is he doing? I don't know how to use the magic!"

"Shh . . . ," Prewitt warned. "Look at the trees."

All around them, the canopy was creaking and bending, growing more agitated. The crackling, snapping sound of trunks splitting open, and mouths yawning wide, echoed through the woods.

For the first time, the Troll blinked, bark closing across its mossy eyes. "No one can heal me," it creaked. "Only my mother Spirit, the Wild Woman, and she has left the realm."

"Ah, but you see, the child before you is the daughter of Firebird Queens. The Firebird's own magic courses through her veins. You know that there is no greater power."

The Tree Troll's head turned back toward Calliope. It pressed its face close to hers, its oaken breath stirring her lashes. "If you *truly* are the girl whose hope saved Lyrica, answer me this: Why did the Firebird Song leave me broken?" Its burned legs rattled. "Why are the Spirits still in disarray? Nature is in balance, and yet they have not returned."

Calliope chewed her lip. "I wish I knew the answer. I don't know why the Song didn't fix everything." She felt a pang as the nursery and its locked door loomed suddenly in her mind. Calliope swallowed around the burl in her throat. "Maybe some things just can't be fixed. Not even by hope." She wrapped her hand around the Feather.

The Troll's gaze fell upon it, and its long fingers unfurled from the Bookkeeper's veiny leg. "The Firebird Feather. You *are* who the Bookkeeper says you are."

The Bookkeeper was already on his feet, backing silently away toward the far end of the bridge.

Calliope looked around at the snapping trees. They were bending close. She didn't know how to use the magic. She didn't know how to heal the Troll, but she had no choice. She had to try.

"Cal," whispered Prewitt. "You can't. It's dangerous."

"We're already in danger," said Calliope. "We have to cross the bridge. We *have* to get to Ilsbeth."

Prewitt threw a glare at the retreating Bookkeeper. Why hadn't he just given the Troll a story? What was he so afraid of?

Calliope took a deep breath, and then she reached out her hand, nerves prickling in her fingers. Could she really heal the Troll? She had no idea how to use magic, and trying felt like wading into the sea without knowing how to swim. Ilsbeth's words rang in her head: *Humans cannot touch Spirit magic. If Calliope tries, she will not survive.*

Calliope swallowed. It was *because* of Ilsbeth that she had to try.

She lightly pressed her fingers to the charred bark of Sapling's leg. The moment she touched it, the *sound* of its magic filled her, tender chimes ringing in her mind. Sorrow overtook her heart as she let the *sound* come.

Calliope gritted her teeth and refused to fight it, letting it weave through her, and to her astonishment, *power* strummed through her fingers.

The Tree Troll sucked in its breath, and a wisp of mist seeped into its barky nostrils. The branches at its legs began to soften, and the wick of life gleamed freshly green at their centers.

"It's working." The Troll's voice was full of disbelief, and its eyes turned down to its changing legs.

It was true, but Calliope was paying a price for the magic. The *sound* and the sorrow that came with it filled her so completely that it threatened to overwhelm her. It was a loneliness so heavy and wretched that it seemed as if her chest would collapse beneath the weight, and without warning, the locked nursery door rose up in her mind. She felt it threatening to open, to reveal all the pain she had hidden behind it.

"Cal!" Prewitt's face twisted in horror.

"Cal, remember your hope," he shouted.

Calliope tried. She strained for focus, but the door in her mind would not be ignored. It demanded opening, but she pushed against it. *Not now! Please, not now! There is no hope in that place. There's only sadness. Only pain.*

She bent double, gasping, fighting to keep the door closed, to grasp the magic and push it through her fingers and into the

Troll's leg. But the more she tried, the weaker she felt. The edges of her vision began to blur, and the energy drained completely from her limbs. She stumbled and collapsed, wet black dirt spilling from her eyes and onto her cheeks.

Prewitt ran forward, falling down beside her. She was not moving.

The Tree Troll rattled on its burned legs, fury turning the ivy at its brow a fiery red. A snarl ripped from its lips, and it swung toward the Bookkeeper, who had nearly reached the end of the bridge. "Liar!"

The Bookkeeper tried to run, tried to reach the stairs beyond the bridge's edge, but he did not make it.

The Troll caught him in its grip, thin fingers curling around his scrawny throat. "You claimed the girl had the Firebird's magic!"

Prewitt watched, panic burning his stomach. The Bookkeeper's face was turning purple. "Pay it!" he yelled. "Pay the toll. Give the Troll your story."

The Bookkeeper's eyes bulged, and he strained for breath, kicking and wriggling in the Troll's grasp.

"Bookkeeper, please! If you don't do this, we're all going to die! We'll never find the books. We'll never save Lyrica."

The Bookkeeper stopped fighting, and his body went limp. His eyes were dull with defeat. "All right," he gasped with the last of his air.

The Troll's grip loosened slightly. "You know that I will not accept just any story. You must give me the one you least want to tell. Tell me the story of what happened on the Nymph Isles."

The Bookkeeper's beard trembled. "No, please. Any but that."

The trees bent toward the Bookkeeper, mouths wide. "If you wish to cross the bridge, that is my toll."

The Bookkeeper's frown deepened, and for a moment, it seemed he would refuse, but then, to Prewitt's great relief, the Bookkeeper began to tell his story.

"We had nearly given up hope when the Isles appeared to us." He spoke in a rush, and the Troll breathed deeply through its nostrils, as if inhaling every word.

"Go on," it said.

"For months, my children and I sailed the northern seas. I knew where the Isles *should* be, but I was running out of time. The seas were growing stormier by the day. Just when I had decided that perhaps my years of research had yielded false information, the Nymph Isles *appeared*, the sparkling shores more beautiful than I ever could have imagined.

"I had been right all along. The Nymph Isles were hidden, a mystery, because they had been concealed by the Ancient Spirits. Looking out at the Isles, I saw spirits everywhere, in numbers that I could not have imagined. Mermaids swam, dark and curious, in the depths around our ship, and a dragon—yes! A dragon! Flew through the sky. The Spirit of the Suffering Sea herself waited on the back of a kelpie nickering and stamping in the shallows. She beckoned me, and I took a dinghy to meet her.

" 'Why have you come to our shores?' she asked. And I told her: to find the prophecy that will save Lyrica from the Demon and its servant. 'Perhaps Lyrica should not be saved,' she said. 'Perhaps the time of Firebird Queens is at an end, and a new era of Spirits has come.' But I was not swayed by her suggestions. I spoke eloquently, using my knowledge to prove my worth, and in the end, she welcomed me like a king.

"Only I was allowed on the shore. My son stayed behind in the boat while I trod the realm of spirits." Pride lifted the Bookkeeper's chin. "I was guided to a lake that led to the Hall of Mosses, a great palace beneath the Isles where I met the leader of the Ancient Spirits of the Isles—the one who had led the abandonment of the kingdom a thousand years prior: the Great Forgeman. He had once been a Spirit of the Mountains, and it was he who had seen the future in his Forge that would tell of the rise of the Spectress and the fall of humankind.

"Other men would have been overawed before such power, but I did not cower. I asked for the prophecy and spoke my case for Lyrica, and the Forgeman acquiesced. I held it in my hands, a victor, but then . . ." He hesitated.

"Go on . . ." The Tree Troll's eyes were closed, and it held its breath, waiting for more.

"It was then I realized I had been cursed. From the moment the prophecy's black shell touched my hands, I began to age. With a grim smile, the Forgeman told me that every minute I stayed on his shores, I would lose a year. It was a cruel curse. I wasn't young to start with; what years did I have to give? 'For your pride,' the Forgeman said. But what pride had I shown? It wasn't pride that had brought me to the Isles. If anything it was humility. It was courage, and knowledge, and yes, even hope."

The Bookkeeper shook his head, still baffled, but then his eyes sparked with a new light, and he leaned forward, straining against Sapling's fingers. "They thought they had tricked me. They did not plan for me to ever leave the Isle alive. But they misjudged my cleverness, my resourcefulness. I sacrificed what they did not expect, what no one else would be willing to give, and I returned to the kingdom victorious and saved us all."

He leaned back, and there was relief in his face. "There. I have paid your toll. That is the story that I have never told until this day."

The Tree Troll withdrew its fingers, and the Bookkeeper fell to the warped branches of the bridge.

The Troll had breathed in the story, and now, with a creaking sigh, it released it. A cloud of billowing green spilled from its nostrils and swelled into a figure. There on the bridge beside them was the Bookkeeper, younger, taller, but undeniably him.

The Tree Troll's voice was full of power. "Every story has many truths, but the storyteller tells only one. Now watch, as I do what Bookkeepers fear most, and reveal the part of the story you do not wish to be told."

17

The Bookkeeper ran across black sand, cradling a conch shell darker than the night sky above. His feet slogged, and his voice was ragged and panicked. "Milo! Milo!"

A young man paced the shore, delicate hands worrying waves of thick blond hair. A dinghy waited nearby, salt water nudging its stern, lodging it deeper and deeper into the sand.

He turned at the sound of the Bookkeeper's cries, and his face slackened. "Father! What's happened to you?" His gaze flicked to the black shell, and his blue eyes widened. "*Feathers!* You found it! You were right! There really *is* a prophecy!"

"Of course I was right." The Bookkeeper bent, shoving the boat into the water, his back cracking. "Don't just stand there. Help me! We have to get out of here."

As he spoke, dark spots spread across the Bookkeeper's scalp, and a new line creased in his brow.

Milo gasped. "What is happening to you?"

"There was a price. We knew there would be."

Milo leaped into the boat, pulling the Bookkeeper over the side.

"Row! Row!"

Milo obliged, his breath coming in pants.

The Bookkeeper cast a glance over his shoulder at the disappearing shore. "Faster! Faster!"

"I'm trying!" Milo's muscles strained as waves bullied the hull. "The sea—she's fighting me!" Puce seaweed stretched up like tentacles, tugging at the oars until the handles snapped with a sound like breaking bone.

"I can't go back there. I can't!" The Bookkeeper's voice was shrill. "Look at me!" He pulled at his cheeks.

"We never should have come," Milo wailed. "The Nymph Isles Spirits will never let us leave. Why did we think they would?"

The Bookkeeper clutched the shell, his eyes squeezed shut.

"We have to send the ship away," sobbed Milo.

"No!" The Bookkeeper's eyes were wild. "I *will* take this prophecy back. I have not come this far to be thwarted. There *must* be a way." He glared up at the sky as if the answer would appear in the stars, and then his mouth spread, and he pointed a gnarled finger at his son. "Call the North Wind."

"The North Wind?" Milo shook his head, uncomprehending.

"Quickly, before we're swept back to the shore and I lose more of my life."

Milo's brow scrunched, and he muttered under his breath. "The East Wind demands a drowning, the South Wind trades in secrets, the North Wind . . . the North Wind . . . I don't remember. What was it again?" His eyes suddenly lifted. *The North Wind steals your future.* His head bobbled. "I don't want to give up my future, Father."

The Bookkeeper raised the conch shell. "I *must* take the prophecy back to Lyrica. It is the only way to save the kingdom."

"But . . . couldn't I take it?"

"Don't be absurd! You are not yet the Bookkeeper. You do not have any authority. Who would believe *you* returned from the Nymph Isles?"

Milo sagged.

The Bookkeeper reached out, resting his hand on Milo's shoulder. "I've always been able to count on you." He forced a warm smile to his lips. "My clever, capable son. You must assist me now. Do not waste this chance to save Lyrica, to do what is right. Let me take the prophecy back."

Milo hesitated, and the Bookkeeper tried a different tack. "You *are* my apprentice, are you not?"

Milo nodded.

"Then you are sworn to obey, whatever I ask." The shore loomed, the black sand wet and fresh as funerary dirt.

"I know, but—"

The Bookkeeper slammed his hand down on the bench. "I am your father, Milo! If I return to the black sands, my life will be over in minutes. Don't you care whether I live or die?"

Milo ran his hands through his hair. Then he nodded. "Yes—yes, Father. Of course I care. I'll try."

He turned his face to the onyx sky, and curious constellations watched as he called in a tentative voice, hardly more than a whisper. "North Wind? I'm Milo, son of Thomas, the Royal Bookkeeper. If you will come and save us now, I will . . ." He hesitated.

"Go on," hissed the Bookkeeper. "Say it. For Lyrica. For *me*."

Milo swallowed. "I will give you my future."

The words hung. The waves stilled.

For a moment, nothing happened, and then the Wind struck. Water exploded around the dinghy as the boat pushed forward against the tide.

"It's working! It's working!" Milo laughed, giddy and light. The ship drew near once more.

Two ropes hung down into the water, metal hooks beating a rhythm against the hull. Milo stood, grasping them and securing the dinghy. "We can go home now!" His voice was jubilant.

The Bookkeeper nodded, his eyes bright, as he clutched the shell to his chest. "Go on, let's leave this cursed place and never return!"

A sudden gust of wind struck Milo. He stumbled, groping for his father's arm.

The Bookkeeper fumbled the shell. "No!" He pawed the air, only just catching it before it splashed into the sea.

The Wind flung water, shrieking and gusting, and the dinghy drank its fill of the tide, the hull sinking perilously low.

The Bookkeeper turned just in time to see his son fall backward into the water. Milo kicked and thrashed and fought the sea, but it was no use. Kelp wrapped him in greedy arms, claiming him for the deep. His eyes were moons as he sank, and his mouth screamed.

The Bookkeeper stood, frozen and horrified, as his son sank. Then he turned back toward the ship, holding the prophecy close.

18

Ilsbeth lay in total darkness, a damp blindfold wrapped tightly around her eyes. Her hands and feet were bound, and panic shrieked in her skull. It commanded her to struggle, to fight, to thrash and kick until she was free, but she would not listen. She stayed perfectly still, forcing her breath to steady and her mind to settle.

That was the first rule of capture. Stay calm. The second was to *pay attention*. Information was the key to survival.

She cursed herself for barging into the Bookshop.

She had noted the Bookkeeper's reaction to the drowning man in the tide pool, had seen his wrinkled face fill with horror and something else—what was it? Recognition? Disbelief? Confusion?

He had stumbled away, pushing through the crowd of screaming people toward the Bookshop.

Ilsbeth had been about to turn back, to see what would happen to the drowning man, when she had caught the glint of flames off a silver mask. Every muscle had tensed as she scanned the crowd and found the others. Four total.

She should have taken a moment to strategize. But instead, she had acted on instinct. Maybe it was the adrenaline, or the excitement of destroying the false Spectress, that had made her feel more powerful than she was.

You are *powerful*, she reminded herself. *It was a bad strategy, but that does not mean you are weak.* She could have beaten them if only she had taken a moment to think.

Instead, she had sidled up to the door, peering through the half-moon window. She had watched the robed figures as they crept across the atrium toward the thick curtain that hid the Bookkeeper's room. They had slid long-bladed daggers from their boots, and she had been filled with indignation.

No one was going to sneak up and attack an old man. Not with her around. She had hurled herself through the door, flinging out her whip. It had cracked, sending a dagger flying from a figure's hand. The dagger had struck the bronze railing with a loud *tong*.

The Bookkeeper's ashen face had peered through the curtain, and realizing that he was in danger, he had ducked back inside.

Two of the masked figures had attacked Ilsbeth at once while the third retrieved their knife and the last one slipped through the curtain.

It had taken only a moment to disarm them. They were adequate fighters, but they had been no match for her. She had sparred with the Guardians of the Glade, with Ardal himself—the greatest warrior of spirits or men. For the first time since the Firebird had returned, she had felt joy, full and alive in her blood.

But she had miscalculated.

She had judged them all the same, but the fourth masked figure had been nothing like the others, and Ilsbeth had been surprised by their skill. By the time she recalibrated, it was too late.

"Give the girl some water." A woman's voice interrupted Ilsbeth's thoughts.

A tin cup pressed against her lips, and lukewarm liquid dribbled into her mouth. She let it spill from her lips, keeping her body limp.

"She isn't drinking it." A man's voice.

"She'll drink when she's thirsty. Leave her." The voice was commanding, confident. *The Silver Shag*, Ilsbeth was certain.

"She's only a kid. Can't we at least—"

"I said, '*Leave her.*' We will be at the Cape soon. Then all we will need to do is wait for the Queen to come."

"What if she doesn't?"

"She *will*." Her words were steely, and the man did not argue again. Boot steps thudded up wooden stairs, and then there was silence but for creaking planks all around. It felt to Ilsbeth as if the world were tilting and rolling beneath her.

Was the Silver Shag right? Would Calliope come?

Will my father? The thought surprised her. *I do not need my father to come. I do not want him to.*

What about the Glade Girls? asked another rebellious thought. They were probably safe in their beds, tucked away after the chaos of the night. She felt a pang of jealousy and cringed. That wasn't what she wanted—coddling and safety— so why did the images of her sisters content and warm in their beds with their mothers and fathers at their sides make her feel . . . ?

She didn't know what she felt. She could normally fight her feelings away, but here, with no place to run, no way to escape, they had finally caught up to her.

Still, Ilsbeth refused to let them weaken her, to let the possibility of someone coming to rescue her keep her from doing what she could to save herself.

She began to work at the knots at her wrists. She ignored the pain of the rope biting into her skin, twisting and bending her fingers in ways they did not want to bend, until at last, she was able to get her fingers directly on the knot. She dug her nails into the fibers, struggling with them until the binds began to loosen.

Finally, her hands were free. She reached up, yanking the blindfold off.

She blinked against the dim light. She was in the belly of the wrecked ship. It creaked and groaned, tilting and swaying. There must be a proper name for the space, but if there was,

Ilsbeth did not know it. She unbound her legs, trying to calm herself, but now that she could see, she knew that being untied did not make her free. There was no place for her to go.

She tried to steady herself, but the ship pitched and she stumbled toward the space where a great hole gaped in the ship's side. She fought to keep the fear from settling in her skin. There was nothing separating her from the water. She could have walked straight into the sea. Goose bumps prickled all along her arms. *Spirit magic.*

She reached reflexively to her waist, but her hand came up empty. Her whip was gone.

She backed away, trying to put space between her and the sea, and she bumped into a crate. She turned to see more and more crates all around. They overflowed with warm blankets, soft-woven sweaters, brightly knit jackets, pants, shirts, and socks. There were rattling glass jars of fruit and preserved vegetables, and some kind of red meat swung from hooks overhead.

She ducked, moving across to the other side of the space, but before she had gone far, she froze. *Someone was watching her.* She held perfectly still, waiting for them to make a move, but they did not, and after a moment, she realized her mistake. It wasn't a person at all but a painting. It was so lifelike that she had to lean close and press her fingers to the paint to be certain that it really was just an image. It was a man. There was something familiar about him, but she was certain she'd never seen him before. He was young, with long blond hair and laughing blue eyes that crinkled gently in the corners. He had been captured in a posture of ease, leaning back in a wooden chair outside a house made of shells. One hand shielded his eyes from the gleaming sun, and the other held a book.

Ilsbeth turned away and saw a stack of other paintings, but she let them be, searching instead for anything that could be used to make a whip or turned into another weapon.

Several large wooden barrels were chained to the floor. The chains were thick, far thicker than necessary for the size of the barrels, and it was clear that the Silver Shag had gone to great lengths to be certain the barrels would not tip over or spill.

Ilsbeth moved to investigate. The metal hoops were engraved with words that Ilsbeth could not read, but she understood the symbol burned into the wood beneath the chains: a black skull.

Ilsbeth pressed her ear to the barrel, expecting to hear some kind of liquid sloshing, but instead she heard a strange rattling. What could be inside that would require so much protection?

She reached down, trying to heft the chains away from the barrel head. Her muscles strained, and when pulling made no headway, she shoved. They fell to the planks with a horrible *clang*, and she waited, holding her breath, but the ship went on creaking, and the sound of laughter filtered down through the thin boards.

She reached out and lifted off the head of the barrel. It was filled to the brim with glistening ice-blue pearls. Ilsbeth narrowed her eyes, trying to make sense of it. Why would pearls be chained, and why were they labeled with a skull? She reached out to pick one up.

"Those don't belong to you."

Ilsbeth whirled, grasping for her whip and coming up empty.

The Silver Shag stood before her, blue eyes shining behind her ornate mask. She strode across the planks, reaching out. "The barrel head. Give it to me."

Ilsbeth handed it to her, and the Silver Shag pressed it into place.

Ilsbeth kept her face even as she watched, noticing how the woman's lip curled as she looked at the barrel.

"Don't you want to know what they are?"

"I *know* what they are," said Ilsbeth.

"Mmm . . ." The Silver Shag looked down at Ilsbeth, her arms folded across her chest. "You are one of those children, aren't you? The ones they call the Glade Girls?"

Ilsbeth glared at her.

The Silver Shag drummed her fingers against her biceps. "You are no stranger to spirits. What would you say if I told you that these pearls are a gift from a Spirit? That they will take away the suffering, pain, sorrows, and fear of the kingdom?"

Ilsbeth did not answer.

"Speak," barked the Silver Shag.

Ilsbeth gritted her teeth. "I would ask what the Spirit expects in return."

The Silver Shag's eyes widened, and Ilsbeth could see that the answer surprised her.

"Why, power, of course. The people of Lyrica are not as wise as you. They are desperate for relief. They will take the pearls, and a Spirit Queen will rise."

"The Queen will not allow this," said Ilsbeth.

"Your Queen will not be there to stop it."

Ilsbeth's spine tingled, and she understood the Silver Shag's plan. Ilsbeth was a decoy, meant to draw Calliope away from the Royal City.

The Silver Shag nodded. "Your Queen will come to save you, her friend, and in return, she will lose her kingdom forever."

Ilsbeth did not hesitate; she ran toward the stairs, bounding up them and shoving hard on the hatch. It opened, and a waft of salt air blew back the loose strands of her hair, but before she could take another step, the Silver Shag grabbed her shoulder, pulling her backward, dragging her away, just as two more masked figures loomed from the deck.

Ilsbeth could do nothing more than struggle as the blindfold was forced back across her eyes, and her hands were rebound, tighter than before. She was shoved down onto the heap of blankets, and the Silver Shag's lips pressed against her ear. "This story is playing out the way *I* choose. You are powerless to change it, Glade Girl."

The Silver Shag's boots thudded up the steps, and the wooden hatch slammed shut. Voices drifted unintelligibly from above.

A wave of nausea struck her, and Ilsbeth began to shake. The ship groaned beneath her, and the sea beat at the boards, splashing through until Ilsbeth was soaked and trembling.

The image of her father came unbidden. She saw him breaking through the boards, bringing with him a flock of avenging falcons. She pushed the image away. *I do not need him to come. I can save myself.* But the thought was weak, and it was quickly overpowered by doubt.

What if the Spirit magic failed and the ship began to sink? She had always imagined that she would die fighting. It was unbearable to think of sinking into the sea, bound and sightless.

A new feeling flooded her. It was something she had never felt before, something so unfamiliar and awful that she thrashed and tugged and yanked at her bonds until her muscles shrieked, but the feeling came nonetheless, slipping into the unprotected spaces of her heart.

It was the feeling of helplessness.

19

Calliope was limp in Prewitt's arms. Her face was ashen, and there was dirt on her cheeks.

He brushed it gently away. "Cal?" She didn't move. "Cal, the Troll is gone now. We can cross the bridge. We can go find Ilsbeth."

She didn't answer.

Prewitt looked up and saw the Bookkeeper still sitting in a heap on the bridge. When the story had been completed, the green mist had wound across the bridge and new growth had filled the gaps and holes, making it strong once again.

Sapling had reached out, grabbing the limb of a tree as he had hauled his burned legs up into the branches. "The toll has been paid. Truth has been told. You may cross my bridge. But be warned; you gave me hope, a cruel lie for your own gain. The next time I see you, the toll will be your life." Then the trees had carried it off, and the forest had fallen into silence.

Prewitt felt a bit sick from what the green mist had shown. The Bookkeeper had let his son die so that he could take the prophecy back to the Royal City. Prewitt knew his own father loved the kingdom just as much as the Bookkeeper did. The duty to protect it was something he talked about all the time. But even so, Prewitt knew that there was no duty, no love stronger than his father's love for his family. He never would have done what the Bookkeeper had. He would have found some other way to get the prophecy home.

Prewitt didn't want to talk to the old man now, didn't want to look at him at all—what he'd done was too awful—but Prewitt knew that he had no choice. Calliope needed help, and he couldn't carry her on his own. It took several times calling the Bookkeeper's name before the old man looked up.

Prewitt had expected to see sorrow in the man's face, or at least regret, but instead, the Bookkeeper's eyes were red-rimmed and angry. "How dare the Troll attack me that way," he spat. "I did not deserve it. That was not the *true story*. I was there. I know what happened." He turned his face to Prewitt. "Now you see why the Trolls are our enemies," he said. "That is why the bridges must stay hidden so that people can continue to tell their stories how they choose."

"I don't care about the bridges," snapped Prewitt. "Because of you, Calliope is hurt."

The Bookkeeper's mouth fell open. "Me? What did I do?"

"You told the Tree Troll that Cal could heal it, instead of giving it the story like it asked."

"Well," said the Bookkeeper, looking slightly abashed, "I

believed that she could. She was *so close* on the beach; I saw it in her face. She needed only to reach out and grab it. I thought that perhaps, given the right opportunity and incentive, she might succeed." He stood and came to look down at Calliope. "We must hope that the library at Castaway Cape still stands and that we will find the books we need."

He shook his head, disappointment tugging like fishhooks at the corners of his mouth. "Hurry up then, Bargeboy; stop gawping at me and help me pick the girl up."

The late-morning sun was already hot, and sweat beaded across the Bookkeeper's bald head as they finally came to the edge of the woods. They set Calliope down, and took a moment to catch their breaths.

The Bookkeeper turned to Prewitt. "We do not know what will meet us at the Cape. This is a place of crime and chaos. Need I tell you the stories—"

"No," snapped Prewitt. "I don't care. All I care about is getting Calliope help. That's what you should care about, too."

The Bookkeeper thrust his jaw forward. "Certainly, I care. Why do you think I'm so determined to find the books? It's all about helping *her*." He sighed. "I thought the Song would be enough, that it would turn her into something special."

Prewitt glared at him. "Calliope doesn't need to be *turned* into anything. It was her hope that called the Firebird back, but you made her feel like that wasn't enough."

The Bookkeeper blinked. "I am trying to keep the kingdom safe. That is not a crime. Now"—he took a breath and waved his hand at Prewitt—"take a moment to gather yourself.

Your emotions are out of control. I know you are the Bargeboy, but this is no time for barging. Cover her hair, quickly. We don't want her recognized."

Prewitt stared down at Calliope. Her black curls were wild around her cheeks. He took off his cap and pressed it down onto her head, gently tucking her curls underneath. Then he slid the Feather from her sash and hid it inside his jacket. "Don't worry, Cal. I'll give it back as soon as it's safe, I promise."

The Bookkeeper held up a hand. "All right, Bargeboy. Time is of the essence. Let us go, and when we reach the wall, you will let me do the talking, do you understand?"

Prewitt nodded. "I just want Cal to be okay."

Together, he and the Bookkeeper lifted Calliope back up and carried her out of the woods.

A stone wall towered so suddenly before them that they nearly crashed into it. They walked about a hundred feet along the wall until they reached a stone archway that housed a heavy metal gate.

"Hello, friends!" bellowed the Bookkeeper, looking up toward the top of the gate.

Two men stood guard on the wall. The sun shone in their eyes, and they raised their hands to their brows as they squinted down at them.

"What do you want, old man?" asked one guard.

"I have need of a doctor for my granddaughter. She fell ill on our journey from Madrigale."

"We cannot help you," said the other guard.

"But you have to!" cried Prewitt.

The man on the left eyed Prewitt suspiciously. "Isn't that the Bargemaster's jacket?"

Prewitt looked down at himself. Why hadn't he thought to remove it?

"Keen eyes, my friend," shouted the Bookkeeper. "Yes, it is a Bargemaster's coat. We found it in the wreckage of a boat that ran adrift in the reeds outside our village."

"I see," said the man, pursing his lips. "Well, the city of Lyre is only half a day's walk from here. Follow the wall east until you reach the road. You can find the girl a doctor there."

Prewitt's mouth fell open. "We don't have a half day! She needs help now!"

"Quiet, boy." The Bookkeeper gave him a sharp glance. Then he cleared his throat. "I'd like to speak with the Reckoner."

"The Reckoner?" The guard raised a brow, exchanging a glance with his companion.

"Yes," said the Bookkeeper. "He is an old acquaintance of mine."

The second guard's face changed, and where before he'd been wary, he was now all smiles. "Why didn't you say that in the first place?" He turned his head and motioned over the wall. "We've got a visitor for the Reckoner," he shouted.

To Prewitt's surprise, the gate ground open, and the Bookkeeper beamed. "The power of words, boy. You just have to know the right ones, and any door will open for you."

Prewitt didn't answer. He didn't care. He only wanted to get Calliope inside and find someone who would help her— even the Reckoner.

The gate shut behind them, and the guard who had shouted ran down a set of stone steps, slinging his arm across the Bookkeeper's shoulders.

Prewitt looked around, taken aback by what he saw. Castaway Cape wasn't a prison at all, at least not in the way he'd expected. It was a city. People were not chained or bound, but walking freely. Their faces were bright as they chatted with one another, but the moment they saw the newcomers, they hushed.

Prewitt noticed a girl perched on the side of a stone fountain. She stared at him, unblinking.

He frowned. He still wasn't used to seeing girls his age. How had she escaped the Spectress?

Her choppy blond hair was tucked behind her ears, and she sat with a pencil in her hand and a stack of parchment in her lap. Her eyes never left him as he and the Bookkeeper carried Calliope across the light-brown dirt.

"So, the Reckoner is a friend of yours, is he?" said the guard with a wink, and something about the way he said it made Prewitt feel suddenly uneasy.

The Bookkeeper inclined his head. "Sebastian and I are well acquainted, yes. We, ah, were schoolmates once. He would be quite upset if my grandchildren or I were harmed."

"Well, by all means then, you must see him."

"What about my sister?" Prewitt demanded.

"In a moment, in a moment." The guard waved them on, and they walked a few more feet before stopping. The guard nodded toward a spike with a purple coat on it. "There you are, Grandfather," he said, laughing. "Say hello to your old friend, the Reckoner."

The other guard guffawed, and people all around stopped and turned to watch.

Prewitt's heart raced, and he wished Calliope would wake. He wished he could have stopped her from using the Spirit magic. He wished they'd never left the Royal City, but even as he wished it, he could hear Calliope chiding him, reminding him that they had come to save their friend.

The Bookkeeper squinted, struggling to see without his spectacles. When he finally did, his face twisted, and he let out a breath. "You aren't guards at all! Imposters! Heathens! Tyrants!"

The man sneered. "Call us what you will. But the Reckoner is not in charge anymore. Castaway Cape is free."

"Then why are you guarding it?" asked Prewitt.

"Oh, we're not keeping people in, boy. We're keeping strangers *out*. Especially strangers from the *Royal City*."

The Bookkeeper huffed. "We're not from the Royal City. I told you we're from Madrigale!"

"Yeah, yeah, sure. You think we can't recognize a Royal City accent when we hear one? It's been a long time, but our memories aren't that short." The guard reached out and grabbed the Bookkeeper by the collar. The Bookkeeper dropped Calliope's legs, his hands in front of his face.

Prewitt collapsed to his knees under the weight of Calliope's limp body. "Please!" He looked around at the gathering crowd. "You have to help us!"

"Not until you tell us who you really are," hissed the guard. His lip curled and his tone was threatening.

A man came striding across the courtyard, tugged along by the girl Prewitt had seen watching.

"What's going on here?" the man barked.

The guard dropped the Bookkeeper's collar, looking abashed. "This man said he knew the Reckoner, so I—"

"This girl needs help," said the newcomer. "Can't you see that?"

"I just thought—"

"Never mind what you thought. This is not who we are. We don't treat people like this, especially children. Return to your post."

The guard slunk back to the wall, climbing up the steps to join his comrade.

"I apologize," said the man. He was tall and slim, with light-brown hair and full, smiling lips. "We haven't had any visitors in many years. I'm afraid the guards are a bit overzealous."

"I should say so," said the Bookkeeper, dusting himself off.

The man bent and gently picked Calliope up. "Follow me."

The buildings were connected in long rows, some many stories high. They were each made of the same dusty clay. Bright flowers grew in pots along windows and in doorways, and sun-bleached awnings cast shade between the streets. Rooftop gardens were lush and green, and clothing hung from lines strung between upper-story windows, waving in the breeze.

The streets were bustling and noisy. Children ran across the connected gardens, screaming and laughing. Stalls were set up beneath the awnings, and craftspeople sat painting, carving, and building.

The Bookkeeper had said that Castaway Cape was a place of chaos, but Prewitt could see no chaos anywhere. None of these people looked like criminals at all, certainly not people who had done anything bad enough to get locked away forever.

"In here," said the man, and they followed him through an arched doorway and into a tidy house.

It was nothing like Prewitt's cramped home on the tiers. The space was open. Purple flowers hung in baskets from the ceiling, and a low table inlaid with rose-stamped tile stretched across the floor surrounded by brightly colored cushions. The girl hurried to rearrange them and the man lay Calliope down. The hat fell from her head, and her curls spilled onto the floor, but the man's face did not register anything but concern.

"Wait here." He disappeared through an arched doorway, and they heard him bound up a set of stairs.

The girl sat cross-legged, the stack of parchment on her lap. More paper and pencils were scattered on the floor as if it were a place she sat often. She bent her head over the parchment, jotting something before looking up. Her tongue poked out of a space where a tooth was missing on the right side of her mouth.

"Where are you from?"

The question caught Prewitt off guard. "The Royal City," he said automatically. Then he remembered that the Bookkeeper had said they were from Madrigale. "Or, we used to be from the Royal City, but we . . . moved."

The pencil scribbled. "What happened to your friend?"

"She's not my friend. She's my sister," said Prewitt, proud that he had at least remembered that.

The girl raised her brow. "You look the same age."

"We're, uh, twins."

Both brows lifted, and the girl wrote something more.

The man thundered back down the stairs, his arms full of supplies. He set them down and knelt beside Calliope, easing his arm beneath her head.

"Chichi, go and get some cool water from the basin."

The girl tucked the pencil behind her ear and ran across to the other room. When she came back, she was carrying a jug full of water. It sloshed down across the dark-gray weave of her dress. She set it beside her father and then plopped back onto the floor, pencil poised.

"What's your name?" she asked.

"Huh?" Prewitt's attention was on the man. He had dipped a piece of linen into the water and squeezed it out before tenderly placing it across Calliope's forehead.

"Your name! You must have a name. I'm Chichi, and that's my father, Reynard."

"Oh, um, it's . . ." Prewitt tried to think of a name. Only his father's came to him. "It's Meredith."

"You sure?"

Prewitt nodded.

"You don't seem that sure."

"My friend is sick."

"I thought she was your sister."

Prewitt flushed. "She is."

"If you say so." More scribbling.

"Chichi, stop pestering our guest. No one thinks clearly when they're worried."

Prewitt nodded. "I am worried." At least he could tell the truth about that. "Is she going to be okay?"

"Well, I don't know. I think so." Reynard lifted Calliope's hand, pressing his fingers to the inside of her wrist. "Can you tell me more about what happened to her?"

"Um . . ." Prewitt hesitated.

"She fell ill on our journey," said the Bookkeeper. He was wandering the room, bending close as he investigated things. "She must have been overcome by the heat."

Chichi tilted her head. "It's not even midday."

"Chichi . . . ," Reynard warned.

Chichi put the pencil to her teeth, charcoal blackening her gums. "I'm only trying to help."

"We're doing just fine, thank you."

Chichi sighed, bending over the parchment and jotting down something else. She looked back at Prewitt, her eyes scanning him from the top of his head to his boots as if she could find answers to every one of her questions. He squirmed beneath her gaze.

Reynard reached into the basket of items and pulled out a tiny vial. He untwisted the top and waved it beneath Calliope's nostrils.

Her head jerked back, and Prewitt flinched.

"It's all right," said Reynard. "See? She's coming round."

Calliope's breaths came quickly, and her eyes flashed open, darting wildly. "Where am I?" she gasped.

Prewitt moved close, worried that she might say something that would give them away. "It's me—*Meredith*." He gave her a look, hoping she'd understand, but she shook her head, confused. "Meredith?"

"She may be a little disoriented for a moment or two," said Reynard, pushing himself to his feet. "But she should be all right. I can't see anything wrong with her. Nothing that rest and sustenance can't cure, I shouldn't think. Let me get you all something to eat."

He left the room, and Calliope's head turned on the pillow. "What's going on?"

Chichi leaned forward, listening, and Prewitt glared at her. "My sister could use some water," he said.

Chichi looked pointedly at the pitcher.

"She can't drink it out of that, can she?"

Chichi rolled her eyes and flung down her pencil; then she jumped up and stomped out of the room.

Prewitt quickly caught Calliope up to speed. He told her

about the Bookkeeper's story, about the drowned man who had been the Bookkeeper's son, and about the awful thing the Bookkeeper had done.

She shook her head, not wanting to believe it. "I've always known that he would do anything for the kingdom," she said. "But that's horrible. It's so sad."

She glanced around. "Are you *sure* this is Castaway Cape?"

Prewitt nodded.

"It isn't what I expected."

"I don't think it's what any of us expected," said Prewitt.

Chichi came running back with a glass. She sloshed water into it and thrust it at Calliope. "What's not what you expected?"

"Life outside our village," said Calliope easily. "We didn't know what it would be like. Things are so different at home."

Reynard returned with a tray of sliced meats and cheeses and a basket of warm rolls.

"Are you a doctor?" asked Calliope, nibbling on a roll.

Reynard laughed. "Not at all. We don't have a doctor on Castaway Cape. We had one for a while, but he died not too long after the Spectress came to power."

Calliope pulled the roll away from her mouth. "I'm sorry."

"We've all suffered," said Reynard.

"We've all survived," chirped Chichi. They smiled at each other.

"I have some things I need to do," said Reynard. "You're welcome to stay here as long as you need, but we do have two rules that you must obey."

He held up a finger. "First, there are torches that line the edge of the city; no one is allowed beyond them for their own safety. The winds are treacherous near the cliff's edge, and those who have disregarded the boundary have been swept off and met their deaths on the rocks below."

His face was grave as he held up another finger. "Second, no one is allowed outside after dark." His tone was grave, but he gave no explanation for the second rule. Instead, he slapped his hands on his knees and let out a laugh. "All right, all right, enough seriousness for now. I have to get going."

He looked across the room at the Bookkeeper, who was peering around the corner into the kitchen. "Can I help you find something before I go, Grandfather?"

The Bookkeeper startled and looked back at him. "Ah, yes. I was wondering if perhaps you had a library here? All the books in our village were destroyed, but the Cape seems to have been untouched by the ash golems."

Reynard smiled. "Not completely, but we have worked hard to rebuild our life here. We *do* have a library and quite a large collection. I can take you if you'd like."

The Bookkeeper's face lit, and he almost ran to the door.

Reynard laughed.

The Bookkeeper was halfway onto the street before he remembered Calliope and Prewitt. He turned back, hesitating.

"Don't worry, Grandfather," said Reynard. "Chichi will watch over the others, won't you, Cheech?"

The girl nodded, her face solemn, but the moment the Bookkeeper and Reynard had gone, she whirled.

"I know who you *really* are," she said.

"You do?" asked Prewitt.

"Not you," said Chichi. *"You."* She pointed her pencil at Calliope, and her mouth spread into a wide grin.

"You are the Queen of Lyrica."

20

"**But how did you figure out who** I am?" Being called the Queen still made Calliope feel like an imposter, and she would have corrected Chichi, but she found herself smiling.

Prewitt rolled his eyes. "Firebird feathers, Cal. You could have at least *tried* to deny it."

"Why? I don't think Chichi is going to tell anyone. Otherwise, she would have said something while her father was here."

"I *knew* you weren't twins," giggled Chichi. "Have you seen yourselves?" Then she pointed at Prewitt. "You! You didn't even know your own name. Remember when you said you were from the Royal City but that you'd moved? Moved!"

Prewitt scowled as Chichi's riotous laughter made her fall backward onto the cushions. Her feet kicked the air as she wiped away a tear. "Of *course* I knew you were lying!"

"But that still doesn't explain how you knew who I am."

Chichi sat up and leaned forward, eager. "The first thing I needed to figure out was *why* you'd lie. Why keep your identity a secret? You obviously didn't think you'd be safe here, and *who* would anyone in Castaway Cape want to harm? The only person I could think of was the Queen who banished them here—only she died the night of the Terrible Thing. But her daughter survived, and rumor has it that her hair is just the same as her mother's, and her grandmother's, and pretty much every other Firebird Queen ever."

Calliope reached up to touch her curls.

Chichi nodded at Prewitt. "And you! In the courtyard, the sun shone on you, and I saw something shimmering beneath your jacket, just *there*." She jabbed the place where the jacket had been patched after it had been singed by the Spectress's fireball.

"Hey!" said Prewitt, flinching away from her pencil tip.

Chichi rushed on, flapping her hands in her excitement. "I've heard the stories. Everyone has! About the Firebird returning and the Princess finding the lost Firebird Feather. *That's* what you have under your coat, isn't it?" She reached for Prewitt's jacket and he jerked back.

"I knew it!" crowed Chichi. "Let me see! Please? Please! Just for a second?"

Prewitt shook his head, but Calliope smiled. "It's all right, Prewitt."

Prewitt pulled out the Feather and Chichi leaned close. "I can't believe it. This actually came from the Firebird itself? Can I hold it?"

Prewitt reluctantly passed her the Feather. She held it reverentially, running her fingers gently along its length. She gave it back to Prewitt who handed it to Calliope, and she tucked it into her waistband and pulled her tunic down over it.

Chichi knelt, her pencil at the ready. "You *have* to tell me *everything*. I want to know what it was like when you fought the Spectress. Did you really go in with an army of girls? What happened when the Firebird came back? Some people say that you let the Spectress go. Is that what happened?"

Calliope held up her hands. "I'll tell you anything you want to know, but first you have to help us."

Chichi frowned. "Help you?"

"We're looking for our friend. That's why we're here. The Silver Shag took her." She reached into her pocket, pulling out the fledgling's message, and handing it over.

Chichi's eyes scanned it. *"Bring the Bookkeeper to the fort at Castaway Cape before the full moon wanes or the girl will die."* She looked up, frowning. "The Silver Shag couldn't have written this. She wouldn't kill anyone—especially not a little girl. The Masked Rampage only does good."

Prewitt scoffed. "Is that why they're running around the kingdom, telling everyone that the Spectress is still alive?"

The door creaked open, and the three children jumped as a woman came in holding a wicker basket. A light-blue scarf was wrapped around thick blond hair that fell in waves across her pale forehead. Her cheeks were rosy, and she smiled warmly when she saw Calliope and Prewitt on the cushions.

"Mama!" Chichi jumped up, running to the woman. "You're back!"

"I see we have guests!" said the woman, pulling off her scarf. "I heard a rumor that the Cape had visitors, but I had to see it for myself." She smiled at them, and her eyes searched the room. "I was told there were three of you."

"Yes," said Chichi. "Their grandfather is with them. He went to look at the book collection with Daddy."

"I see." The disappointment was evident in the downturn of the woman's mouth. "Well, I'm sure I'll get to meet him later."

She set her basket on the table, and Calliope couldn't help but gasp. Inside were several intricate loaves of bread. Chichi's mother smiled, picking up a loaf and handing it to her. "Fresh bread made just this morning."

Calliope held the bread to her nose, breathing in the yeasty scent.

Chichi giggled. "Haven't you seen bread before?"

Calliope shook her head. "Not like this!" She handed the bread to Prewitt, who gave it an appreciative sniff before placing it back in the basket. "People are still afraid to bake bread where we're from," said Calliope.

Chichi's mother frowned. "That's too bad. Someone should do something to help them feel safer."

"The Princess is trying," said Calliope. "But they won't listen." She chewed her lip. "How did you all return to normal so quickly? I thought you were . . ." She trailed off, not wanting to offend them.

"Let me guess," said Chichi. "You thought we were all criminals?"

Calliope and Prewitt nodded.

"Well, we're not. It was my great-great-grandfather who was sent here for life."

Calliope stared at her. "What do you mean?"

"Most of the people who live here have never committed a crime," said Chichi's mother. "Those who did are quite old." Her eyes narrowed. "It was the Reckoner's belief that crime should be cut off at the root."

"The Queen would never have allowed that," said Calliope.

Chichi's mother tilted her head. "But she did." Her voice was hard. "At any point, she could have set people free. But instead, she let the Cape suffer under the Reckoner's rule."

"Suffering made us strong, though," said Chichi, gazing worshipfully at her mother's face.

Chichi's mother sat down on the cushion beside Chichi and wrapped her arms around her. "That's right," she said. "It's a part of our story, which is why we will keep on telling it." Chichi's mother rested her cheek on the top of Chichi's head. "Our stories are our strength," she said.

Calliope's heart panged. It felt lonely watching them together. She swallowed, refusing to let the feeling grow. "Why don't you leave now? The Spectress is gone, and the Reckoner is dead. You don't have to stay here anymore. Why do you keep it guarded?"

Chichi's mother tucked her hair behind her ear. "This is

our home. It may not have been our choice to be here, but we made it what it is. We belong to each other here. Who would understand us beyond the wall? They think we're criminals. Do you suppose they would be kind to us?"

Calliope saw Chichi's face fall. She grabbed her parchment stack, hugging it close.

"Enough of this dreary talk." Chichi's mother stood. "I want to hear all about what's brought you to Castaway Cape. Give me just a moment to put away this bread, and then you'll have my undivided attention." She moved into the kitchen, and they heard her opening and closing cupboards.

"Why don't you ask my mother about your friend?" said Chichi. "She'll tell you the same thing. The Silver Shag would never—"

"If the Silver Shag is so good, then why are she and the Masked Rampage telling people that the Spectress is still out there?" demanded Prewitt.

Chichi chewed on her pencil. "Maybe it's true."

"It isn't," said Calliope. "The Spectress is gone. The Firebird returned. You held the Feather yourself."

"That doesn't mean the Silver Shag is lying. She and the Masked Rampage help people. I wouldn't be alive if it weren't for her."

Calliope shifted against the cushions. "Why? What did she do?"

Chichi's entire face lit, and she leaned forward. "She saved everyone on the Cape. I wasn't born yet when the Spectress came to power, but my father said things were awful here. So many people died from the first ash golem attacks, before they knew that the fires were dangerous. They were trapped inside the wall with the monsters." Chichi shuddered. "The Queen's guards died then, and the Reckoner, too. People tried to leave, but the Spectress's men were waiting on the other side of the wall.

"There was no food, and everyone was suffering and afraid. Daddy says that things were so bad that people started fighting one another. But then, a little less than a year after the Spectress rose to power, the Silver Shag came and changed everything.

"For so long, people had been told they were weak, that they were prisoners, but the Silver Shag convinced them that they had power, that they could create a new story." Chichi held up a fist, shaking it as she reenacted the scene, making her voice defiant. " 'These walls that were meant to weaken you will be your biggest strength.' "

Chichi dropped her fist, grinning. "She was right. The walls kept the Spectress's men out."

"But if everyone was stuck inside, what did they eat?" asked Prewitt. "Nothing grew in the Royal City. Just weeds and poisonous things. We almost starved."

Chichi nodded. "Here too. But the cormorants came."

"Cormorants?" Calliope stared at her, remembering the bird that had dropped the pearl. *Sentinels of the Sea*, Marisa had called them.

Prewitt made a face. "You ate cormorants?"

Chichi fell over, laughing hysterically. "No, no, no!" she said, giggling. "They gave us fish! But more than that, it was the cormorants who brought us the Silver Shag. Daddy says they carried her out of the sea during a really bad storm."

Prewitt tried to imagine it, the black-winged birds lifting a masked woman from the depths of the sea.

Calliope turned to him. "Prewitt," she said. "I think I know which Spirit is working with the Silver Shag."

"You do?"

Calliope nodded. "The Spirit of the Suffering Sea. It all makes sense now! The monsters on the beach—they weren't made of ash and fire; they were *water*."

"The Suffering Sea?" Chichi picked up her pencil, not able to keep the curiosity from her face.

Calliope nodded. She told Chichi about cormorants being the Sea Spirit's sentinels, and she explained about the pearls. "Every sad, painful story she steals gives her more power. That's why the Silver Shag is keeping people afraid. She plans to use their stories to help the Spirit of the Suffering Sea take the throne."

Chichi was unconvinced. "Why would the Silver Shag do that?" she said. "You heard what I said. The Silver Shag only does good. She helps people."

Calliope shook her head. "They were in the Royal City last night, Chichi. I saw their masks. I know you don't want to believe it, but they took our friend."

Chichi's jaw was set. "You're wrong."

Calliope and Prewitt tried again to reason with Chichi, but

she wouldn't hear it. Instead, she got up and went to join her mother in the kitchen.

Calliope sighed, falling back against the cushions and staring up at the ceiling.

Prewitt leaned close. "Don't worry, Cal. We'll find Ilsbeth on our own," he whispered.

Calliope hoped that he was right.

21

The sun was curving back toward the horizon before Calliope's energy returned.

She had tried her best to sleep, but rest would not come. Instead, she lay with her eyes closed, listening as Chichi came back too curious to stay away, and began pestering Prewitt with questions about the Royal City. She felt the fabric of his jacket, noted the calluses on his hands, and counted the number of freckles across the bridge of his light-brown nose, writing everything down.

"Why do you do that?" asked Prewitt.

Chichi looked up, her tongue sticking out, and she considered for a moment before she replied. "For a long time, I thought I wasn't good at anything. I'm not pretty like my mother or smart like Daddy, and that bothered me. But then one day I realized that there is something I do that other people don't. I *notice* things."

Her blue eyes sparkled. "That's what makes me special. It's how I am going to make a difference."

She picked up the sheaf of papers, flipping through them, and Prewitt saw they were filled with drawings and words that he couldn't read for himself.

"I've written all about our lives here," said Chichi. "Mama says our stories are our strength. She says we must always remember every part of them. Once people read our stories, once they get to know us each as people, and see that we're just like them, they won't be afraid of us or think we're criminals anymore. We'll be able to leave the Cape."

"Then what will you do?" asked Prewitt.

"I'll travel the kingdom and write about people everywhere. Won't that be exciting?"

Prewitt didn't think writing about people's day-to-day lives would be especially exciting, and he said so, which only made Chichi laugh and write something down.

By the time Reynard and the Bookkeeper returned, the flush had returned to Calliope's golden cheeks, and her eyes had regained their shine.

The Bookkeeper pulled a wagonload of books through the door and sat down heavily among the cushions.

"I'm sorry you couldn't stay," said Reynard. "But the library will reopen in the morning, and you can go back and keep looking for . . . well, whatever it is you seem to be looking for."

The Bookkeeper sniffed. "I never thought I'd see the day when *I'd* be kicked out of a library."

"Find anything good?" asked Calliope, hoping he would understand what she meant.

The Bookkeeper shook his head. "Not yet."

Of course, Calliope knew that the books and the library had been a ruse, but she had begun to hope that maybe there *could* be answers in Castaway Cape.

The Bookkeeper bent his head close to the page of an ancient-looking book. "If only my spectacles hadn't broken," he grumbled.

"Perhaps we can find you another pair somewhere," said Reynard.

But the Bookkeeper was already lost in the text.

Chichi's mother came into the room, carrying a stack of empty bowls. "You must be Grandfather," she said, beaming at the Bookkeeper.

"Pardon? Oh, yes. I am indeed."

"Will you be joining us for supper?"

The Bookkeeper didn't look up. "Who could eat when there are words to devour?"

"Anyone who is truly hungry, I'd expect." The words held a chill that made Calliope and Prewitt exchange a glance.

But the smile was back on Chichi's mother's face as she waved them all through the front door, handing them each an empty wooden bowl as they crossed out onto the street, leaving the Bookkeeper behind.

Prewitt pulled Calliope close as they followed Reynard toward the courtyard. "Maybe we'll get a chance to slip away and look for Ilsbeth. If we can find her on our own, we can set her free and we won't have to give them the Bookkeeper at all."

Calliope nodded, her eyes darting around, taking in the city. The atmosphere was warm and friendly and in such contrast to the Royal City that Calliope found it unsettling. What had made such a difference here? How had people found a way to move on after so many years of hardship?

In the courtyard, rows of tables had been set up and arrayed with platters of smoked meats, heaps of cheeses, bowls of bright decadent sauces, and thickly iced cakes melting in the evening sun.

Hundreds of people stood in a wide circle around the courtyard, side by side.

"What are they doing?" asked Calliope.

"You don't do this in the Royal City?" asked Chichi, pulling them into the circle.

"People are too afraid to gather like this," said Calliope, and she felt a pang of guilt as she recalled their frightened faces before the bonfire.

"No one here seems afraid at all," said Prewitt.

"Shh." Chichi held a finger to her lips. "It's starting!"

Reynard stepped forward, and the people quieted. He waved an arm, and everyone looked up to the sky.

Calliope grabbed Prewitt's elbow. "Now's our chance," she whispered. But before they could break away, a shadow passed over the courtyard, and they saw what the crowd had been waiting for.

Cormorants filled the sky until there was no sky to be seen. They flew overhead, their wings a wild frenzy, and they settled in a mass along the wall.

Everyone turned their faces toward them as Reynard lifted his voice. "Before the Masked Rampage, before the Firebird returned and the darkness was vanquished, there was nothing to eat, and the cormorants brought us fish. Let us thank them."

The crowd bowed to the birds and the birds lifted their wings.

"Before the Masked Rampage, we were outcasts," shouted Reynard. "But the Silver Shag kept us safe. She reminded us that we could be strong together."

Shouts rose from the crowd. "Long live the Silver Shag!"

Reynard lifted his bowl, and around the circle, hundreds of other bowls lifted as one.

"Together we starved!"

"Together we starved!" the crowd chanted.

"Together we feast!"

The birds raised their necks and took to the sky once more, and the crowd broke apart. They moved toward the tables, chatting as they filled their bowls with food.

"This happens every day?" asked Prewitt. It was bizarre to think that these people had lived through the same darkness as the Royal City, had suffered the same fear and torment, and yet, they had moved forward, had returned to some kind of normal, while the rest of the kingdom was still haunted and broken.

Chichi nodded. "Morning and night. It helps us remember what we've come through. My mother always says that our whole story, good and bad, is what makes us strong. It's all a part of who we are, so we mustn't ever forget."

The children filled their bowls and found a place on the edge of the courtyard to eat.

Calliope watched the people of Castaway Cape talking together and laughing.

Chichi's mother came and sat with them in the grass, her legs crossed and a large bowl of fruit in her lap.

A group of small children chased one another along the top of the wall with gleeful shrieks.

Calliope looked around for their parents, but no one seemed to be paying much attention.

"Don't worry," said Chichi's mother. "They won't fall, but if they do, there are a dozen people who will come running to pick them up again."

Calliope frowned. "Wouldn't it be safer if their parents made them get down off the wall? Then they wouldn't fall at all."

Chichi's mother popped a cherry into her mouth, spitting the pit into the grass. "Falling is part of living. A parent mustn't rob a child of that."

Calliope frowned. She hadn't ever thought of it that way before. She had always assumed that if her mother were there, she would make sure she never fell or made a mistake, but maybe that wasn't what a mother's love looked like after all. Her eyes welled. She would never know for sure.

Someone waved Chichi's mother over, and she left her bowl in the grass and went to join them.

"Chichi," said Calliope, choosing her words carefully. "Do you know who the Silver Shag and the Masked Rampage are? Do they live here?"

Chichi didn't look up from her parchment.

"Please, if you know, you could help us find our friend."

Chichi shook her head. "Your friend isn't here!"

"But if you tell us who the Silver Shag is—"

"I don't know who any of them are," snapped Chichi. She jumped to her feet, gathered her parchment together, and ran off to join her mother.

Before Calliope or Prewitt could sneak away to find Ilsbeth, dusk had fallen.

The streets were empty as Reynard hurried them back to the house.

He arranged cushions for Prewitt and the Bookkeeper downstairs, and then he led Calliope up the steps to Chichi's bedroom.

The girls crawled under the covers together.

The moment Reynard shut the door, Calliope turned to Chichi. "Please, if you have any idea where she could be, you *have* to tell me. She's in danger!"

The other girl rolled away from her.

Calliope sighed. She lay, staring up at the ceiling. They were running out of time. If the Silver Shag and the Masked Rampage were at the Cape, they must realize that Calliope was there.

Why hadn't they come to find her? What were they waiting for? Her thoughts were like wild birds, flitting through her skull, wings flapping.

It had been terrifying to wake up in Castaway Cape without any memory of how she had gotten there. One moment, she had been falling, the Troll's sorrow and her own mixing like poison in her body, the *sound* of magic a knife in her skull, and the next, she had opened her eyes in Chichi's living room.

Now that she knew that it had been the Spirit of the Suffering Sea who had tricked her people on the beach, Calliope was even more anxious. She had a horrible feeling that if the Spirit offered pearls to the people, they would accept them gladly. They were tired of being afraid, of being sad, of all the pain of the last twelve years of loss. They wanted to move forward, and Calliope understood. She herself had wished she had taken a pearl. It would have been so easy.

How could she defeat the Sea Spirit? She had felt its magic on the beach, and it had been stronger by far than the Troll's. Without knowing the secret of the Queen's magic, Calliope knew that she would never be able to defeat the Ancient Spirit. She pulled out the Feather, letting its glow play on the ceiling.

The cries came through the window and caught her like a blow to the stomach.

Help us!

Save us!

Free us!

With all the worry about Ilsbeth and the Sea Spirit, Calliope

168

had nearly forgotten the voices, but they had not forgotten her. Their wails were more urgent than ever.

They pulled her from the cushions and yanked her out the door and down the stairs.

The dust was soft between her toes as she padded through the streets.

Torchlight flickered, lighting the path, but she would have known the way without it. She had only to follow the cries. They were a cord that pulled her heart, tugging her on and on.

She walked beyond the torches, until the city was behind her, and followed the voices until she could hear the sound of the roaring sea. She was about to take another step when she nearly fell off the edge of the Cape.

She wobbled, her heart in her ears and the wind in her hair. Looking over the drop-off, she suddenly saw for herself what made Castaway Cape both a prison and a fortress, for the Cape *was*, and then, just as suddenly, it was not. White chalk cliffs dropped hundreds of feet straight down, and at the bottom, broken boats lay like vulture-picked carcasses.

She blinked, adrenaline rushing in her ears, the voices tamed for a moment, and she sucked in her breath. Among the wreckage was the hulking form of a ruined ship, and she knew at once that it was the one Jack had described. In the moonlight, cormorants roosted along the deck and across the railings.

She squinted and saw something white within the broken hull, fluttering like fabric. Her heart picked up pace, and she held in a cry.

Ilsbeth! She looked around for some way down from the cliff, but there wasn't any.

She had to go find Prewitt so they could figure out together how to get to the ship.

She turned around and let out a shriek.

A face pressed close to hers, a face so shocking that she nearly toppled backward off the cliff.

22

Night ended the watermen's search for Prewitt and Calliope.

They had found their tracks into the woods and followed them a short distance, but then the tracks had ended, and there was nothing, no sign of them at all. It was as if they had vanished. None of them spoke their worries aloud; instead they continued their search in vain. They swept the woods until twilight crept down the trees and pulled curtains across their path, and Jack, the two watermen, and the Bargemaster were forced to return to the castle.

They gathered in the kitchen, a low fire snapping in one of the hearths.

Meredith took off his cap, crumpling it in his hands. "None of you can breathe a word of this to anyone. There's more at risk here than you know. With the Queen gone from the city, the throne itself is at stake."

Old Harry rubbed his eyes. "None of this is a coincidence. The Queen is smart. She wouldn't have left the city without good reason."

"Good reason or not," said Cedric, "the city is in danger."

The Bargemaster nodded. "I sense it, too. The best thing we can do is keep this between us until—"

He broke off, turning his head.

They all heard it, the distant *bang* of a door being flung open, the echo of voices.

The Bargemaster got to his feet, sharing a concerned look with the watermen. They hurried down the castle corridors, the commotion growing louder until they finally pushed through the doors to the throne room.

A dozen people stood in the dark, all shouting at once.

Meredith lifted his hand, and when that did not calm them, he held his fingers to his lips and whistled, long and shrill.

They stilled.

Moonlight fractured through the cracked stained glass, casting worried faces in lurid light.

"Tell me what's wrong," said Meredith, his voice soothing.

A fat woman stepped forward, wringing her hands. "My daughter is missing."

Jack recognized her at once as Fi's mother.

Meredith frowned. "How long has she been gone?"

The woman shook her head. "I don't know!" Her breaths were short and fast, and tears streaked her cheeks. "I only turned my back for a second—just a second!—and then she was gone."

Meredith looked at the others. "You've all come to help find her?"

"Help? We're not here to help!" sputtered a man. "All our daughters are missing."

Meredith's face turned gray, and his hand dropped from his sword hilt. *"All of them?"*

"It's the Spectress again!" A small man squeaked. "I know it!"

There were nods around the group.

"The Spectress is gone!" said Meredith. "The Firebird returned and defeated her."

"You lie!" said the man, blinking droplets of sweat from his eyes. "We all saw her! We all saw what happened when the Queen started the fire! The ash golems came."

There were shouts of agreement, and the group moved toward the Bargemaster, their anger growing.

"We will find your daughters," said Meredith, raising his hands. "Please, stay calm."

"Stay calm? How can you tell us to stay calm? Haven't we been through enough? When will our suffering be over? When can we stop living this nightmare and finally get some peace?"

Fi's mother saw Jack, and her face reddened. She shook a finger at him. "That boy! He knows something. He was pounding on my door, trying to get my Fi to come out."

"Yes!" Another man nodded. "He came to our door, too." He squinted. "I've seen you with the Queen, haven't I, boy?"

"They're all working with the Spectress!"

Meredith stretched a protective arm in front of Jack. He

turned his head, speaking out of the side of his mouth. "Get somewhere safe before this spirals out of hand."

Jack didn't question him. He turned and ran from the throne room, Urchin gripping his shoulder with all twenty claws.

He raced down the city steps to the water. That was where he always went when things upset him. But even the sound of the waves couldn't soothe him tonight.

He was worried about Ilsbeth, about Prewitt and Calliope. What had happened to them all? What had happened to the Glade Girls?

Angry shouts carried down the tiers, and he hurried along the beach toward the cove.

He waited for the sea to breathe, and then he slipped into the water and let it carry him down to the passageway. He heard the crack of a whip, and his heart leaped. *Ilsbeth!* He ran forward, expecting to see her twirling and spinning, water splashing beneath her soles as she struck out at broken crates.

But when he got to the cove, his feet slowed, and his mouth dropped open. It wasn't Ilsbeth at all.

There, standing in the moonlight, were all seven of the missing Glade Girls.

23

Prewitt sat bolt upright, his heart pounding.

He scanned the room. What had woken him? The Book-keeper snored beside him, a stack of books open on his chest, but around the room, the unfamiliar shapes of the furniture felt oddly threatening.

Prewitt pushed himself to his feet. *Calliope.* The hairs on the back of his neck raised, and his stomach churned. Reynard had insisted that the girls sleep in their own room at the top of the stairs, and he hadn't wanted to argue. But now he padded toward the second level, groping his way along the textured wall. His eyes began to adjust to the dim glow coming through the sky-light, and he moved more quickly up the star-studded steps.

When at last he made it to the top of the stairwell, he paused. There were three doors. Two to the right, and one at the far end. He was about to tentatively tap on the first door, when he saw something strange smudged across the clay bricks at his feet. He bent and dread pooled in his chest.

There on the floor was a familiar orange smear: a fire flower petal.

How had it gotten there?

He scanned the landing and—there!—another petal farther down the hallway, just outside the last door. He tiptoed toward it, leaning, listening.

No sound came from inside. He reached out and pushed the door open, his heart a crescendo in his ears.

Moonlight streamed from above, and all around, there were paintings.

He had never seen anything like them. Spirit creatures stared from canvases of all shapes, and he knew at once that they were the missing paintings from the shell cottage.

There could be no doubt. Reynard had been in the Royal City. *He was a member of the Masked Rampage.*

Prewitt spun on his heel. He had to get Calliope, had to find Ilsbeth and leave.

He turned down the hallway and nearly cried out when he saw Chichi standing there in the dark, the whites of her eyes shining.

"What are you doing?" she asked.

Prewitt blanched. "What are *you* doing? Where's Cal?"

Chichi didn't answer. A thousand questions burned in her eyes.

"Chichi!"

"She left."

"Left! Where did she go?"

Chichi shook her head. "I don't know. I asked her, but she didn't answer. I told her not to go anywhere—it's against the rules—but she acted like she couldn't hear me. It was like she was listening to something else, but I couldn't hear anything. Where do you think she went? What do you think she was hearing?"

Prewitt smacked a hand against his forehead. "The voices! She told me they always start after dark. I should have remembered! I should have kept her safe!"

"Voices? What voices? Tell me!" Chichi's tongue stuck out through the gap in her teeth, and she looked like she might explode if she didn't get an answer.

Prewitt ignored her, trying to think.

It must have been the sound of Calliope leaving that had woken him. But where would she have gone? Where was Reynard now? What if he or the Silver Shag found her?

He thought back to what Calliope had told him in the Bookshop. She had mentioned that the voices came from across the sea, that they always took her to the water.

Prewitt yanked out his book of maps, his gaze sweeping over the jutting Cape; then he snapped it closed and shoved it back inside his jacket.

He pushed his way around Chichi.

"Where are you going?"

Prewitt didn't answer.

"You *can't* leave! No one is allowed outside after dark!"

Prewitt whirled, glaring at her. "You knew all along, didn't you?"

Chichi flinched. "Knew what?"

"That your father is one of them—the Masked Rampage."

Chichi shook her head. "No! You're wrong."

"I *saw* the paintings, Chichi. They're from the Royal City. Your dad was there last night."

Chichi avoided his gaze.

Prewitt hissed through his teeth and continued on down the stairs.

Chichi grabbed his arm. "There are rules!"

"You keep saying the Silver Shag is good. So, what's with all the rules? What's she trying to hide? Why doesn't she want anyone to go outside after dark?"

"She's keeping us safe."

"Yeah, sure. Go ahead and keep believing that."

Prewitt tried to shake Chichi off, but her grip tightened.

"Wait!" she hissed.

Prewitt tried to pull away. "Let go of me!"

Chichi clapped her other hand across his mouth, yanking him back to the stairwell. "Something isn't right . . . *Someone's here.*"

There was a muffled thud and then a scuffling sound.

Prewitt's eyes widened, and Chichi flinched beside him.

"Get off me! How dare you touch me!" the Bookkeeper's voice rang out.

"Where's the *Bargeboy*, old man?" Someone else. A voice Prewitt didn't recognize.

"Bargeboy? I don't have any idea what you're talking about! We're travelers from—" A thud, and the Bookkeeper howled.

Prewitt and Chichi exchanged glances.

"Find him. Now. We don't need him running after the Queen."

Chichi dragged Prewitt up the stairs. She pulled him through the hall toward the room of paintings and yanked him inside, shoving him toward a ladder leaning against the wall. "Go, *go!*"

They heard the sound of boots thundering up the steps.

"Go!" Chichi hissed a third time.

Prewitt didn't argue. He climbed up through the skylight to the rooftop.

When he looked over his shoulder, Chichi's back was turned toward him.

"Daddy? What's going on? Who's that with you?"

"Chichi? Why aren't you in bed?"

"I heard a noise."

Reynard sighed. "Have you seen the Bargeboy?"

Prewitt tensed. What would Chichi say? Would she give him away?

"The Bargeboy? Who's that?"

"Don't pretend, Chichi. I know you know. You probably knew before I did."

"Where's the Queen?" said Chichi. "I woke up and she wasn't here."

Her father didn't answer for a moment, and then he said, "She'll be fine. We saw her going toward the edge of the Cape. We'll get to her before she can get into trouble."

"What's going on?" Chichi asked again.

"Rampage business. It does not concern you."

"But how come—"

"Go back to bed, Chichi."

"I want to know what's happening!"

"You'll know soon enough."

Chichi's questions trailed away as she was shooed back to her room.

Prewitt ducked, peeking through the leaf cutouts on the rooftop.

After a minute, two men appeared in the street below, dragging the Bookkeeper between them.

They were cloaked and their faces were covered with silver masks.

"Get off me! You can't do this to me!"

The Bookkeeper gave a strangled yelp, and Prewitt caught the threatening flash of a dagger in the moonlight.

Chichi pulled herself up onto the roof, crawling over to join him. Her breaths were shallow, and her eyes were wild as she took in the scene below.

The cloaked figures scanned the street, their masks gleaming, and then they hurried away, hauling the Bookkeeper with them, his feet dragging in the dirt.

"Come on," said Chichi. "We have to find out what's going on."

She led the way across the rooftop gardens, and together they scampered building to building, staying in the shadows, as they followed the men at a safe distance.

Prewitt's mind moved even faster than their feet. Reynard had said they'd seen Calliope going toward the Cape's edge. *We'll get to her before she can get into trouble.* What did that mean? They had the Bookkeeper now; would they set Ilsbeth free and let them go home?

Chichi muttered to herself as they tiptoed through the gardens, still asking questions—even when there was no one to answer.

They reached the final rooftop. They could see the dark edge of the Cape beyond the glowing line of flames, and past that, shimmering moonlight on the star-strewn sea.

Cloaked figures were gathered in the darkness, and Prewitt searched for Calliope. *Please don't be here. Please don't be here.*

But she was.

And when he saw her, his body went limp.

She was teetering on the edge of the cliff, and *someone* was gripping her shoulders, someone with a silver mask and strong white fingers.

Prewitt heard Chichi's breath catch, and her body strained forward as she watched. Her eyes moved back and forth across the scene as if trying to read a language she didn't understand.

Prewitt saw the jagged rocks waiting like wreckage-mangled teeth at the bottom of the cliff, and his eyes caught on tattered sails, a wrecked hull, a deck covered in shifting birds. *The shipwreck!*

He turned toward Chichi, but her eyes were focused on the figures below.

More silver masks flickered in the torchlight, and curving bird beaks hooked down above shadowed mouths. Long black cloaks snapped in the wind, sending dust swirling around boot-clad feet. No one spoke.

They were waiting—for *what*?

Prewitt scanned the rooftop. He didn't know what he was looking for, didn't know what he could do, but he had to do *something*. He wanted to shout his frustration. Why, why couldn't he be *swayed*? Why couldn't he have spirit-like speed, or supernatural fighting ability? Yes, he was the Bargeboy, the other half of the moon, but what good did that do him now? All the hours, all the work he'd put in with his father were no use to him here. He wasn't a warrior. If he raced down to the cliffside, he would be captured, too, and then he wouldn't be able to help Calliope at all.

Reynard and his partner dragged the Bookkeeper beyond the torches. "We have the old man."

The figure holding Calliope's shoulders straightened, and with a sweep of their arms, they moved Calliope away from the edge of the cliff.

Prewitt let out his breath, but his nerves still jittered. *Run.* He thought as loudly as he could.

But of course, Calliope didn't run. She stomped forward, her hair a whorl of black in the wind. "What are you doing? Let him go!"

"But isn't this why you've come to Castaway Cape, Calliope,

Queen of Lyrica?" a woman's voice, languid and unrushed, came from the shadows.

The Masked Rampage swiveled, their heads bowed in reverence as a new figure treaded forward.

The edges of her cloak were threaded with silver, and her mask was intricately etched, but it was the way she stood that told Prewitt everything. She was not the tallest person present, but she held herself as if she were. There was no hesitation in her, not in movement or in voice.

There wasn't a doubt in Prewitt's mind. They had found the Silver Shag.

Calliope didn't flinch. She glared at her, face set. "I don't know what you're talking about."

The Silver Shag threw back her head, laughing. "There's no need for pretense. I know who you are, and I know why you've come. After all, it was my note that brought you here." Her voice was vaguely familiar, and Prewitt frowned, trying to place it. "You brought the Bookkeeper to save your friend just as I knew you would."

The Bookkeeper's head craned toward Calliope, and betrayal lifted his gray brows. "So we aren't here for books after all. I've been led like a sheep to the slaughter."

Calliope's shoulders drooped to her toes. "They were going to hurt Ilsbeth." Her voice was so quiet that Prewitt wouldn't have caught her words had the wind not carried them.

"A sheep?" The Silver Shag laughed again. "I doubt you've ever been a sheep in your life."

The Bookkeeper turned his eyes toward her, contempt twisting his mouth. "The infamous Silver Shag. How flattering that you've gone to so much trouble on my account."

The Silver Shag inclined her head, and beneath the curved silver beak, her mouth was a dangerous smirk, but she did not speak.

"Only cowards hide behind masks," taunted the Bookkeeper.

The Silver Shag's eyes flashed. But she did not take the bait. She nodded at two of the cloaked figures. "It's time."

The Bookkeeper cried out as he was dragged forward, his feet kicking up dust.

"Stop it! Leave him alone." Calliope tried to go to him, but one of the Masked Rampage grabbed her arms, holding her back.

"At least give me Ilsbeth!" she cried. "That was the deal!"

"I made no such deal." The Silver Shag nodded once, and the Bookkeeper was hauled to the cliff's edge.

He flailed and thrashed. "You can't do this! Don't you know who I am?"

"We do," said one of the figures, and then he shoved the Bookkeeper off the cliff.

Calliope screamed, and from his hiding place overhead, Prewitt bit his cheek to keep from crying out.

Beside him, Chichi trembled, but she didn't look away.

The Bookkeeper seemed to fall in slow motion, limbs flailing, beard trailing like a puff of smoke in the dark.

Immediately, the masked figures turned as one. Raising their arms, they tipped off the cliffside.

Prewitt jumped to his feet as the Masked Rampage took flight.

Their arms spread, their cloaks embraced the wind like wings, and they rode the air like the cormorants they worshipped. Then they dove, unfurling a large white sheet, and caught the Bookkeeper just before he hit the rocks.

Prewitt let out his breath as they drifted the rest of the way down, landing lightly, before hauling the wretched Bookkeeper toward the wrecked ship.

"Did you see that? Did you see?" Chichi was trembling, but Prewitt caught the excitement in her eyes. They were still her heroes—even after everything she'd seen.

The Silver Shag stepped in front of Calliope, looking down at her.

"Why are you doing this?" asked Calliope.

"I'm changing my story," said the Silver Shag. "In order to do that, I must give the Spirit of the Suffering Sea what she wants—the throne of Lyrica."

"I won't give it up." Calliope's face was fierce.

"I know. Which is why we are taking you to the Nymph Isles. It is the one place that can hold you."

Understanding registered on Calliope's face. "That's why you wanted the Bookkeeper. Because he's been to the Nymph Isles and returned. You wanted to know how he did it, to make sure I wouldn't be able to do it, too."

The Silver Shag's eyes narrowed, but she didn't answer.

"But why? Why are you helping the Sea Spirit? What did I ever do to you?"

The Silver Shag lifted her chin. "You are the daughter of Firebird Queens, and that is enough. They did not value what was important. They cannot be trusted to keep the kingdom safe. After all, they forgot to protect the Feather. They forgot the power of the Song. They forgot their magic and the meaning of hope."

Calliope swallowed. "But I remembered the Song. I called the Firebird back. Look! I have the Feather!"

"It's too late. The damage has already been done. You have the Feather, but the kingdom is still broken."

"I'm doing my best to fix everything."

"Your best is not enough."

Calliope flinched.

"Soon there will be a new Queen, a Spirit Queen, and perhaps she will do better."

"But this is your kingdom, too! You can't let the Sea Spirit take over. You can't let it steal people's stories."

For a moment, the Silver Shag seemed to hesitate; then she said, "She won't *steal* them. She only offers to trade them . . . If people are foolish enough to give their stories away, what fault is that of mine? The Sea Spirit has promised not to touch the people of Castaway Cape." The Silver Shag looked out across the water. "She has made many promises."

Prewitt watched as the Silver Shag turned back toward Calliope, her mask shimmering in the torchlight.

"Tonight, I will set things right."

Before Prewitt could do anything, before Calliope could so much as scream, the Silver Shag dragged her over the cliff.

Prewitt raced across the rooftop and down the steps at the far side of the building. "Cal! Cal!" He ran past the torches, screaming her name into the wind.

The rest of the Masked Rampage followed the Silver Shag off the cliff, and a dozen masks flickered below as the Silver Shag hauled Calliope across the rocks and onto the wrecked ship.

Prewitt took a deep breath. *I'm coming, Cal.* He bent his knees, ignoring the wave of nausea that rose up at the thought of the sharp rocks below. He was about to jump when Chichi grabbed his arm, eyes wild. "Don't! You'll die!"

Prewitt shook her off. "I can't do nothing! I can't! No one returns from the Nymph Isles, Chichi! The Spirits hate humans. If they take her there, who knows what will happen to her!"

He looked back down at the rocks. The sea had begun to rise, not as a tide rises, slowly and in inches, but all at once. It wrapped like a hand around the ship and wrenched it from the rocks.

Now was Prewitt's only chance. Maybe jumping would help his *sway* come. He'd met Spirits, been close to the Firebird itself. He was the Age of Hope. All that had to add up to *something*. He bent his knees, sucked in his breath, pulled back his arms, and—

A massive hand gripped the back of Prewitt's neck, yanking him backward. "Don't be reckless, boy."

Prewitt fell onto his backside, tailbone throbbing. He looked up. Towering above him, leather cloak flapping, was the Falconer.

"They have the Queen!" Prewitt cried, pointing out at the ship. "And Ilsbeth, too!"

The Falconer's thorn bush brows met, and his glower intensified. "Ilsbeth," he growled, turning toward the sea. He caught sight of the vanishing ship and spat a word that Prewitt had never heard before. "That craft is Spirit guided. We'll never catch it now."

Even as he said it, the ship disappeared beyond the horizon.

Prewitt rounded on Chichi, who was watching the ship with a dazed expression. "If you had helped us, none of this would have happened. This is all your fault! Do you still think the Silver Shag is good?"

Chichi's face crumpled, and tears splashed onto her round cheeks, trickling into the creases beside her nose. She shoved her fists into her eyes and collapsed in the dirt.

Prewitt rubbed the back of his neck. "Don't cry, Chichi. I'm sorry I yelled. I'm just . . ." He sighed. "We'll figure it out. It's okay."

Chichi shook her head. "It's not okay."

Prewitt put a hand on her shoulder. "Look, I know the Silver Shag was your hero. But—"

"No!" Chichi pulled her fists out of her swollen eyes. "The Silver Shag isn't my *hero*." She burst into tears once more.

"The Silver Shag is my mother."

24

The Silver Shag gripped Calliope's shoulders as the white cliffs of Castaway Cape shrank against the starry sky.

After she finally released her, Calliope ran to the railing, looking down into the black water. The *sound* of the Spirit's magic was so loud that every muscle in Calliope's body tensed with the effort of pushing it away. It was the same hollow chord that she'd heard at the bonfire, the one that pounded through her with its ice-cold emptiness.

Calliope wanted to jump, to run away, but she knew that if she jumped, the Spirit magic would overcome her and she would never survive.

"There's no point in jumping," said the Silver Shag, echoing Calliope's thoughts. "The sea is on our side."

Calliope hesitated. Maybe the Silver Shag was right, but she had to try, didn't she? She had to find a way back to the city. She had to keep her people safe.

"Don't forget. We still have your friend. If you care about her, you'll do as you're told."

As if on cue, one of the Masked Rampage climbed from the hold, dragging Ilsbeth with him.

Chunks of hair had pulled loose from her normally smooth ponytail, and she licked her lips, groaning.

"Ilsbeth!" Calliope raced across the deck toward her.

The man shoved Ilsbeth forward. "Not such a fighter now, are you, girlie?"

Ilsbeth blinked, taking in the moon overhead, then turned and threw up on the man's boots.

He cursed in disgust, and the Silver Shag laughed. She nodded at one of the others. "Get the child some water and a bit of bread."

Ilsbeth wobbled, feeling weak and unsteady. She reached for her whip, but again her hand came up empty. Another wave of nausea struck her, and she fought to stay on her feet. Calliope caught her, holding her upright.

"You'll feel better with something in your stomach," said the Silver Shag, moving toward the prow. "And even if you don't, bread's better coming back than bile." Her lips curved, and she pushed back her hood. Blond hair tumbled around her shoulders, and her eyes closed as she soaked in the cool breeze.

Her demeanor had changed entirely, and behind her mask, her eyes were almost giddy.

The Bookkeeper glared at her. "You are out of your depth, Silver Shag. You may think I will tell you how I returned from the Nymph Isles, but I will not. You've wasted your time acquiring me."

The Silver Shag only smiled. "Get some rest, Bookkeeper."

The deck was soon still, scattered with resting men and women in silver masks and black birds with their heads beneath their wings.

The world was quiet, but the ship was loud, a chaotic symphony of flapping sails and creaking, crunching boards. It sounded to Ilsbeth as if it would fall to pieces at any moment and strand them in the sea. She groaned, leaning over a bucket.

Calliope rubbed her back, and for once, Ilsbeth was too weak to stop her.

"I am sorry," said Ilsbeth.

Calliope blinked. "What do you have to be sorry for? You've been through so much."

"I should not have gotten captured." The bucket muffled Ilsbeth's words.

"It isn't your fault, Ilsbeth." Calliope stared out at the water. "It's mine. This all started after I tried to force people to confront their fears. I never should have lit that fire. There must have been another way, but I couldn't see it."

Ilsbeth's head lifted, and she wiped her mouth on the back of her hand. "It is not your fault, either. I, also, thought the fire would help."

"But I'm the . . ." Calliope paused. She still couldn't call herself the Queen. "I'm in charge," she said instead. "Everything is my fault."

Ilsbeth sighed. "It is hard to lead. It is hard when you must make a choice with confidence even though you do not know how it will turn out."

"It's lonely," whispered Calliope.

Ilsbeth nodded. "Yes."

"Sometimes I just wish I had parents to make the choices for me," said Calliope. "At least then I could feel . . ." She trailed off.

"Safe," said Ilsbeth.

Calliope almost smiled. "Yes," she said. "Safe."

They sat side by side, the ship rocking beneath them.

"At least they didn't take Prewitt," said Calliope. It was her one consolation. She knew he'd worry, knew he'd do whatever he could to find her, but a part of her hoped he would just go home to Meredith and Marisa.

Her head ached with the *sound* of Spirit magic, and she massaged her temples.

"If only I had my whip, I could fight them all. I could defeat them." Ilsbeth's eyes narrowed at the Silver Shag's back.

Calliope shook her head. "We'd still be stranded in the middle of the sea." She groaned and pressed her hands over her ears. The *sound* was so loud. It made it impossible to think. After a moment, she looked up to see the Bookkeeper watching her.

He glanced around and then scooted closer, leaning forward. "You could stop this, Highness. *Reach out and take the magic.* You did it before. You have the power."

Calliope shook her head. "I don't! You saw what happened before."

"But you're growing stronger." The Bookkeeper's eyes shone. "When the *sound* of the magic first hit you on the beach, you almost fell from shock, but look at you now. Soon, the *sound* won't affect you at all. Reach out!"

Ilsbeth's jaw tensed. "Do not listen to him. Spirit magic is not to be used by humans."

"The Queen is *more* than human. She was chosen by the Firebird itself." The Bookkeeper turned to Calliope. "Do not let the Firebird down."

Calliope looked at the Feather. If she failed, she would only hurt herself, but if she succeeded, she might be able to protect the kingdom. She turned to Ilsbeth. "What choice do we have?"

"None at all." The Bookkeeper wrung his hands. "I *cannot* return to the Nymph Isles. Do it quickly. The air is changing; the Isles are close."

Calliope felt it. Cool mist hung in the sails, and her breath swirled in front of her.

"You're right. I have to try."

Ilsbeth didn't argue, and she did not allow her face to give anything away, but fear writhed in her gut.

Calliope stood and moved portside, purpose in every step. She was doing her best to feign confidence, but Ilsbeth saw the truth in Calliope's white knuckles on the gunwale. She got to her feet, steeling herself for whatever happened next.

Calliope stretched out her hand, grasping something that Ilsbeth could not see. Her dark hair blew back, and her eyes shifted, turning a deep, unsettling blue-black.

The Bookkeeper leaned forward, and Ilsbeth saw the hunger in his eyes. She reached to her empty belt, and her fingers itched. Her traitorous stomach rolled, and she fought to keep her legs steady. She was useless here.

Calliope leaped onto the railing, balancing as the ship swept across the sea. The hollow *sound* vibrated through her blood, an overwhelming, ominous chord, ice-cold and haunting. She swallowed her fear and *reached*.

The water lifted to meet her fingers, and she fought to tame it.

The Silver Shag strode across the deck. "Stop! Someone stop her!"

But it was too late. Calliope stepped forward.

The Silver Shag gasped.

The waves rose to meet Calliope's feet, and she did not sink. She turned toward the shipwreck, reaching out a hand, and pushed with all her strength. The ship broke free of the Sea Spirit's magic with a horrible *crack*. Calliope felt a surge of joy. She had done it! But the moment was short-lived.

The *sound* crashed into her, filling her with emptiness so heavy, so absolute, that she could not feel anything else. *I'm alone*, she thought, and that loneliness brought the nursery door rising in her mind. It threatened to open, and Calliope pulled away. *Be hopeful*, she thought. *Be hopeful!* But it was too late; the magic had already overtaken her.

The Masked Rampage was fully awake now, cowering on the deck. "We're sinking!"

Water filled the ship, dragging it down, and everyone reached for something to hold on to.

Ilsbeth fought for balance. "Calliope!" she shouted, but Calliope could not hear. Her eyes could not see.

Ilsbeth looked around. She pushed across the deck as it sank farther, the water up to her knees. She tried not to let her fear slow her down. Instead, she breathed in the moment and allowed it to sharpen her.

Black water began to trickle from Calliope's eyes. Spirit magic was taking over, and soon, Ilsbeth knew, Calliope would lose herself to it entirely, just as the Spectress had lost herself to the Demon.

Ilsbeth scanned the deck.

"What do you need?" The Silver Shag was at her side.

Ilsbeth did not take the time to be surprised. "A rope."

The Silver Shag nodded. She waded across the deck and came back with a length of thick brown rope.

Ilsbeth took it, holding out her hand. "A knife."

The Silver Shag hesitated only a moment, and then the cool handle of a dagger was in Ilsbeth's hand. She slashed through the end of the rope and began to unravel it. When the ends were loose, she turned toward the sea. She fought against the tug of the waves at her waist, and she silenced the terror that assured her she was about to drown.

Ilsbeth took a breath and let it out. The cries of the Masked Rampage drifted away. The whip was heavy and awkward, but in her hand, it had new life.

"Calliope!" she shouted again.

Calliope turned toward her, but she was not herself. Her face was twisted and furious, and there was no kindness in her eyes.

The ship sank farther, and Ilsbeth gripped the gunwale with one hand to keep from being swept away.

Using all her strength, she flung out the rope with her other hand, and it struck Calliope hard in the temple.

Calliope looked at Ilsbeth, her eyes clearing, and in that instant, she was herself once more.

Then she slipped beneath the blue-black sea.

25

"I don't understand why my mother would do this," said Chichi, shaking her head. She had thought she knew people, had thought that watching them could tell her everything she needed to know about their stories. But she had missed the truth about the person closest to her.

Every night Chichi had begged her mother to tell her the story of how she had become the Silver Shag, and every night her mother had held her close and whispered, "Only you know who I truly am." Then she would tell the story of the night she had drowned. How cormorants had brought her to Castaway Cape and given her a new life. She had taken up the silver mask and fought against the Spectress's rule to create a safe haven within the walls of the Cape, and then she had gone outside and delivered kindness and essentials to people who desperately needed them.

It was Chichi's favorite story. *Stories are our strength.* But what if they were all a lie? Mothers weren't supposed to lie to their children. If they couldn't trust their mothers, who could they trust?

The Falconer cleared his throat. "People do unexpected things when they're desperate, and your mother sounded desperate to get to the Nymph Isles." He gazed out at the water, and his voice grew hard. "But, desperate or not, she made a mistake taking my girl with her."

Prewitt rubbed his cheeks. "If only we had one of those capes that the Masked Rampage was wearing. Then we could at least follow."

Chichi wiped her eyes. "The cloak couldn't take you across the sea. They don't fly, really. They *glide*. They use the air currents, and can go a certain distance, but the wind's too unruly to trust it to take you very far—at least, that's what my mother said." Her face fell. Maybe that had been a lie, too.

The bird on the Falconer's shoulder screeched, and Prewitt stood up straighter, an idea forming. "Chichi, do you know where we can get a cloak?"

Chichi's brows met. "I just told you—"

"I know! But what if there were a way to use them *in spite of* the wind."

Chichi brushed her bangs from her eyes. "I think I could find some. I know who makes them."

"What are you thinking, Bargeboy?" The Falconer paced the cliffside.

"Is it true that your falcons are the fastest the kingdom has ever known?"

"Yes."

"Can they fly *against* the wind?"

"They can fly through anything."

Prewitt's mouth spread into a grin.

"What? What are you thinking?" asked Chichi.

The Falconer stopped pacing, his brows raised in understanding. "I see. It could work."

"What could?"

Prewitt explained his plan, and the Falconer told Chichi what they would need. Then she raced away through the dark streets.

Once she was gone, the Falconer stood at the edge of the cliff. He flung his head back and whistled. The sound was piercing. It rode out across the wind and lifted into the night sky, calling, beckoning.

Prewitt shivered, and the whistle died away.

They waited together in silence, the hulking man and the boy in the red jacket. Each minute was longer than the last, but finally Chichi returned, a cloak draped across her arms and a bundle at her back. They knelt on the edge of the cliff, working in the dim, flickering light of the torches, and as they did, the peregrines came. They dove from all directions, fluttering down into the dust at the Falconer's feet.

When they had finished, Prewitt bent to pick up the cloak.

"No."

Prewitt looked up.

The Falconer's gaze was fierce. "You are not coming."

Prewitt gaped at him. "What do you mean?"

The Falconer took the cloak from Prewitt's hands, shoving his thick arms through the sleeves.

The blood rushed to Prewitt's cheeks. "It was *my* idea."

"My birds will not guide you."

"But I can't do *nothing*!"

The Falconer scowled through his brows. "You want to help, Bargeboy? Warn the Royal City. Tell them that the Masked Rampage is coming—and the Sea Spirit is on their side."

Chichi and Prewitt watched the black shape of the Falconer fade into the night sky.

"How am I going to get back?" moaned Prewitt. "How am I going to warn everyone? If the Spirit of the Suffering Sea gets to the city, if they take her pearls, they'll lose their freedom forever. She'll rewrite their stories, and they won't be *them* anymore."

He paced beneath the torchlight. "I can't let that happen, not without at least telling them the truth. They deserve a *real* choice."

"We have horses," said Chichi. "If we could sneak one beyond the wall somehow, you could ride to the Royal City."

Prewitt shook his head. "It would take too long. Besides, I don't know how to ride a horse."

Prewitt wondered if he could make it back across the Tree

Troll bridges. The Troll had been clear that if it saw them again, the toll would be death. Had it only been talking about the Bookkeeper? Or had it meant the children, too? Prewitt couldn't take the risk.

He reached into his jacket and pulled out his book of maps. The white cliffs of the Cape snaked west along the Lyrican Sea for many miles before cutting into a shape that Prewitt had often thought looked like a hat, the Royal City perched at the top.

The only way that he could see to return home would be to take the road beside the clifftops, but even with a horse, it wouldn't be fast enough.

He ran his finger along the page, tracing the line where the cliffs met the water. Waves crashed on the rocks below, and he peered down at the broken boats.

An idea came to him.

It wasn't a good idea. It was dangerous and foolish and might get him killed, but if it worked, it would get him home in time to warn the city.

He turned to Chichi. She sat with her knees tucked up under her chin, biting her fingernails and blinking forlornly at the moonlit water.

"Chichi, can you get me another cloak?"

She stared at him as he explained his idea, and then she nodded and pushed herself to her feet, dusting off her pajamas and running away without asking a single question.

Prewitt waited, his nerves on edge as the moon crept across the sky. He wondered what was happening to Calliope and

Ilsbeth. He wondered what the Royal City would do if they knew that the Sea Spirit wanted to take over the kingdom. Would they care that her pearls came with a cost? Perhaps it would seem like a fair price to pay to forget their traumas.

How could Prewitt convince them that it wasn't? How could he make them see that things could get better? He was mulling these questions over when Chichi returned. She had put on a cloak of her own. It was so long, it dragged behind her like a train as she ran toward him. "I almost got caught! I had to hide behind Widow Andra's sofa. Luckily, she's nearsighted and can't see well in the dark. It's her cat that saw me." She handed Prewitt a cloak. "I thought for sure it was going to give me away!"

Prewitt pushed his hands through the sleeves.

"I'm coming with you," said Chichi. "If my mother has really lied to all those people, if she's a villain instead of a hero, then I have to do what I can to make it right. Let me help you warn everyone."

"All right," said Prewitt.

Chichi blinked. "You aren't going to try to talk me out of it?"

"Would it work?"

Chichi shook her head.

Prewitt's mouth quirked. "Then let's go."

They stood on the edge of the cliff. Prewitt's heart hammered in his chest, and his knees were weak. He turned to Chichi to ask if she had any tips, but before he could, she spread her arms and leaped. She was grinning ear to ear as she fell, and Prewitt heard her squeal as the cloak caught the air. She tilted her arms and leaned this way and that, experimenting as she swooped up and down.

Prewitt took a couple of steps back, and then he ran and jumped into the air. For a moment, he was certain the cloak had failed, and his stomach and heart tangled themselves in his throat, but then he felt the cloak catch, and he was *flying*.

If he hadn't been so worried about Calliope, so afraid for his family in the Royal City, he would have let himself enjoy the thrill of the moment. But instead, he allowed his father's voice to bring him down to earth.

If you don't put in the work, you won't be ready when the adventure calls.

He landed harder than he expected, skinning his knees on the rocks. Prewitt winced as he got up, running his hands through his hair. He looked around. He had spent the summer rebuilding the ships in the harbor. His hands had blistered and calloused, and his skin had burned and deepened from hours in the sun, but he had learned how to work.

Maybe he wasn't *swayed*. Maybe his father was right and *sways* weren't even real, but he could do *this*.

He set his jaw and began.

It took over an hour, but Prewitt finally found a catboat with an intact sail and damage minimal enough to be fixed if he had the right tools. He climbed across the rocks, moving from vessel to vessel, searching the wreckage until he uncovered what he needed.

He heard himself barking orders at Chichi just as his father had with him, and he tried not to get frustrated when she groaned and sat down.

She rubbed her eyes. "This is hard. I'm so tired. Aren't you tired?"

Prewitt realized that he wasn't. Day after day he had gotten up early and gone to bed late. He'd worked with his father and stayed on his feet past the point when he thought he no longer could, and somehow, without realizing it, he'd gotten strong.

Finally, the moment came to find out if the catboat would survive the sea.

Prewitt readied the sail and held his breath. The wind struck it, and the boat groaned, sliding from the rock with a great splash that soaked them both.

The boat held.

Prewitt let out a whoop. He had done it!

But it was only the beginning; he knew he couldn't let the victory steal his focus.

He sailed the little boat away from the cliffs, putting all his father's teachings to work. The wind was against them, but the water was calm, and as he turned the catboat westward, Prewitt found that he was, too. He sailed close-hauled, with the sail trimmed tightly, and turned the catboat so that the keel was angled into the gale. Then he tacked as his father had taught him, letting the wind play at the starboard and then at the port.

He heard his father's orders in his mind as loudly as if the Bargemaster were there at his shoulder, and he piloted the catboat slowly through the night sea.

The adventure had come at last, and he was ready.

Ever since he'd heard of *sways*, he had wished for one himself, had wanted it so badly that it ached. But it wasn't a *sway* that was helping him now.

Work is your magic. He had rolled his eyes when his father had said it before, but now he thought he understood. Maybe there was magic in ordinary things—perhaps human determination, dedication, and hard work could be just as powerful as Spirit magic.

Prewitt swallowed, looking out into the darkness. He certainly hoped so, because that was all he had.

26

The rippling moon shrank away as Calliope slipped into the black embrace of the sea.

She was herself once more, but her energy was gone. She sank, her arms and legs heavy as stones. Her eyes drifted shut, and the golden light turned to darkness.

Help us!

Free us!

Save us!

I'm sorry, she thought as she sank down into the cool water. *I don't even know how to save myself.*

Calliope was surprised when she opened her eyes. The moon was bright, and the deck chafed beneath her back, but her head was gently cradled in someone's lap. She blinked, and then coughed.

Above her, Ilsbeth's lips drew tight. "You must not try to use Spirit magic again. It is destroying you."

Calliope groaned. Her chest ached, and chills shook her body. "What happened?"

"You fell into the water. The Silver Shag saved you."

"The Silver Shag?" Calliope glanced over and saw the Silver Shag standing a few feet away. Her mask shone. "Thank you. I thought I was going to drown."

"It was not drowning that nearly killed you." The Silver Shag's voice was cool. "It was the Spirit magic."

"I should be able to do it. The Queens had the power before. That's what the Bookkeeper said."

The Silver Shag laughed. "If I had a stone for every time the 'Bookkeeper said,' I would sink to the bottom of the sea."

The Bookkeeper let out an offended squawk. "There *were* stories about the Firebird Queens' magic. It is not my fault that I do not remember the details. Am I to be blamed for the burning of the books and the destruction of the knowledge? Calliope is the daughter of the Firebird Queen. There is no reason she cannot use the magic. She only needs to find the way. She must lean into it and not hesitate. She must do what it takes for Lyrica."

The Silver Shag's eyes glittered. "You know all about *doing what it takes*, don't you, old man?"

The Bookkeeper frowned. "I don't like what you're insinuating. I have certainly given what I could to the kingdom, but you would make it out that I have done something wrong in executing my duty."

"There's something ahead!" one of the Masked Rampage shouted from the crow's nest, pointing out across the water.

The Bookkeeper turned toward the railing. He squinted hard, and after a long moment, his face turned white with terror.

Sparkling moonlight meandered across the waves until it met a deep black nothing. The darkness stretched from water to sky, obliterating all light as if a hole had torn in the universe and shadow itself was drinking the sea.

Help us!

Save us!

Free us!

Calliope sat up. Her heart pounded, and her head reeled with the new intensity of the voices. She finally knew where they were coming from. Somewhere, within the darkness, thousands of people were suffering, crying out for her to save them.

The Bookkeeper shook his head in consternation. "This cannot be the Nymph Isles. What has happened to them?"

"Maybe the Isles aren't there anymore," said Calliope, wrapping her arms around herself. "Maybe something happened to the Spirits."

Help us!

Save us!

Free us!

Spirits or not, *something* was there in the darkness, something that had called her across the sea.

The Bookkeeper whirled on the Silver Shag. "Turn the ship around."

"I don't take orders from you."

"You don't know what happened here, what this place took from me!"

"But I do." The Silver Shag reached to the back of her head and pulled on the silk ribbon. The silver mask fell to the deck, revealing her face at last.

The Bookkeeper squinted, trying to see her clearly, and then he staggered backward. "Sina." The name was a breath.

Calliope gaped at the woman, standing tall before them, blond hair blowing across her face. It was Chichi's mother. She hadn't heard anyone say her name at Castaway Cape, and yet, it was familiar. *Sina . . .*

"You always try to control the story, don't you, Father?" said Sina, sharp eyes on the Bookkeeper.

Calliope blinked. *Sina.* Yes, she remembered, it was the name of one of the Bookkeeper's children. *Sina and Milo.*

"You tried to control it all those years ago when you forced us from our home and erased our mother."

"It was too painful. I couldn't talk about her, couldn't see her paintings hanging on every wall. I couldn't live with those stories."

Calliope swallowed, the memory of her own mother sharp in her mind. She had felt the same way living in the castle.

"It was painful for me, too," spat Sina. "I needed to talk about it. All I had left were stories, but you forbade us from talking about her at all. You even made the Queen take Mother's paintings from the castle. I begged the Queen not to, but she said that her Bookkeeper knew best. Just as she believed the Reckoner knew best."

Calliope didn't want to believe it was true. Her mother must have had a reason that she trusted her advisers, but she would never know what it was. That part of the story was lost, like the broken branches of a bridge.

"Sina." The Bookkeeper stretched out a wasted hand, and the Silver Shag flinched back. "I thought you were dead," he whispered.

"I have a new name," snapped the Silver Shag, and she grasped the handle of the dagger at her belt.

"Don't hurt him!" cried Calliope.

The Silver Shag turned on her. "You defend him? You must not know what he did."

"I do," said Calliope. "I know that Milo drowned, but hurting the Bookkeeper won't bring your brother back."

"Is that why you've brought me here?" said the Bookkeeper. "Why you attacked me in the Bookshop? Vengeance?"

"I brought you here to change the story," said the Silver Shag. "To get Milo back."

"That's impossible," said the Bookkeeper. "No one can get him back now."

The Silver Shag spoke through gritted teeth, her breath hot and white. "When we found the Isles, I did what you told me. I stayed on the ship. But I saw *everything*. I saw you flee, tripping and falling across the beach. I saw you get into the dinghy, and I saw the sea fight against you, trying to keep you on the Isles." Her voice grew louder. "I saw you force Milo to summon the Wind and give away his future."

"Force? I never—"

"He would have done anything you asked! He loved you, and you took advantage."

"I didn't know it would mean death," said the Bookkeeper.

"You could have saved him," Sina said. "But I watched you choose the prophecy. You kept it from falling into the water instead of saving your son."

"The Wind was too strong! It had already blown the ship away, and the dinghy was tied. You know that."

"What I know is that when I tried to turn the ship around, to go back, you did nothing to help. You did nothing but lie on the deck with that shell pressed against your ear. The prophecy was all you cared about." Sina laughed. A mirthless sound. "You tried to get me to listen. As if I would care.

"I knew then, that if I wanted to get my brother back, I would have to do it alone. The Wind could not stop me. The sea would not frighten me. I dove off the ship and into the water, and I began to swim back toward the Isles through the ice that numbed and the sea that tried to drown me, too. But I would not be drowned so easily. The Spirit of the Suffering Sea admired my will and let me live. She promised me my brother, if I swore to be her servant and help her win the crown of Lyrica."

The Bookkeeper's eyes were full of pity. "Oh, Sina. My girl. Death is not a story that can be changed, whatever the Sea Spirit told you. She has tricked you." He reached for her, and the Silver Shag stepped back, her grip still tight on the dagger.

"You're wrong," said Sina. "My brother is alive. The Suffering

Sea saved him. He waits, somewhere, here on the Isles." Her eyes turned to the black cloud on the sea.

The Bookkeeper shook his head. "You're being foolish, Sina. You are dooming the kingdom. The daughter of generations of Bookkeepers is forsaking her duty for selfishness."

The Silver Shag stiffened. For a moment, it seemed she would shout at him, but then she regained her composure and pointed the dagger toward a barnacle-coated dinghy on the starboard side of the ship. "Get into the boat."

"What?" The Bookkeeper balked.

"The Wind was offered a future. A future it shall have."

The Bookkeeper tugged at his cheeks. "You cannot mean to force me onto the Isles. You know what it will do to me!"

Calliope heard the fear in his voice. She pushed herself to her feet, nearly falling, and Ilsbeth grabbed her elbow, her other hand tight on the length of rope.

"Admit that you were wrong," hissed the Silver Shag. "Tell me that you shouldn't have uprooted us from our home and silenced the stories of my mother. Tell me that you wish you had given *your* future instead of his."

The Bookkeeper pulled his shoulders back, and with a great effort, he looked into his daughter's eyes. "I cannot say what I do not believe to be true."

Disbelief fell like a slap across her face.

"I know it is hard to hear, but if I had done anything differently then, the kingdom would have fallen." The Bookkeeper pointed a wizened finger at Calliope. "The Queen lives because

I got that prophecy back to the Royal City. Because I was willing to make the difficult choice, instead of the kind one, the Spectress was defeated and the entire kingdom was saved."

The Silver Shag shook her head. "After all this time, you still can't admit you were wrong."

"I wasn't wrong. You just didn't like the decision I made."

The Silver Shag turned her back on him, and three members of the Masked Rampage grabbed him and forced him into the dinghy. He struggled for a moment and finally went limp.

The Silver Shag stood at the gunwale. "Spirit of the Suffering Sea, arise!"

The water was crystal clear, dark seagrass erect in the black seabed. The numbing air was calm, and white clouds hung like ghouls. Beyond it all, the darkness waited.

The Sea Spirit came.

A wave rushed toward them from the darkness. It rose up, shifting into the form of a woman, skirts made of fishing nets. Her body was water, whirling and spinning, never settling. Her hair was kelp, dripping and gray-green, and her eyes were smooth fragments of green sea glass. Where her mouth should have been, broken pieces of bone-white shells grinned.

My Silver Shag. Her watery arms opened wide.

"We have a deal," said the Silver Shag. "You promised that if I brought you the girl, and helped you take the throne of Lyrica, you would give my brother back to me."

Calliope strode forward. "The throne of Lyrica is mine! The Firebird gave it to me!"

The Sea Spirit rose and fell, and the shells of her mouth slid into a garish frown. *Can you take away your people's pain? Can you change their stories and ease their suffering? With me as Queen, they will forget about the Dark Age of the Spectress's rule, and all the things they have lost will be but a dream. I will write them a new story. Don't you want them to be happy?*

Calliope moved to the railing. "Of course I do! You're the one who has been spreading lies and making their fears worse. You tricked them and brought all the painful memories back."

The taste of bitterness on their tongues shall make my gift all the sweeter.

"You want to give them a new story, but what you're giving them isn't happiness. It's a lie."

Help us!

Save us!

Free us!

Calliope pressed her hands over her ears, and she felt Ilsbeth move to stand beside her.

The ship rose and fell, and the Sea Spirit suddenly dissolved into the sea, the fragments of her face drifting to the sandy floor. Then, with another wave, she rose again, her face whirling back into a guise of humanity.

The Sea Spirit held out her hand. Floating in her palm was a single, perfect blue pearl.

Sweet child, you are suffering, too. I can feel that your sorrow is great. Let me take it from you. Let me give you a new story. Let me free you from the burdens you bear. The words broke gently against the railing.

Calliope's head hurt so badly, and the cries were so loud, that for a moment, she was tempted. It would be so easy to reach out and take it, to not have to worry about everyone and everything anymore. Didn't she deserve to be happy, too? Didn't she deserve peace? If her head was clear, then her heart might be, too. Maybe then the Queen's magic would work and she would be able to keep her people safe.

She swallowed, remembering what Marisa had said: *Taking a part of someone's story, even a painful part, is not a kindness.*

She shook her head. "No," she said. "I will not take your pearl."

You will regret your decision, seethed the Sea Spirit.

"What about my brother?" said the Silver Shag. "Don't forget our deal!"

The Spirit inclined her head, and a wave swept over the side of the ship, carrying Milo with it.

The wave broke, leaving him limp on the deck.

"Son!" the Bookkeeper cried from the dinghy. He tried to stand, but one of the Masked Rampage shoved him down again.

Milo did not move.

The Silver Shag fell to her knees. "Brother!" She patted his cheeks and glared over at the Sea Spirit floating near the railing. "You told me that you saved him!"

Do not worry. He only sleeps. For many years I've kept him with me in the deep. He will wake when the kingdom takes my pearls and I am on the throne. The true Queen of Lyrica.

"This was not our deal!"

215

You are free to take him as he is.

The Silver Shag sat back on her haunches.

"The throne of Lyrica is mine," said Calliope, and rage pushed the voices from her ears. "The Firebird gave it to me."

The Sea Spirit turned her glass eyes toward Calliope.

"Do it," hissed the Bookkeeper from the dinghy. "Use the Queen's magic. Do it now!"

The girl does not know how to use the magic. I saw her try. Whatever magic the Firebird gave her ancestors is not in her. The rule of Firebird Queens has come to an end.

Calliope's heart plummeted. She wanted to argue, to tell the Spirit that she was wrong, but she wondered if it was true. She had never wanted to be called Queen, had felt that the word didn't belong to her. Maybe that was because it didn't.

Ilsbeth stepped in front of Calliope. "I will take care of this." The rope was tight in her fist as she faced the Sea Spirit head-on.

You cannot fight me, child. I am the Ancient Spirit of the Suffering Sea.

"I am Ilsbeth, daughter of the Halcyon Glade, and I have fought my share of Spirits."

The Spirit laughed. She sank down into the water, disappearing beneath the waves, and Ilsbeth scanned the surface, waiting, every muscle tensed.

The Spirit struck from behind. The force of the tidal wave was like nothing Ilsbeth had ever felt before. It was a battle she could not win. But she tried. She held her breath and pushed and kicked and struck out, but it was all useless. She was tossed end over end and swept into the darkness.

Her body was scraped raw as the waves dragged across the black sand of the Nymph Isle shore, and she finally broke free, jumping to her feet with a scream, fury white at the edges of her vision. Calliope crawled from the water, the Firebird Feather casting an aura a few feet around her.

Ilsbeth waded back into the water. She struck it over and over with her fists. "Face me! Come back and face me!"

There was a splash nearby, and Ilsbeth's eyes prodded the dark, trying to see what had made the sound. Something slid past her ankles—something with scales.

Calliope grabbed her arm, holding the Feather out, and they saw the mass of sharp-toothed eels writhing in the shallows. There were thousands of them, so many that they could not see the bottom.

"Get out of the water!" shouted Calliope, and Ilsbeth did not argue.

Nearby, the dinghy drifted against the shore of the Isle, and the Bookkeeper cried out. "No, no, I can't come back here!" He grabbed a broken oar from the bottom of the boat and shoved it against the sand. The dinghy slipped back, bobbing in the shallows, and the Bookkeeper sobbed, trying without success to row himself away.

Ilsbeth looked around, squinting to see more of the Isle in the dark, but it was no use. She could only see what the Feather's glow revealed.

She turned to Calliope and saw that her hands were pressed to her ears, her face contorted with pain.

Ilsbeth strode toward her. "Tell me what to do."

"The voices. They're so loud." Calliope's words came in gasps. "Someone here needs my help. I know it. I have to find them."

Ilsbeth didn't ask any questions. She turned on her heel and marched to the edge of the water, glaring at the Bookkeeper. "Stop moaning and be helpful. You have been here before. Tell me what I need to know to get the Queen safely across the Isle, the landscape, the dangers, what we will encounter once we leave the beach."

"I don't know!" he wailed. "It wasn't like this before. Not this—this darkness. Something has happened to the Spirits."

"The land will still be the same," snapped Ilsbeth, "and the Spirits may still hide in the dark. Tell me what you saw when you were last here."

The Bookkeeper continued to fight the current, splashing futilely with the broken oar. "There were three distinct Isles. This must be the largest of the three, the one at the center, but I am not certain. Beyond the beach, you should find a forest. It was lush and thick with lichen and ferns, and full of wild creatures that shifted form. On the other side of the forest was a knoll. There, I was guided around steaming pools of bubbling water and warned not to touch them.

"I was led to the entrance of the Hall of Mosses. It spreads below the Isle, made up of living things, fungi and moss, coral and seagrass. Some of the rooms were completely filled with water where spirits swam. There were pathways beneath the water, connecting the three Isles, but I was led past them and taken to a cavern where I met three Ancient Spirits: another Sea Spirit, the Spirit of the Sea of Discontent; Myca, the lord of things that grow in the shadow; and the Great Forgeman who sees the future.

"I did not see his Forge, but I understood that its fire must have been the cause of the boiling pools that I had passed. The Forgeman gave me the prophecy, and together, the three Spirits cursed me. I fled and saw nothing more."

Ilsbeth nodded once. "It will have to be enough." She left him fighting with the oar. A current suddenly caught the dinghy, and he was swept sideways into the darkness toward the next Isle. His cries faded against the groan of the sea.

Ilsbeth joined Calliope. "I am ready. Let us go and find the source of your voices."

Calliope nodded and led the way into the dark.

27

Calliope forced herself toward the sound of the cries, holding the Feather high. Without its light, they would have been lost forever. A sense of foreboding draped itself across Calliope's shoulders as she and Ilsbeth trudged across the frozen black sand.

Calliope's teeth chattered, but she was glad for the cold. It sharpened her drowsy mind and kept her body moving. She still felt exhausted from trying to use the magic, but she refused to let her weakness keep her from finding the voices. They spurred her on, step after laborious step, until the glow from the Feather lit the edge of a forest.

But it was nothing like the Bookkeeper had described. The trees were black corpses in the sand, and harsh wind blew flurries of ice around their stripped trunks. They creaked like gallows, and lifeless limbs stretched, pleading toward the girls.

Calliope and Ilsbeth did not speak as they entered the forest and made their way through the nightmare wasteland. It was unnerving only being able to see a few feet ahead of them, and Ilsbeth was on edge. Anything could attack; any monster could appear. The cold bit at her fingers and gnawed at her ears, but she refused to be distracted. Her whole body was alert, ready for any hint of an ambush.

But it did not come. There was no sign of life anywhere—no plant, no creature, no spirit. At last, the trees thinned, and then there was only sand, shimmering like the ashes of lost stars as it rose and fell beneath their crunching feet.

The air suddenly changed, and the gleam from the Feather was softened further by a warm mist that wafted toward them, dampening their cheeks and clinging to their hair. At first, they could not tell where the mist was coming from, and it grew thicker, making it hard to see their own feet.

Ilsbeth's arm suddenly flung out, and Calliope halted. She had nearly stepped into a pool of water. Its surface was pristine, black and shining, and Calliope was amazed that Ilsbeth had seen it.

Steam rose from it in swirling clouds.

Calliope crouched for a moment, the surface flaring in the golden light of the Firebird Feather. She held her other hand above the water, her chilled fingers tingling in the warm steam, and the cries intensified, so loud that she nearly fell face-first into the pond.

"Ilsbeth! There are people trapped under the water. I can hear them!"

Calliope was about to plunge her hand into the pool when

Ilsbeth grabbed her wrist. "No! This must be one of the pools that the Bookkeeper spoke of. If there is a Forge beneath, the water will scald you."

Calliope stared back at the black surface. The voices tugged her, begging her to find them. "I can't abandon them, Ilsbeth."

"Fine. I will test the water first." Ilsbeth let go of Calliope's wrist and took a breath, steeling herself, but before she could touch the surface, Calliope stepped into the pond.

"It's okay," said Calliope. "It's just warm."

Ilsbeth sighed, clearly irritated. "You must be more careful. We do not know what is beneath the surface."

"I don't understand," said Calliope. "There isn't anything, just mud." She took another step forward, and then she was falling, tumbling through dense, steam-filled air before landing hard on her side on damp stone.

She pushed herself up, cringing. Above her head, the surface of the black pond broke as Ilsbeth flung herself through. She landed in a crouch, then immediately straightened, whipping around in a circle, her hands up and her eyes wary.

There before them stood a great Forge. A stone hearth curved in a circle, rising up and over an enormous pit. Huge bellows were propped on the hearth, and within the pit, a pulsing glow emanated from sizzling hot charcoal.

Ilsbeth grabbed Calliope's wrist, a warning look in her eyes.

Calliope followed the sharp tilt of Ilsbeth's chin and saw a man draped over the edge of the Forge.

The Forgeman.

His cheek rested on the rock, and, for a moment, Calliope thought that he was a statue. He was as still as stone, and his bare arms were dark gray and cracking. He wore a brown leather apron tied around his waist, and on the floor beside him lay an enormous steel hammer.

Ilsbeth circled the man once, and then she bent, reaching toward the intricate wooden handle of the hammer.

There was a grinding sound as the Forgeman's head rotated, and Ilsbeth froze, caught in a tawny gaze.

"Eight flowers seeded by the light of the moon, watered by sorrow, shall grow too soon." The man's voice was warm and round, and his tone was gentle, but Ilsbeth did not relax. Her teeth bared and she glared up at him.

"I have been waiting for you, child of the Halcyon Glade."

Suspicion narrowed Ilsbeth's eyes. "How do you know who I am?"

"I see many things in my Forge. But the coals grow cold, and my eyes grow dim."

He turned to Calliope, and it was clear that the movement took effort. He looked like a statue because he very nearly was. His head grated on his neck, stone against stone.

Help us!

Save us!

Free us!

Calliope pressed her hands to her ears. "Where are they?" she demanded. "Where are the people you're hiding?" Her gaze swept the chamber. "What have you done with them?"

Waterfalls cascaded on all sides as if pouring down from the outer edges of the pond. The Forgeman stood with great effort and lumbered forward. "If perfect hope she can achieve, then all that's broke may be redeemed. I knew you would hear them, daughter of the Firebird Queen, child who called the Firebird back to Lyrica."

"The prophecy," whispered Calliope, recognizing the words. "It was your prophecy that helped save the kingdom."

"Yes," said the Forgeman, "and now, it is your turn to save us." He trundled farther on, the ground trembling with every ponderous step, and finally stopped before the tumbling water. He held out his giant hands, and the water split over his palms, creating a gap just wide enough for them to see through to the other side.

Behind the waterfall was a pathway into the sea beneath the Isle, and there, nestled in the sand, a few feet away, was a small black stone.

Help us!

Save us!

Free us!

Calliope frowned. Somehow, the voices were coming from the stone itself. "I don't understand!"

"What is it?" asked Ilsbeth, staring down at it.

The Forgeman's face was sad. "It is the Suffering Stone, the heart of the Spirit of the Suffering Sea, and it is destroying us."

Calliope moved closer, and the pain of the voices was almost too much to bear. She reached for the Firebird Feather, for any comfort it might bring, but she felt none.

"All the stories stolen by the Sea Spirit are kept within this stone. When she stole the stories, she grew stronger, but she underestimated what carrying the magic of humankind would do. Just as humans cannot carry Spirit magic without destroying themselves, Spirits cannot carry human magic."

Ilsbeth frowned.

"Speak, daughter of the Glade."

"What magic do humans have? I have never seen a human use magic. Only Calliope."

"That is because you have been looking for the wrong kind of magic," said the Forgeman. "The magic of humanity is in their ability to take sorrow, suffering, hardships, and trials, and transform them, like an oyster turns a grain of sand into a pearl. But, just as not every oyster creates a pearl, not every human finds a way to make their story into something more—although all have that magic within them."

Ilsbeth frowned.

Calliope looked down at the stone. Dark tendrils of black mist swirled around it, pouring like ink into the surrounding water. "You mean that when the Spirit of the Suffering Sea took their stories away, she took the magic that would have made them who they were supposed to be?"

"That is correct. She took their power and grew strong, but her heart became heavy and brittle beneath the weight of the stolen stories. Her actions had created a great darkness, and she understood that she had cursed herself. She did the only thing she could. She removed her heart and hid it here beneath the Isles."

His head hung heavy on his neck, and he gave a great sigh. "The darkness spilled into the water and across the land, and it poisoned us, stripping away our magic. I'm the only Nymph Isles Spirit with any magic remaining. All life is nearly gone from the Isles."

"It is what you deserve." The words were bitter on Ilsbeth's tongue. "You created the Nymph Isles to escape the Demon and the Spectress and abandoned humankind."

"We kept our distance to save ourselves, but we did not abandon you. We have sent many magical gifts to aid Queens past."

"If you wanted to help us, then why did you leave?" asked Calliope.

"I see the future in my Forge, a series of possibilities. I prepare for all. If you had failed, my brother and sister Spirits would have been saved. If you succeeded, then we would return."

The Forgeman's eyes beseeched her. "But instead, we are trapped here, weak and dying. Only the Wind and the Sea are free to move; the rest of us are tied to the land, which has been poisoned by stolen stories. You are the only one who can save us: a child who can hold both human and Spirit magic. Only you can carry the heart away and remove the darkness from the Isles."

Calliope tugged on her curls, staring down at the stone. The pain of the voices was excruciating, and getting closer, picking it up, seemed impossible. "Even if I could take it, where would I go? I thought the only way to leave the Isles was to give up my future. Isn't that why the Sea Spirit wanted me here? Because I can't leave?"

"Yes. When the other Ancients and I built this realm, we knew it would have to be protected. We were trying to avoid the darkness the prophecy forewarned." He shook his head. "But darkness came another way."

He looked at Calliope, and his eyes were sad. "Unbeknownst to the Spirit of the Suffering Sea, we used the last of our magic to build a door." The Forgeman pointed to the black sand that stretched into the darkness. "Take the stone and follow the pathway to the next Isle. There, upon the shore, you will find a Spirit Door. It was made to take the stone away and will only allow the person carrying the stone"—he bowed his head toward Ilsbeth—"and her companion, to pass through. Once you are on the other side, you will find yourself in the great desert beyond the mountains where the Sea Spirit cannot follow."

Calliope twisted the Feather between her palms. "You said that only a person with the power to harness both Spirit and human magic can carry the heart, but I don't know how to use Spirit magic. Every time I try, I get hurt."

"You are the daughter of the Firebird Queen. You called the Firebird back to Lyrica. Have you forgotten your power so easily?"

Calliope looked up at the Forgeman. "Is it hope? Is hope the power? Will you help me? Will you tell me the secret?"

The Forgeman's solemn eyes held hers. "You have all you need."

Calliope frowned. *You have all you need.* She looked down at the Feather. It was all she had. If it was all she needed, then why wasn't the magic working? Why did she keep hurting herself?

The Forgeman dropped his hand, and the curtain of water closed. "If you do not help us, the darkness will destroy the Nymph Isles, and the Spirits that lived here will be gone forever." He looked at Calliope. "Ours is a world of humans and Spirits. We are all children of the Firebird, and the world runs off our collective magic. Many of the Spirits have already left the realm; if we are destroyed, then balance will never be restored. Darkness will fall across the land, and all that was good will be gone."

He dragged his stone legs across the floor and sat heavily on the edge of the Forge. "You are the child who will unite us. You must use your magic to remove this darkness and save us all."

Calliope squeezed her eyes shut. She wished she knew that she could do it, but she was afraid. She had tried to use the magic, and it had nearly destroyed her—*how* could she carry the stone and survive?

The Forgeman made one last attempt, the words coming slowly, his breaths labored. "You do not need to *use* magic, only to carry it. If you will take the stone away and remove the darkness from the Isles, then I will give you my allegiance and the allegiance of all the lesser spirits in my domain. I, lord of the mountain, of rocks, and gems, land, and stone, one of the Ancient Children of the Firebird, do swear it. If you risk yourself to save us, I will recognize you as Queen from now until the end of your last generation." He held his hand to his heart and bowed his head.

Ilsbeth sucked in her breath, and Calliope saw the shock in her eyes. No Spirit had ever recognized a Firebird Queen. The Sea Spirit believed that once Calliope was out of the way, she could claim the throne without any repercussions. But the Forgeman's allegiance could change that. He was one of the most powerful spirits of all. Having him on her side could keep others from rising up against her people. She would be able to return and promise her kingdom safety with even more certainty. They could stop living in fear once and for all.

Here, at last, was something she could do that would make a difference. This was more than planting flowers.

"I'll try," she said. She looked down at the Suffering Stone, and she felt the power of it, the great darkness of stories stolen and left to rot. "I don't know if I can carry it, but I will try."

"Thank you, child." The ground shook as the Forgeman stood. "Now, I must warn you that once you pick up the Suffering Stone, the weight of its darkness will be unbearable, and you will not be able to hear or see the world as it truly is. You must be strong. Do not turn away from the path, and most of all, do not take the heart into the water. You must get to the door without any of the Sea Spirit's creatures following. If they see the door, they will try to close it, and if it closes, there will not be enough magic to reopen it."

Calliope felt panic rising within her. What had she agreed to?

"I will go with you," said Ilsbeth. "I cannot carry the stone myself, but I will keep you safe." She reached for her whip, but again, her hand came up empty, and she felt the shock of its loss anew.

"Once more to a child, our fates are tied." The Forgeman's words shook the walls, and the charcoal in the Forge shifted as it burned hotter.

"The Firebird chose you, Calliope, daughter of Queens. You carry its Feather. Do not forget what you have already done. Your story has given you all the magic you need. Harness it and find your true power."

Calliope's hand drifted to the Feather. She thought of all the times she had failed so far. She thought of the magic that had coursed through her and taken her over, how it had pulled her energy away and left her fragile and weak. The memory filled her with fear.

The Forgeman stepped toward the Forge. "I have magic enough for one more gift." He reached for a piece of burning charcoal, lifting it in his bare hand, and he placed it on a steel anvil. With great effort, he raised his hammer. "Goodbye, Queen Calliope of Lyrica. May we meet again."

He gave a great groan, and the hammer fell. The earth shook, and the stones cracked beneath his feet. The Forge burned brighter than the sun, and the acrid smell of metal sharpened the air.

For the first time, Calliope heard the *sound* of the Forgeman's magic. It was as if he had been holding it back, saving it for one final act. The *sound* of it was like the blast of ten thousand trumpets, and it vibrated through her, lifting her hair at the roots and trembling inside her soul.

Tears welled in her eyes as an emotion of complete surrender filled her, and then the *sound* cut off, and the feeling was gone.

The Forge was dark.

The steam began to evaporate, and the air cooled.

Goose bumps raised across the girls' skin, and Calliope shuddered as she lifted the glowing Feather and saw the Forgeman.

He had turned entirely to stone.

Ilsbeth swallowed. "Your gift," she said, glimpsing something shimmering beneath the Forgeman's left hand. She moved closer, and when she saw what it was, she couldn't keep the shock from her face. "It is . . . I do not understand."

"It's a whip, Ilsbeth!" Calliope's eyes shone. "The gift isn't for me at all. It's for *you*."

"For me? But why?" Ilsbeth reached out a tentative hand and picked up the golden whip. It thrilled through her fingers, its energy racing up her arm. She looked at the Forgeman's face.

He could see the future. If he had given her the whip, it was because he knew she would need it.

She tightened her grip on the handle and set her jaw. She turned to Calliope. "I am ready."

Calliope nodded, wishing she had the same confidence as Ilsbeth. Together, they walked through the waterfall, leaving the petrified Forgeman behind.

They stood, looking down at the Suffering Stone. Tendrils

of black shadow leaked from a web of cracks and trickled across the sand, seeping into the dark water that arched all around them.

Calliope held the Feather high, and they peered down the pathway. There was no sign of the door the Forgeman had spoken of.

What if there wasn't a door at all? What if the Forgeman had lied and it was all a trap?

The pathway stretched into the darkness, walls of water forming a tunnel at the bottom of the sea. The Forgeman had said that the path would lead them to the next Isle, but Calliope had no way of knowing how far they would need to walk, or how long she would have to carry the stone.

"What will happen when I pick it up?" she whispered, staring down at it.

Ilsbeth's eyes scanned the black water, and every muscle in her body tensed. "I do not know."

Calliope swallowed, and then she bent toward the heart of the Suffering Sea. She gritted her teeth and picked up the stone.

28

Help us!

Save us!

Free us!

The voices were a cacophony in her mind, but it was Calliope's heart that felt them most. She hunched beneath the weight of their sorrows.

Ilsbeth pressed a cool hand to Calliope's shoulder. "I am here."

Calliope heard her as if from across a great distance, but it was impossible to feel comforted.

Her feet were leaden, and each step felt impossible, but Ilsbeth guided her on, encouraging her with empty promises. *We are almost there. The door is close. Soon we will be home.*

Calliope tried to believe her. She focused on the glow from the Feather. *You have all you need.* What did she have?

The inky blackness wound around her fingers, pulling her, dragging her back. It was a terrible weight, too great to bear, but she bore it anyway.

Your story has given you all the magic you need. What had the Forgeman meant? What had her story really given her other than heartbreak and loss?

Step after step, with the stone in her palm, and her heart full of the painful cries of generations of lost stories, she walked down the path. "How much farther?"

"You are almost there," said Ilsbeth, hoping it was true, but she still could not see the door. There was only darkness beyond the glow of the Feather.

Around them, the black water was eerily calm, and the sand *shush*ed softly beneath their feet. Ilsbeth wondered what would happen if the Sea Spirit realized her heart was being moved.

Calliope groaned, and Ilsbeth fought the urge to take the stone away, to carry it for her, just for a while. It was infuriating to be forced to watch and do nothing more useful than promise it would soon be over.

She squeezed Calliope's shoulder. "You can do this, Highness. You are almost there." Over and over she promised it, and over and over Calliope only nodded, tears streaming down her cheeks, her muscles straining against the weight of the Suffering Stone.

"Soon, we will walk through the doorway. Soon, this will all be over. Soon, we will be home." *Soon. Soon. Soon.*

Calliope's hands shook beneath the stone. It weighed almost

nothing, but the emotions within were so heavy, she could feel herself breaking beneath them, and doubts began to attack her mind.

She wasn't strong enough. She didn't have what she needed. The Forgeman had made a mistake. She wasn't special or chosen. The Firebird had abandoned her. Her own mother had abandoned her.

She knew she had to drop the stone. If she did not, she was certain she would die beneath the weight of it. *I cannot do this on my own!* she thought. *What can hope do for me now?* The doubts were relentless, but she walked on in spite of them.

The sound of shattering glass made her freeze. It was a sound she'd heard over and over.

Calliope . . .

Calliope nearly dropped the heart.

"What is it?" said Ilsbeth. "What is wrong?"

Calliope's eyes darted, searching the water surrounding the tunnel.

Calliope, my daughter . . .

"Mother?"

Calliope saw her at last, floating in the wall of water beyond the pathway where the light from the Feather just reached. Dark hair rose and fell around her mother's shoulders, and her velvet robe billowed. Scattered on the seabed at her mother's feet were broken pieces of glass, and Calliope knew at once that they had come from the storm glass that her mother had broken on that Terrible night so long ago.

Her mother stretched out a hand, and blood seeped from her palm as if she had only just cut it. Sharp-toothed sea serpents swarmed around her, and black kelp wrapped around her throat.

Calliope rushed toward the wall of water. "Mother!"

"Calliope, wait!" Ilsbeth's grip was hard on Calliope's shoulder. "Remember what the Forgeman said. You cannot trust what the Suffering Stone makes you see. You must not take the Spirit's heart into the water."

Calliope jerked away. "But it's my mother, Ilsbeth! Can't you see her?"

Ilsbeth searched, and her eyes caught on the eels, swarming toward them. "We must get to the Spirit Door, *now*."

Calliope shook her head. "I have to help her!" Even as she said it, her mother cried out again. *Daughter! Give me the heart! Let me change my story. Let me return to you, and together we will save Lyrica.*

Calliope held out her hand. "Here! Here, Mother! Take it!"

"That is not your mother," hissed Ilsbeth. "Your mother cannot be returned to you. Do you not remember what the old man said? Death is a story no one can change."

Calliope tried to wrench away from Ilsbeth's grasp. "Why are you saying that? She's not dead, Ilsbeth. She's right there. I can see her! She can help me! I can't carry the heart on my own, Ilsbeth. I can't!"

"You *must*."

The eels swarmed closer, their yellow eyes on the stone

in Calliope's hand. Ilsbeth saw the inky darkness seeping between Calliope's clenched fingers.

Calliope's eyes flashed. "You don't want me to have help." Her tone was bitter. "You want me to be miserable, because you're miserable. Your sisters abandoned you, and your father never came to rescue you, but that doesn't mean *I* have to suffer, too."

Ilsbeth flinched and stepped backward. "I don't need *anyone* to rescue me."

The stone, my daughter. Give me the stone.

"Yes, Mother!" Calliope reached into the water and placed the stone in her mother's outstretched hand. For a moment, Calliope felt relief.

But then she saw the truth: the sea serpent's sharp teeth, and the stone lodged between them.

Her mother was gone. She had never been there at all, and now the heart was in the sea.

The stone cracked further in the serpent's jaws, and the pathway began to flood.

"We have to get across to the next Isle!" said Ilsbeth, grabbing Calliope's arm. "We have to get to the door!"

"We can't get through without the heart!" Calliope scanned the water, trying desperately to find the eel that had taken the stone, but it was no use. The water around them was a teeming, writhing mass of slithering black sea serpents.

She turned to Ilsbeth. "I have no choice. I have to go after it."

"How? You cannot survive underwater." Ilsbeth searched

Calliope's face, and she suddenly understood what Calliope planned to do. "No. You cannot use Spirit magic."

"I have to! There's no other way."

"It will destroy you!"

Calliope pulled the Feather from her waistband. "I have to try. For Lyrica. For the Nymph Isles. For *you*. I'm so sorry about what I said. I didn't mean it."

Ilsbeth shook her head. "You owe me no apologies."

The tunnel was flooding fast, and Ilsbeth tried to keep herself from panicking.

Calliope threw her arms around her, and for once, Ilsbeth did not shy away. "You have to get to the Spirit Door, all right? You have to find a way to keep it open long enough for me to get the stone."

Ilsbeth nodded, and her hand was tight on the handle of the golden whip. "I will not fail you."

Calliope took Ilsbeth's cold hands in hers. "If I don't make it back—"

Ilsbeth shook her head. "You are Calliope, descendant of the first Firebird Queen. You are the Age of Hope. You *will* come back with that stone, and I will be holding the door."

Calliope nodded, then took a breath and stepped into the sea, drawing the Spirit magic to her.

Ilsbeth saw the change in Calliope's eyes. "Remember who you are," she shouted. "Remember!"

Her cry died away, the light from the Feather disappeared, and Ilsbeth was alone in the dark.

For so long, she had refused to be the leader of the Glade Girls, and when she had finally accepted that she was, they had no longer needed her. She had felt alone and helpless, and had wondered what her purpose was when there was no danger to fight, no family to hold together. She had felt out of place in a new home where she did not know who she was supposed to be. And then she had been kidnapped.

She had been truly helpless for the first time in her life.

But the Forgeman had given her the golden whip. He had given her a new purpose. She held the whip up, let its light gleam around her. Perhaps she did have her own kind of magic after all.

She turned and raced along the flooding pathway, splashing through the rising water.

Sea serpents swarmed around her ankles, and she kicked out at them, forcing her way forward until at last she saw light. She had made it to the end of the path, and reached the shore of the other Isle!

The open Spirit Door was lodged in the shallows. The doorframe was made of black metal studded with dark seashells, and red-capped mushrooms grew in a semicircle at its base.

Water lapped against the doorway as if it were closed, but Ilsbeth could see through to the other side. Across the threshold, the desert stretched out forever, and the full moon bloomed among the stars. Silver light streamed through the doorway, kissing the wet black sand of the Nymph Isle.

The tide rose ever higher, and Ilsbeth flung her whip out, striking the serpents. They exploded in a shower of light, but others soon took their place. They wrapped around her legs, trying to pull her under, and she fought them back.

Their teeth sank into her flesh, and she roared as she drove them away. She struck out, over and over, and over and over they returned. The water pushed against her, and the sand swallowed her feet. Slippery kelp draped itself around her and tried to yank her from the door.

The golden whip cracked, and Ilsbeth prayed that Calliope would come.

29

The Glade Girls formed a circle around the pool at the center of the cove, facing up toward the full moon.

Jack sat on a broken crate a few feet away. Ilsbeth's fledgling fluttered down to the barrel beside him. It looked around at the girls, tilting its head this way and that, as if trying to understand why Ilsbeth was not there.

"It's all right," whispered Jack. "She'll be home soon." He had been shocked to find the girls in the cove, but Fi had quickly explained that Ilsbeth had found them all during the bonfire and told them that if ever they needed her, they should go to the cove.

They had all come, hoping that it would be true.

But the cove had been empty, and they knew that Jack had told the truth. Ilsbeth was gone.

Now, the air in the cove was alive with energy. The tallest

girl, Hazel, turned her dark head toward Fi. "Can we do it without the Wild Woman?"

Fi folded her hands. "We do not need the Wild Woman to guide us; we only need to *see* where Ilsbeth has been taken. Then we will go and find her and bring her home."

The others made eye contact, and they all clasped hands.

Questions buzzed in Jack's mind, but he kept them to himself. It was clear that he was not a part of this group, and he didn't want to bother them unless they asked for his advice.

The girls spoke in perfect unison, their voices rising to the moon above.

"We are the daughters of the Halcyon Glade. Show us where our sister has been taken. Show us where she is now." They repeated it three times, and then their heads bent toward the water.

For a moment, there was nothing, only seven faces staring back at them, and then the water changed. Their reflections vanished into darkness, and the air sharpened with sudden, frosty cold. Their breaths came in white clouds, and black ice crept over the surface of the pool.

Jack hugged himself tightly, looking across the black water.

No one spoke, and then there was a *crack*, and a burst of light, and Ilsbeth's figure appeared in the surface of the pool. She held a golden whip in her hand, and she flung it out again and again, with flashes like lightning.

The girls shifted, but they did not break the circle. They watched as their sister fought, and listened, without speaking, to Ilsbeth's grunts and screams, the sharp bursts of air as she struck out at sea serpents with vicious teeth. Waves crashed into Ilsbeth, knocking her off her feet, and they watched as she clung to an iron doorway so that she would not be swept away by the rising tide.

It was horrible to watch.

"She is tiring," said Fi. "Her strikes are weak, and I can hear her feet are slowing."

They all knew it.

Ilsbeth's muscles shook, and she was sucking in water, choking as it attacked her lungs. Her breathing grew ragged, and there was agony in her screams.

The eels tore at her flesh, and her dress hung in ribbons, but she did not leave the doorway. She continued to fight as if her life depended on it.

The Glade Girls looked up from the water, into one another's eyes. Their sister was going to fall, and all they could do was watch.

"We cannot travel through the moonlight," said Fi. "But she may be able to hear our voices."

They turned back to the pool and began shouting into the darkness.

Ilsbeth fought until her back was against the door, striking out again and again with the whip, and when it was finally wrested from her hand, she punched with her fists. She kicked and she fought with everything in her until she could not fight anymore.

She knew her body was breaking, but it was not until her mind broke that she knew she had lost.

I cannot do this. I cannot fight the sea.

I am all alone.

She fell to the ground.

Ilsbeth. Someone called her name. *Ilsbeth, Ilsbeth.*

Their voices rang all around her, coming through the doorway. Was it only exhaustion bringing her sisters to her mind?

You are not alone, they cried. *We are with you! Get up! Keep fighting! Do not give up.*

Ilsbeth forced herself to stand. She was their leader. She could not quit. This was just like training in the Glade, her sisters by her side. They had experienced something terrible, but it had made them strong. Together. They were magical because they had been through something that bonded them. If human magic was the ability to take something terrible and transform it, then she and her sisters had more power than she had ever known.

She only had to keep the door open for a little longer, just a few moments longer. "I hear you!" she shouted. "I hear you!"

They urged her on and her doubt receded. She had been so afraid of the sea, of its wild expanse. Of loneliness that could sweep her away. But now, she fought without fear. She had trained for fire, but now she faced water. She kept her head above it, and she met the serpents as they came, beating them back until she could beat them back no longer.

Until there was nothing left to give.

Then she fell down into the water, and her sisters were silent.

Someone was shouting, cursing as they ripped the serpents off her. They lifted her up, pressing her to their chest as the tide receded.

The smells of hay and leather were warm in Ilsbeth's nostrils, and a soft-gloved hand pressed to her cheek.

"Ilsbeth." It was her father's voice, strangled and tortured.

She opened her eyes, blinking up at him. "You're here," she whispered.

"I will always come for you," said the Falconer gruffly. "That is what a father does."

Ilsbeth swallowed, and a tear squeezed from the corner of her eye. "I did not think you cared."

The Falconer couldn't speak. He pulled her close, rocking her back and forth until her head went limp. He let out a wail, the sound ripping from his chest, and he sobbed.

Nearby, the Bookkeeper clung to the sides of the dinghy. It had been swept back and forth between the Isles with the change in the tide. He watched the Falconer with his daughter for a moment before clearing his throat.

The Falconer's sobs caught, and he blinked at the old man. "You! You know things. Books and—and learning. Help her—please!"

The Bookkeeper shook his head. "She needs to return to the Royal City."

The Falconer whistled, but his birds had gone. The darkness had frightened them away and sent him crashing down into the water. He knew that even the sound of their master would not bring them back into it.

He turned to the Bookkeeper. "Tell me how to leave. There were rumors that you came here before. That you are the only man to have ever set foot here and returned home. Tell me how you did it!"

The Bookkeeper shook his head. "I paid a price I should not have paid."

"Tell me!"

The Falconer listened, and when the story was finished, he nodded, pressing himself to his feet, his daughter limp in his arms.

He moved to the water. "North Wind! I summon you!"

A frigid blast struck him, but he faced it without flinching.

"Take my daughter away from here."

"You must give up your future," whispered the Bookkeeper.

The Falconer looked down at Ilsbeth's face, and his voice was gentle. "I offer it gladly."

The Wind's howl calmed, and its frigid breath was gentle on his cheeks. Then Ilsbeth was lifted into the air.

The Falconer watched with empty arms as the white slip of her tattered dress disappeared into the darkness.

"I love you, daughter," he whispered.

Behind him, the Spirit Door slammed shut.

30

"Chichi, wake up! We made it!" Prewitt shook Chichi's shoulder. "I can see the light from the Bookshop!"

Chichi rubbed her eyes and sat up. She saw the silhouette of a crooked tower in the distance, and at the top, a pulsing, dim red light.

"There's the Bookshop!" She jumped to her feet. She had always wanted to see it.

The wind suddenly changed, and Chichi wrapped her arms around herself, shivering, as Prewitt ran to let out the sail. The catboat picked up speed, and they raced toward the quiet harbor.

"I did it." A grin spread across Prewitt's face. "I sailed us here all by myself. Wait until Dad hears."

Movement on the horizon caught his eye, and his smile faded.

The wrecked ship glided across the sea toward them. Stars glittered through shredded sails, and cloaked figures gathered at the gunwales, faces flashing silver. Cormorants flew low across the water like a dark cloud.

But none of these had been what caused Prewitt's breath to catch.

It was the Spirit that made his fingers clench the rudder. A giantess of seawater swelled across the waves. She wore the moonlight like a silver cape and tugged the wrecked ship behind her, a child's toy on a string.

"Hurry!" shouted Prewitt. "We have to get to the castle! We have to warn them not to take the Spirit's pearls!" The catboat sailed into the harbor, and they bounded onto the dock, feet pounding.

Prewitt hit the sand and was halfway across the beach before he saw the figure sprawled small and lifeless in the tide pools. His heart squeezed. *Ilsbeth.* It was the white dress that gave her away, and he ran forward, heels flinging up sand.

"Ilsbeth!" She was coated in grime, and her hair was loose around her shoulders. Her skin was a mess of cuts, but her face was peaceful in the moonlight. What had happened? How had she gotten there? Where was Calliope? Prewitt's gaze swept the night sea as if he could find the answers in the waves.

The Spirit was nearly there. He turned to Chichi. "Go to the castle. Get my mother, Marisa. Tell her Ilsbeth's been hurt."

Chichi gaped down at Ilsbeth.

"Chichi!"

Chichi jumped and then she nodded, her eyes wide. She turned to go, and Prewitt called after her. "Warn them, Chichi! Tell them the Sea Spirit is coming to steal their stories!"

He waited with Ilsbeth, growing more and more anxious as the wrecked ship drew near. He knew he had to think of a way to stop the Spirit on his own, but all he could think about was Calliope.

Dread filled his entire body. He wanted to pat Ilsbeth's cheeks, to try to wake her, to ask her what had happened, but even unconscious she intimidated him.

Prewitt heard the jangle of bells, and a falcon screeched, swooping toward him. Prewitt raised a protective arm, but it was only the fledgling. It fluttered down beside Ilsbeth's head, nuzzling her cheek with its beak.

"Ilsbeth! Ilsbeth!" The Glade Girls appeared, racing across the sand, Jack in tow, and they crowded around her.

"Out of the way!" Marisa barged through, a chaos of skirts as she flung a large bag onto the sand.

"Oh, you poor dear," Marisa soothed as she assessed the wounds. "What did the Silver Shag do to you?" She was pointedly not looking at the sea, at the approaching Spirit that brought the unknown near. She rolled up her sleeves and got to work.

Chichi watched from a distance, her arms around herself. She looked out at the wrecked ship, at the silver masks coming close. They had always been a symbol of hope, but now, all she felt was confusion. Why was her mother doing this?

"Where's Dad?" asked Prewitt. "We need him!"

"He's securing the castle the best he can." Marisa's eyes lifted, sweeping the group of girls. "Where is the Queen?"

Prewitt shook his head. "I don't know!" He heard the panic in his own voice and tried to force himself to be calm. "I don't know," he said again.

Marisa reached out, tugging him in for a quick hug. "It's all right. I'm sure wherever she is, she can handle herself. Let's just do our best to deal with the trouble at hand. We need to get Ilsbeth off the beach so I can wash her wounds and find some way to get her warm." She pressed her hand to Ilsbeth's cheek. "Her skin is like ice."

She gave orders to the Glade Girls, and they lifted Ilsbeth up and carried her across the sand toward the cove. Jack followed, the fledgling on one shoulder and a puffed-out Urchin on the other.

Once they had gotten Ilsbeth inside, they laid her on blankets beside the pool of water, and Jack hurried to build a fire from broken crates. They watched as Marisa warmed water and did her best to clean and dry Ilsbeth's wounds.

Prewitt pulled Jack aside. "We have to do something."

"What can we do?"

Prewitt told him, and Jack shook his head. "It won't work."

"It doesn't have to work," said Prewitt. "It only needs to give us more time. Cal will come back. She'll save us. I know she will. I know it." He put as much confidence into his voice as he could, then turned to the Glade Girls, who had been listening.

"You do not have to ask," said Fi. "We will come."

"It'll be dangerous," he warned.

Lanna uncoiled her whip. "The Sea Spirit hurt our sister. It is she who should be afraid."

Ilsbeth whimpered, and Fi bent over her. "We'll be back," she promised. She turned her face toward Marisa. "Take care of her," she said.

Marisa reached out and gave Fi's shoulder a squeeze. "I will." Her eyes shifted to Prewitt, and he saw the worry in them. He thought she would beg him not to go, but instead she nodded. "I'll see you when this is all over."

Chichi had not gone with them to the cove. She had stood apart, confusion and shame tangled in her mind. No one at the castle had questioned her when she had barged in, shouting for help. She had been certain they would accuse her, that they would know who she was just by looking at her. She had imagined them saying, "Aren't you the daughter of the Silver Shag? Don't you know what a monster she is? It is your family that has doomed the kingdom!" She had been certain that they would lock her away.

But they hadn't. Prewitt's mother had *thanked* her. The man in the red coat had called her brave.

But she hadn't come to be brave, and she didn't deserve their gratitude. What she wanted was answers. *Only you know who I truly am.* That's what her mother always said, but she didn't know her mother at all.

Chichi had loved keeping her mother's secret. She had felt proud to be a part of that story. If stories were power, then the story of her mother had been what gave her strength. It had helped her whenever she had felt afraid during the Spectress's rule. It had made her believe that anything was possible.

Now, she was ashamed. She had prided herself on noticing things that other people didn't. A derisive laugh burst from her lips. She hadn't even seen the truth of the person who was closest to her! When she got home, she would rip up all her notes and break every one of her pencils. How had she missed what was right in front of her face?

Chichi crouched in the shadows behind a pile of charred driftwood, watching the Sea Spirit drag the wrecked ship onto the beach.

The Masked Rampage jumped over the gunwales, their cloaks fluttering as they landed lightly in the sand. Chichi searched for her mother, and found her, not flying, but walking down the gangway. She and Chichi's father were carrying something—no, *someone*—between them. *Who could it be?*

Chichi squinted. It was a man. He was limp and pale, and his arms dangled from the board he was laid upon.

Her parents set the board gently in the sand, but the man did not move. Her mother crouched down, pressing her hand to the man's cheek. "Milo," she called. "Milo, can you hear me?" Nothing, not a word, not a flicker of a lash.

Who is Milo? Chichi wondered.

"We're home. I brought you home. You won't believe it, but the light from the Bookshop is still on after all this time."

252

There was an emotion in her mother's voice that Chichi had never heard, and she knew that there was a story here, something she had not been told, another thing her mother had kept from her.

The Silver Shag cleared her throat, pushing herself to her feet. "Take the water from his lungs," she commanded.

Not until the throne of Lyrica is mine. Bring the people to me. The Spirit's voice broke on the shore. *Tell them I have come to take away their suffering and change their stories.*

"If I do this, you will give me Milo, and you will allow us to return to Castaway Cape."

I swear it.

The Silver Shag's eyes narrowed behind her mask. "Do not forget your promise. You must not offer a pearl to any of my people. Castaway Cape will keep our stories. Good and bad. They belong to us."

If that is what you wish, but I do not understand why you would want to keep them.

The Sea Spirit waited in the water as the Masked Rampage ran up the city steps, calling people from their homes.

"The Silver Shag! It's the Silver Shag!" People appeared in their doorways, cautious, and uncertain, but when they saw the Sea Spirit waiting on the beach, the blood left their faces, and they turned to go back inside.

"Do not be afraid!" Chichi's mother called out. "The Sea Spirit has not come to cause you harm."

Two men in blue jackets rushed down the steps, led by the man in red who had met Chichi when she burst into the castle.

It was Prewitt's father: the Bargemaster. He had his sword drawn, and his face was furious.

"Where is the Queen?" he demanded. "What have you done with Calliope?"

The Silver Shag did not cower. She faced him, towering and unimpressed. "The last daughter of Firebird Queens has left you. She abandoned the city because she knows that she is no match for the Demon's Spectress and her ash golems. Only the Sea Spirit can save you now."

Chichi flinched. That wasn't true at all. Calliope hadn't abandoned them. She had gone to save her friend. The friend her mother had kidnapped. The one who they had found half dead on the beach. What had her mother done to her, and where was Calliope *really*?

"Calliope would never abandon us," said the Bargemaster. "She may be the last daughter of Firebird Queens, but it was she who defeated the Demon and called the Firebird back. The Spectress no longer has power. I will not let you tell our people any more lies."

"That's right!" said a man with a puff of white hair. "The Sea Spirit is not welcome here, and neither are you."

Blue eyes narrowed behind the silver mask, and Chichi's mother flicked her hand. The gesture was tiny, but the members of the Masked Rampage caught her signal. They fell on the men in blue jackets, disarming them quickly, but the Bargemaster fought on.

People watched from their houses, whispering as the Silver Shag drew her dagger.

She whirled toward the Bargemaster, her cloaks a flurry of black and silver, and her mouth twisted so that it was unrecognizable. Chichi gasped. This was not her mother. This was someone so horrible and frightening that she couldn't bear to watch.

She buried her head in her arms. Why had she come? She didn't want to be here anymore. She had thought she wanted answers, but she had been wrong. Answers had only brought her more pain. She wished she could go back to the way things had been before the Queen had come to Castaway Cape. She wanted to remember her mother as the person she had been. She wanted to be the girl she had been before, the girl her mother tucked in with stories of bravery, and heroism, and selfless acts of kindness. Chichi's shoulders shook with sobs.

Come, child, do not cry.

Chichi startled, looking to see who had spoken.

The Sea Spirit rose and fell in the shallows, waves tumbling in the nets of her skirts. She stretched out her hands toward Chichi, and a pearl gleamed in her translucent palm.

Let the sea take your tears and ease your troubles. Let it give you the story of your heart.

Chichi stood, walking forward, her sandals crunching across broken shells. She wiped her cheeks on the rough backs of her hands and moved closer.

Her mother had said their stories made them who they were, that they made them strong, but her mother had lied.

She reached out and took the pearl.

"Chichi, no!" The cry seemed to come from far away.

Someone grabbed Chichi's shoulders, spinning her around.

Her mother stared down at her, blue eyes horrified behind her silver mask.

Chichi's mouth spread into a smile, and she held up the pearl. "Look, Mama! Look what the Sea Spirit gave me. Isn't it pretty?"

The Silver Shag rounded on the Sea Spirit. "You promised you would leave us our stories!"

The shells of the Spirit's mouth curved up. *How could I know she belonged to you? She wore no mask.*

"Take it back!" ordered the Silver Shag. She snatched the pearl from Chichi's hand and flung it at the Spirit. It caught in the water of her empty chest and sank into the waves.

The Sea Spirit flowed in and out and up and down, her face constantly shifting, and the pearl swept back to Chichi, who picked it up and put it in her pocket.

A mother should not wish her child suffering. You should be grateful that I soothed her troubled soul. I gave her a new story. A better one.

"What did you change? What did you take?" The Silver Shag knelt in front of Chichi, yanking off her mask.

"Look at me, Charlotte. Tell me what you remember. What's changed?"

Chichi tilted her head. She reached out and pressed a finger to her mother's cheek. It came back shining. "What's wrong, Mama? Are you sad? The Sea Spirit can make it better."

"Please, try to remember. Tell me about when the Spectress was around. Tell me the story of the Silver Shag."

Chichi blinked.

"Please, Chichi. Try!"

Chichi's forehead scrunched. "Silver Shag . . ." She sounded out the name. "I don't know who that is."

"What about the Spectress? What about the long years when we struggled and fought and made the Cape a home?"

"The Spectress?" Chichi giggled. "These are such funny names. Are they people you know?"

"Try, Chichi, try to remember." The Silver Shag pressed her forehead against Chichi's. "Please, my darling. Only you know who I really am."

Chichi pulled her forehead away. She plopped into the sand, a mild expression on her face, and stared out at the water.

The Silver Shag looked up at the Sea Spirit through wet lashes. "You have taken my daughter from me," she seethed.

The Sea Spirit stretched out, resting her palm on Chichi's head. Salt water poured down Chichi's face.

No, Silver Shag, I have given you a new daughter, a better one, undamaged and fresh. Can you not see how content she is?

The Silver Shag reached for her dagger. "I will not let you do this to anyone else. I should never have agreed to help you. I *won't* help you."

Then your brother will return to the deep, and you will never see him again.

The Silver Shag knelt in the sand beside Milo. "I'm sorry, brother," she whispered. "Maybe it's good that you can't see me this way. We both swore we would never do to our children what Father did to us, remember? When he took us from the shell cottage, and refused to let us talk about Mother, we promised we would never forget. We would never stay silent just because a story was painful. We wouldn't pretend things weren't happening, or that they didn't hurt. We would tell our stories, no matter what, because they are a part of who we are."

She pressed a hand to his clammy cheek. "But now, I think maybe we were only partly right. Maybe some stories end up taking too much of our focus. I was so obsessed with this one, with vengeance, and getting you back. I let the story of what happened on the Nymph Isles change me. I let it matter more than any others, and now, I've lost my daughter."

There was a commotion, and the Silver Shag looked up.

The Masked Rampage was dragging the Bargemaster and the watermen down to the beach.

She jumped to her feet. "Wait! Stop!"

But it was too late. The people of the Royal City were creeping from their homes and down the steps. "The Silver Shag says it's safe. We can trust her. Look, there she is, standing by the Spirit! Let's go and see her."

The shell mouth curved upward, and the Spirit's glass eyes shimmered. *They come to me because they trust you. You're their hero. You told the lies that made the darkest parts of their stories overtake them, and now they will accept my pearls gladly.*

Waves broke on the sand, and the Spirit's voice grew to a roar. *Come and give me your suffering, and I will be the greatest Queen Lyrica has ever known. A Spirit Queen!*

The Silver Shag lunged, plunging her dagger into the Spirit's face.

The Spirit burbled, as if laughing, and the waves flung the Silver Shag down into the sand near her unconscious twin. She lay in a defeated heap beside her discarded mask.

The Sea Spirit laughed. *You cannot stop me, Silver Shag. The only one with any power to stop me is the last daughter of Firebird Queens, and she will never return.*

31

Calliope was lost in the dark.

Icy water wrapped around her, but she did not feel cold. She felt nothing at all. Spirit magic throbbed through her, cleaning her out, draining her away. Her name disappeared into the waves, and she floated alone, no sorrows or feelings, drifting in and out with the tide.

Time did not matter.

Nothing mattered.

Remember.

A word, echoing, echoing.

Remember.

The girl frowned. A strange light glowed at her waist. She reached for the object tucked there, wrapping her hand around it, ready to fling it away, but something stopped her. She stared down at it, her body bobbing with the waves.

A memory. She closed her eyes and tried to recall it. A warmth flooded through her, and a flash lit the darkness behind her lids. She opened her eyes.

There in the water was a bird, its feathers flaming and its ruby eyes aglow. Their gazes locked and time stood still.

Follow me, it said.

And the girl did. The bird glided through the water, leaving a trail of bubbles like sparks.

She chased it, and then it stopped. It turned toward her, and with a single powerful motion, it beat down its wings. Flames erupted from its tail, and she somersaulted backward in a flush of bubbles. The Spirit magic that had held her released its grip, and she felt dizzy with the sudden return of her senses. Her chest ached with the need for air, and she remembered who she was. *I am Calliope, daughter of the Firebird Queen.*

She blinked, looking around for the Firebird, but there was no trace of it. Had it really been there?

Help us!

Save us!

Free us!

The words crashed into Calliope's mind. The stone! Where was it?

She looked around and saw a flaming orange reef rising from the sand, and at its center was the heart. She reached out and grabbed it. The cries were a cacophony in her mind, and the stolen stories were heavy in her chest, but she wouldn't let anything stop her this time.

She swam toward the shore with everything she had. Her limbs screamed, and her lungs burned, but at last she broke the surface.

"Ilsbeth!" She waded onto the beach of the second Isle. "Ilsbeth, I found it! I got it back!"

She held the Feather aloft, searching. "Ilsbeth?"

"She's gone."

Calliope turned and saw the hulking man standing in the shallows near the Bookkeeper's floating dinghy.

"Falconer? How did you—"

"It doesn't matter." The Falconer's words were choked, and he did not look at her when he spoke. "I came too late."

"But you can't mean . . . Ilsbeth isn't . . ." Calliope couldn't bear to finish.

"No, not yet."

Not yet. The words said too much and not enough.

"Where is she?"

"The Wind took her."

"But we're supposed to take the stone away. The Forgeman will help us if I do. He can stop the Sea Spirit! He can keep the kingdom safe." She looked frantically around for the door, but when she found it, she faltered.

It was closed.

She ran to it, shoving it with her hands, but it would not budge. She fell to her knees in the sand.

How long had Ilsbeth fought to keep the door open?

She couldn't bear to think about it. It was all her fault. She had wanted so badly to believe what the Suffering Stone had shown her.

She looked down at the stone in her palm.

The Sea Spirit would continue to steal people's stories, and the stone would break. The Nymph Isles Spirits would be destroyed, and balance would be lost forever.

Black tendrils spilled from the cracks in the stone and pooled in Calliope's hand. It seemed strange that something so small could hold so much pain and sorrow. Now, darkness would spread, caused by stories that had been taken away but never healed.

Stories are our strength. That was what Chichi's mother had said before Calliope knew who she really was, and at the time, Calliope hadn't understood. She had wondered at Castaway Cape's resilience. They had all suffered twelve years of fear and loss, but Castaway Cape had found a way to move forward, while the people of the Royal City were still frightened and broken. The pain of their past, their tragic stories, had become the Royal City's prison, and it was the people of Castaway Cape who had found a way to be free.

They had overcome their past and become something greater not by forgetting or trading their stories away, but by retelling them, by sharing them the same way they shared a meal, or a smile, or a shoulder to cry on.

Calliope remembered the Forgeman's words: *The magic of humanity is in their ability to take sorrow, suffering, hardships, and trials, and transform them.*

Calliope frowned. Maybe she had been focusing on the wrong kind of magic all along.

Stories are our strength. There was a part of Calliope's story that she had been avoiding, one that she had locked behind the nursery door. She had hidden away the painful memories of her mother's death, trapped them in a far corner of her mind, and refused to let them out. She had been certain that the memories would weaken her. That they would take away her hope and keep her from finding her magic. But what if she was wrong? What if the secret to her magic was somehow there, in her past, in the story that she had been avoiding?

She closed her eyes, and she thought of the door to the nursery. It rose up in her mind, and again, she had the desire to push it away, to flee from the sorrow it would bring, but instead, she let it come, and as it did, she heard a new *sound*.

It rose above the din of the crying voices, a Song she had heard before. It was the Firebird Song. She felt it in her body and knew that hope had found her. It was there, even in the darkest moment of her past.

The Falconer and the Bookkeeper sucked in their breaths. They could not hear the Song, or the voices from the stone, but their focus was on the Feather, which glowed so brightly that they had to look away.

Calliope opened her eyes just as a cascade of golden light swept across the Spirit Door, changing it from iron to simple wooden planks.

The door to the nursery stood in the sand. "It's our way

home!" she cried. She ran forward, pulling the key from her pocket, but neither the Falconer nor the Bookkeeper followed.

She turned toward them, eyebrows lifted. "Aren't you coming?"

"I gave up my future," said the Falconer. "I will not risk my daughter by going against my word."

Calliope turned to the Bookkeeper, still floating in the shallows. He shook his head, rubbing a hand across his scalp. "What if you're wrong? What if the door is only a trick?" Although she tried to convince them, they would not follow, and Calliope went on alone.

She put the key into the lock and turned it, preparing herself for the flood of memories that lay on the other side. She took a deep breath and pushed, stepping across the threshold without looking back.

32

Calliope passed through the Spirit Door, leaving the key in the lock.

Inside the nursery, the musty air was laced with moonlight. The room was full of all the items she had taken from the castle, all the things that had made her think of her mother. Marisa had done as she had asked, and the crown glistened on a silk pillow at the center of the charred nightstand.

Calliope walked with leaden steps toward the wall where the words were painted in her mother's blood. She pressed her palm against them, her head bowed. *I will never forget what happened here,* she thought. *It is a part of my story—a part of me. But I won't be haunted by it anymore. I will accept it because I cannot change it, and I will use it to grow strong.*

"It doesn't mean I'm not sad." She said these words aloud, as if her mother might hear them. "I think this sadness will always be a part of me. But I choose not to allow one chapter of my story to ruin the others. I choose to be happy anyway. Not a fragile, pretend happiness, but a deep joy that goes on in spite of the pain." She smiled a little. It took effort, but it felt right.

She stepped back with a sigh. A weight had lifted from her, and it somehow made the Suffering Stone easier to carry.

Her fist closed around it. It was time to face the Sea Spirit, to prove to her people that she would keep them safe, that *she* was the Queen of Lyrica. Her gaze fell to the crown.

It was beautiful, gilded in gold, and set with pearls, and she knew that it must be very valuable, but its value to her was far more than precious metal and jewels. The crown had been passed down through the centuries, had rested on the head of every Firebird Queen since the very first—including her mother's. That knowledge had caused her pain before, had made her feel like an imposter, but now it made her feel like a part of something. She had thought she was alone, but she wasn't alone, not really. The crown, like the Feather, connected her to all of her ancestors' stories.

Calliope put the stone in her pocket and reached out, lifting the crown from the silk. She did not know what she would do when she faced the Spirit. She still was not sure how to use Spirit magic without harming herself, but she no longer felt that she needed that kind of magic. She had remembered who she was, and what she had done without anything but *hope*. Yes, she *was* the daughter of Firebird Queens, and that would be enough.

It was time to wear the crown, to face the Spirit boldly, and remind her people that she could keep them safe.

She raised it higher, and was about to place it on her head, when the moonlight glinted off one of the pearls. She lowered the crown, tilting it back, and bringing it closer. The pearl was different than the others, not a glimmering lustrous white, but a pale, ice-tinged blue.

Calliope sucked in her breath. There was no doubt.

She reached out and pried it from the setting.

It was one of the Sea Spirit's pearls.

At last, she understood why the magic of the Firebird Queens had been forgotten. Somewhere in the past, a Queen had given in to the Sea Spirit. She had taken a pearl and lost her story, changing the future of her descendants, and the kingdom, for generations.

Calliope clenched the used pearl in her fist and set the crown on her head.

Inside her pocket, the stone cried out—the voices of stolen stories—and Calliope turned toward the door. It was only a door now. The magic was gone. She could see the castle hallway on the other side.

"It's time to take you home," she said to the stone.

She had a plan. It was an impossible plan, one that relied on an impossible hope. But she was the daughter of Firebird Queens, and hope was what they did best.

33

Come to me. Come and trade away your sorrows. Let go of your suffering, your fear, your heartbreak and loss. Come, and I will give you a new story.

The gathered crowd murmured, and a boy tugged at his father's hand, his chin quivering. "Where's the Queen?" he asked.

The Sea's burbling laugh drifted across the shore. *Your Queen has fled. Only I can keep you safe from the Spectress now.*

"Don't believe her," shouted the Bargemaster. His eye was black, and his hands were bound. "The Sea Spirit lies! Everything that happened at the bonfire was a trick. Look around you! Look at the flowers on the tiers. The Queen planted them for you so that you could have hope again. She would never abandon you."

"How can we be sure?" asked Fi's mother. "She was the one who called us down to the beach. She started the fire. For all we know, she's working for the Spectress."

"Anyone can plant flowers," said a man nearby. "That's not what we need. We need protection. We need our children back."

Fi's mother turned toward the Sea Spirit, and her voice was plaintive. "Can you find our children? Can you keep them safe?"

Yes, said the Sea Spirit. *I can keep you safe. Take my pearl, and you will have all you desire.*

"No one else is taking a pearl."

The Spirit's green glass eyes spun, searching for the one who had spoken.

The Silver Shag stood before her, mouth a firm line. She turned to the crowd. "I lied to you," she said. "Do not trust this Spirit. Do not take her pearls." She nodded at the Masked Rampage, and they released the watermen.

The waves at the edge of the beach grew agitated, flinging themselves onto the sand.

Be silent, Silver Shag. I hold your brother's life in my hands. I hold your daughter's story. Would you give them up?

The Silver Shag flinched, but she did not back down.

The Sea Spirit spread her arms. *Come.* She called the crowd, but Prewitt could see that the Silver Shag's honesty had made an impact. People were backing away, pulling their children up the steps.

The waves smashed against the rocks, and the Sea Spirit swelled, rising until she was as tall as the Bookshop.

The watermen and the Masked Rampage approached the Sea Spirit, swords and daggers drawn. A tide swept across the beach, lifting them off their feet and flinging them to the ground.

I am the Sea. Nothing can defeat me.

"We can!"

The Sea Spirit whirled. There in the harbor was the *Queen's Barge.* Prewitt stood at the helm, the buttons on his jacket gleaming, and the Glade Girls balanced on the row benches, whips in hand.

Prewitt had led them all through the tunnels and opened the door to the Sacred Cavern. He had piloted the Barge out into the sea and called commands calmly and quietly as Jack and the Glade Girls rowed, their oars silent and sure. They had come into the harbor and floated close to the Sea Spirit without her noticing, and now, they did not hesitate.

They attacked. The Glade Girls twisted and spun, lashing out at the Sea Spirit from the deck of the Barge.

Fi's mother cried out and raced down toward the beach. "Fiona!" she screamed. The other parents followed, racing forward, coming to join her as she waded out toward the Sea Spirit.

The Sea Spirit's arms fell in great waves across the Barge deck.

"Stop it!" cried a man in a green sweater. "Leave them alone!"

The whips continued their volley of *cracks*, and water splashed all around as the Sea Spirit lost and regained form again and again.

Meredith and the watermen were on their feet, racing into the shallows, swords stabbing into the Sea Spirit's body without effect.

The tide rose with the Sea Spirit's anger, the waves wilder

and more frantic by the moment. She ran the Barge aground and slammed herself down onto the deck. It splintered, and the girls, Prewitt, and Jack were swept overboard and thrown onto the sand, limp and choking.

The Glade Girls were soon back on their feet, and they faced the Sea Spirit with fierce determination.

The waves bashed against the rocks. *Enough of this! I will ask only one more time: Who will take my pearl?*

"I will."

The Sea Spirit's eyes ceased their spinning, the water calmed, and everyone stopped fighting and turned toward the top of the city steps.

The crown shone in Calliope's dark curls as she descended toward the beach.

The Masked Rampage murmured to one another. "How can this be? How could she have escaped the Nymph Isles?"

Calliope made her way down the steps, and the crowd parted.

"Cal, don't!" Prewitt pushed himself to his feet, trying to run to her, but a wave knocked him down. Calliope walked past him and waded calmly into the water.

The broken shells in the Spirit's face arranged themselves into a chaotic grin, and a pearl swept into the sand at Calliope's feet.

Calliope reached down and took it.

The crowd held its breath.

For a moment, nothing happened.

The Sea Spirit watched, head swaying, but Calliope's face was impassive.

Then, there was a cracking sound, and Calliope lifted her other hand, the long sleeve splitting to reveal her closed fist. Black shadows poured between Calliope's knuckles, and she uncurled her fingers.

The Sea Spirit stared down at the stone in Calliope's palm. For a moment, she did not react. The heart was her own, but it had been so long since she had seen it that she did not recognize it.

"My story is the story of a thousand years," said Calliope. "It is the story of generations of Firebird Queens. Your fragile heart cannot hold it." Darkness seeped from the cracks in the stone, and the stolen stories broke free from the Sea Spirit's heart at last.

In that instant, Calliope felt the Queen's lost magic returning to her. It thrilled through her veins. She could hear the *sound* of the Sea Spirit's magic and recognized it suddenly as an echoing fragment of the Firebird Song. She saw clearly how it should have fit, perfect, and in harmony with the sound of nature all around, and yet, it was discordant and broken.

The Sea Spirit wailed. *It hurts! Oh, oh, it hurts!* Great swells smashed into the boats in the harbor and flung themselves violently onto the beach. The tide swept higher, wresting the burned driftwood from the stack and plunging it into the stormy sea.

The Sea Spirit tore the door from the Bookshop and flung it against the foundation of the tiers. She roared and thrashed her arms across the sand. *My heart is breaking! You have doomed Lyrica! Darkness will overcome them all.*

"No! Don't you see? The stories harmed the Spirits because

they were stolen from humans. But they cannot harm us. They belong to us, and I have brought them home."

The tide rose higher, and the crowd panicked, running up the city steps.

The Sea Spirit raged, water spilling from her as she crashed across the tiers. *I will be Queen!*

"*I* am Queen," shouted Calliope, and the title finally fit. "And I am ready to protect my people."

The Sea Spirit turned, hurling waves at her. She pulled back her arm, and a wall of water crashed against Calliope, but the Feather glowed at the Queen's waist, and she was not moved.

The tide rose, and the Sea furied across the tiers.

People screamed and ran for higher ground, but Prewitt made his way back toward Calliope. The water beat against him, trying to wrench him out to sea, and he clung to the mooring rings on the bottom tier. He wanted to call out to her, to help her, but he saw that she was not afraid. The Sea Spirit's magic no longer had any effect on her.

"Sea Spirit." Calliope's voice was full of magic, and her command echoed across the tide. "Take what remains of your heart and go."

Never. The Spirit grew larger, and her tide was so forceful that it swept a boy from the tier. His mother screamed, reaching, but something had already caught him.

Bright orange blossoms clung to the boy, their roots strong.

All around, the fire flowers that Calliope had planted were stretching out and catching hold of people, keeping them from being swept out to sea. The Sea Spirit tantrumed and fought and tried to tear people away, but the blooms held. They had been planted with kindness and watered by hope, and nothing could tear them free.

But still, the Sea Spirit rose, determined and angry.

The Firebird Feather shone brighter, and Calliope's wet hair slapped against her back. She stood tall, balanced on the white-capped waves, untouched by the Sea's temper. "*Spirit*, you *will* leave my kingdom."

The Sea Spirit ignored her, and Calliope's mouth set. She turned her eyes away from the city, away from the devastation the Sea Spirit was trying to cause, and she reached out for the Firebird Song.

It raced through the open door of her heart and strummed across her veins. She drew the sea to her, and it obeyed. She shaped the waves into a firebird and lifted it from the depths beyond the harbor. Where flames should be, dark water swirled, and its eyes were black holes. It soared across the city, brine pouring from its wings.

The Spirit of the Suffering Sea had nearly risen to the castle, bringing the tide with her. Everything below was now underwater.

Give me your stories, or I will wash you away.

Calliope waved her hand, and the firebird dove, crashing into the Sea Spirit. Water attacked water, and the Sea Spirit lost form. For a moment, she was gone.

But then she rose again, trying to continue forward but

unable to hold her shape. She pushed up the steps, but Calliope's firebird stretched its wings before the castle and would not let her pass.

The Sea Spirit rounded on Calliope.

Calliope's hair whorled, her shirt billowed, but no matter how the Sea Spirit raged and stormed and tried to drown her, she could not be moved.

Calliope held out her palm. "Take your heart and go."

I will not! The Spirit struck her one last time, crushing her own cracked heart into sand.

The Sea instantly dropped away, shells and glass swept back with the retreating tide, and only her skirts remained: nets, tangled on the shore.

Calliope let out her breath, and her firebird melted back into the deep. The water at the edge of the beach was once again calm and rippling.

But when she turned toward the city, she heard the sound of people weeping.

The stories had been released from the Suffering Stone and had returned to the children and grandchildren of those who had once accepted pearls.

Prewitt raced forward, flinging his arms around her. "You did it!" he cried, but seeing her face, he frowned. "Aren't you happy? You saved us."

"Listen to them, Prewitt," she said. "We have to help them."

"How?"

Calliope told him her plan. He raced up the steps toward

the castle, passing Chichi and her mother sitting together on the top step.

Chichi didn't notice him. Her own story had returned, and with it, all the pain and heartbreak that had made her take the pearl. She reached into her pocket, but the pearl was gone. In its place was a small, round pebble.

Chichi looked at her mother, betrayal making her eyes sting. "I thought you were a hero."

The Silver Shag sighed. "I'm so sorry, Chichi. I wanted to be. I tried to make that story true. I really did, but there was another story that got in the way." She grabbed Chichi's hand. "Let me tell it to you."

Mother and daughter walked down the beach, hand in hand, and Sina told Chichi her whole story. Sina pointed out the shell cottage, just visible from the western edge of the beach. She spoke of the grandmother Chichi had never known. "People said she was *swayed*," she began.

Chichi listened carefully, too enrapt to ask even a single question.

When Sina finally finished, both had tears on their cheeks.

"I'm sorry," Chichi said, squeezing her mother's hand. "I wish your story didn't have so much pain in it."

The Silver Shag leaned forward, pressing her forehead to Chichi's. "No, no, darling. If any part of the story had changed, I wouldn't have you. You are worth every moment of pain."

Chichi grinned, and her mother pulled her close. "Stories are our strength, Chichi. Don't ever forget."

"I won't," Chichi promised.

Across the water, a thousand cormorants raised their wings and flew off into the night, and on the beach, a drowned man opened his eyes.

34

Calliope stood at the top of the city steps, Prewitt by her side.

"Are you sure?" he asked.

Calliope nodded. "I'm sure." And this time she was. She looked to Meredith, who gave her a small bow, and then he and the watermen began to move through the city, passing out unlit candles.

Calliope held a box of matches in her hand, and she slid one out, striking it.

The crowd flinched as the flame blazed, small and steady, but they did not run. The Queen had vanquished a powerful Sea Spirit; perhaps she really had defeated the Spectress after all.

Calliope sheltered the flame with her hand, and her voice carried across the tiers. "Because of the Spectress, I grew up without a mother. It was unfair, and I was angry." She turned to Prewitt, and he handed her a candle. "I wanted a different story. But now I know that we can't change our stories without changing who we are. It is our stories that give us power. That give us our own special magic."

The wick caught.

"We must share them and remember them."

The flame glowed steady. "It took time, but in the end, my story made me strong."

She turned to Prewitt, nodding encouragement, and he shifted a little, tugging on his jacket before he spoke. "When the Spectress was here, I had to share my dad. I didn't get to go to school, or learn to read, and it rained all the time. I hated it. Rain, and mud, and *fish*. Ugh, fish."

Somewhere along the tier someone gave a hesitant laugh.

Prewitt held his candle out, gaining confidence. "My story had some hard parts"—his wick caught on Calliope's, blazing into life—"but it helped me realize that I have my own magic. It helped me find my purpose." He looked up at Calliope, and his cheeks were hot.

People began to move closer together.

The Glade Girls stood around Ilsbeth, who had finally woken. She lay on a blanket-heaped pallet outside the falconry. She held out her candle to Prewitt, and her flame ignited, bright and steady. One by one the Glade Girls lit their candles. "We lost our families, but we gained another. Our story gave us sisters," they said together.

Jack's candle lit. "I lost my family, too. It hurt so much. But I'm ready to tell stories about them—to remember them. I think maybe sadness helped me understand others better. I think it made me kinder."

One by one, candles lit along the tier as person after person shared their story, and who they had become because of it.

Soon, everyone's candle was blazing, and people were no longer avoiding one another's eyes. Instead, they were talking. Each story was a spark that grew and spread across the tier, warming the city. They shared the tales of their ancestors, of the past, and of the present, and with each story told, a weight lifted and a bond was formed.

Calliope gazed down at the flickering flames and at the faces turned toward one another. As the wax dripped down their candles, the sky began to wake.

Calliope's eyes caught on Ilsbeth.

Ilsbeth had sent the Glade Girls to join their parents, and now, she sat alone, staring out at the sea, her candle burning low beside her. The fledgling had nestled into the blankets, and Ilsbeth's fingers were buried in its feathers.

"You go," said Prewitt. "I'll only irritate her." Calliope smiled at him, and he ran off to find the watermen.

Ilsbeth didn't look up as Calliope came close, but she spoke. "I am sorry I failed you. I could not keep the door open."

Calliope shook her head. "No, Ilsbeth. I'm sorry. I wish I had gotten to the door sooner, but it took me a while to remember who I am."

She sat down beside Ilsbeth, whose gaze was unwavering

on the horizon. After a moment, Ilsbeth said, "Do you think that the Nymph Isles are still out there?"

"I do," said Calliope. She said it with confidence, because she knew that it was true. She could hear its magic as a piece of the Firebird Song. It was all a part of her now.

Ilsbeth looked at her fledgling, and the corners of her mouth tipped down, so slightly that someone else might have missed it, but Calliope knew Ilsbeth's face too well. She reached out and touched Ilsbeth's shoulder.

"He did it because he loved you," she said, her voice gentle.

"I wish . . ." Ilsbeth trailed off, and Calliope never heard what she would have wished, for the horizon flashed suddenly gold and the sun began to rise, an icy wind gusting around them.

In the falconry window, the peregrines screeched and bated, sending up flurries of hay.

"What is wrong with them?" asked Ilsbeth, whipping her head toward the falconry. The spirit chimes clanged in the doorway, and shock spread unchecked across her face.

The Falconer stood on the doorstep, wind blowing his dark hair across his brows.

Ilsbeth blinked. "Is it really you?" she whispered.

The Falconer nodded, and in two steps, he was kneeling at her side. "The Wind brought me back."

His tone was gruff. "Are you all right?" he asked, looking her over.

Ilsbeth nodded, and it looked as if she was struggling to find words; then she said, "You gave up your future for me."

The Falconer looked at her, and his eyes were warm. "My future has been yours since the day you were born."

Ilsbeth buried her face in the Falconer's jacket, and Calliope moved away, leaving the two alone, but when she looked back, there were smiles on both their faces, and she saw an ease between them that had not been there before.

Calliope wondered why the Wind had brought the Falconer back. Maybe it had been moved by the Falconer's willingness to sacrifice for his daughter, or maybe things were beginning to change. Perhaps humans and Spirits could live in harmony after all.

She climbed toward the castle.

She turned to look down at the Royal City. Her people were gathered on the steps, and children played along the tiers. Screams and giggles mixed with a steady babble, and the scent of woodsmoke and fire flower blooms drifted in the dawn.

She saw Prewitt, holding his little sister in his arms. He gestured across the water toward the sunrise, whispering something that made her laugh.

Jack and Old Harry sat side by side with a pile of nets in their laps, and Calliope saw Cedric being yanked down the market tier by an old woman in a red hat. The woman pointed to a derelict shop and then pressed her hands to her hips. Cedric began at once to pull the boards away from the windows.

Calliope turned her head, listening. A *sound*. She turned toward the castle and walked alone through the orchard, the chill of the wind on her cheeks. She watched as it flurried through the trees, rattling silver leaves and teasing a few from their branches.

Her gaze swept the orchard, searching. She knew he was there, knew the triumphant *sound* of his magic.

She found him, standing in the shadow of an apple tree. The Forgeman was no longer stone. The veins in his arms shone like liquid gold, and his smile was warm. He bowed deeply. "Your Majesty," he said. Then he reached up and pulled an apple off a branch.

With a wink, he tossed it to her.

Calliope caught it, and when she looked back, the Forgeman was gone.

EPILOGUE

Autumn fell crisp and golden across the Royal City. The market resumed, and the shops, which had been shut for so long, were open and full. People began to travel across Lyrica once again. They were no longer afraid, for the Silver Shag and her Masked Rampage had returned to them and told them the truth: the Spectress really was gone. Stories of Queen Calliope's magic had spread throughout the kingdom, and it was no coincidence that they had blossomed wherever the Silver Shag had been.

The three nameless girls were finally found. Their parents had thought them lost for good, but when word came that three girls had not yet been claimed by families, they packed their bags and went at once to collect them.

Castaway Cape was given a new name—Cape Refuge— for the people who had been there had discovered their strength in one another. Calliope's first official decree was that the gates be opened for good and that the people who lived there be allowed to return to their cities if they chose, but almost none of them did.

Calliope unlocked the nursery door and put away the key. Although she was not ready to remove her mother's belongings, she would often go in and sit on the bed. Sometimes, Marisa sat with her.

Calliope and Prewitt had gone back to the forest. They had followed the Troll bridges until they found Sapling, and when they did, Calliope had pressed her hand to the Troll's legs, and they had healed. It had bounded off, the sound of its chiming magic no longer sorrowful, but joy-filled and radiant, and Calliope knew that it was on its way to join its family.

On the day the final leaf fell from the apple trees in the royal orchard, Calliope and Prewitt stood on the quay, watching crates being loaded onto a brand-new ship.

Sina barked orders at deckhands, and Chichi swung back and forth on the ropes, a stack of parchment in her lap and a pencil between her teeth.

"Hurry up, Chichi!" Reynard shouted from the deck. "Or you'll get left behind!"

"No!" Chichi bounced up. "Don't go without me! I want to see the Nymph Isles!"

She ran up the gangway, turning to wave at Calliope and Prewitt.

They grinned back at her.

Milo came out of the Bookshop, locking the door and

flipping over the sign. There was no trace of barnacles on his skin, and color had returned to his cheeks. Since waking, all his time had been spent working. He had gone from person to person and written down all the stories that had returned to them when the Sea Spirit's heart had been broken. There were many shared experiences, but each person told their story differently, and Milo wanted to capture them all as truthfully as he could.

Although the books that had been burned could never be recovered, the tales that had lived on their pages breathed once more. As the shelves of the Bookshop slowly refilled, its heart began to beat again, and it woke to a gentle hand on its doorframe. "I'll be back," Milo promised. "Keep the lantern burning." High above, the light pulsed, bright and white.

"I don't know why I let you talk me into this," Sina snapped at Milo as he boarded the ship.

Milo smiled. "Because it's the right thing to do and you know it."

Sina snorted. "Right or not, I still think we should let the old man stay on that island a while longer. The Spirits could have returned him, but they didn't. Perhaps we should take our cue from them."

Milo draped an arm around her shoulders. "We're just going to go and get him. I didn't say you had to be nice. You can torture him all you like once he's home."

Chichi waved enthusiastically back at the city until the ship was too far away to see.

Calliope and Prewitt turned toward the tiers. The Glade Girls whirled and spun on the beach, their whips cracking. A group of children watched with wide eyes. Prewitt saw Pyper among them, a piece of string tight in her fingers. She flicked her wrist, too.

The market was bustling, and the agriculture tiers were finally being tended. Guards in uniform marched on the castle battlements and stood tall at the gates. People had returned to their work with new gratitude and enthusiasm. They held the stories of their ancestors, and because of them, they had a deeper knowledge of themselves. They were finding a way forward, beyond all they had lost and suffered, and although the path to healing wasn't easy, they were walking it together.

As Prewitt and Calliope moved through the crowds, people stopped to talk with them. They pressed the last of the season's fire flowers into Calliope's and Prewitt's hair and tucked warm rolls into their hands.

New, happy memories were beginning to outshine the darkness of the past.

Calliope and Prewitt chatted as they entered the castle.

Golden light streamed through mended windows. Fires burned brightly in the hearths, and new rugs were soft beneath their feet, and for the first time in a long time, it felt like coming home.

ACKNOWLEDGMENTS

Writing books can be hard, but with the right team, it can also be a joy. I'm so incredibly grateful for the just-right group of people who helped me bring this story into the world.

First, thank you to Mary Kate Castellani, my friend and editor, who makes me better as a human and as a writer. And to everyone at Bloomsbury who makes this all possible. It is an honor to create alongside such passionate, beautiful people. Special love to Beth Eller, Jasmine Miranda, Lily Yengle, Ksenia Winnicki, Faye Bi, and Erica Barmash. (And thanks to John Candell and Vivienne To for helping this story put its best face forward!)

Thank you to my agent, Sara Crowe, for always guiding the way, and to everyone at Pippin Properties who works so hard to bring the very best stories to the world at just the right time.

To all my author friends, Alena Bruzas, Ruby Grigg, Lish

McBride, Kendare Blake, Ryfie Schafer, Marisa Meyer, and many, many more, who have championed me and loved me and shown me how to navigate this crazy place called publishing, thank you. And of course, to "Mama" Martha Brokenbrough, a shining example of graciousness and goodness.

Thank you to Heather Campbell who loves me best, and to Miah Flores, my partner and person. Thank you for celebrating even the smallest things as if they were big.

And finally, these books would never, could never, have any life without the bookshops, booksellers, librarians, teachers, reviewers, bloggers, and readers who champion them. For every single one of you, I am grateful. Thank you, thank you for finding *The Firebird Song*, for putting it on your shelves, posting photos, and shouting your love from the rooftops. I wish I could hug each and every one of you! I hope, very much, that you enjoyed *The Spirit Queen*.

S.D.G.